WISTERIA
WEDDING

Wisteria Witches Mysteries

BOOK #13

ANGELA PEPPER

CHAPTER 1

The best type of upcoming event is the one that requires the purchase of a new dress in any color except black.

I was in need of such a dress, so I walked into my favorite clothing store, Mia's Kit and Kaboodle. To my surprise, I found that it was full of lost souls.

Not *lost souls* as in ghosts, which were something I had been seeing regularly since coming into my witch powers, but lost souls as in regular people who didn't know what to do with themselves during the awkward stretch of days between Christmas and the new year.

Several of these lost souls were women about my size, browsing in the dress area.

So much for my plans to get in and out without hand-to-hand combat, or the use of magic. I tried to limit my use of magic to emergency use only, but it was hard to exercise restraint. There were few problems I encountered in life that couldn't be solved by magic. Or, to be honest, made much, much worse.

As I paused just inside the door, the owner of the shop, Mia Gianna, greeted me warmly as usual.

"Zara, you got here just in time. I put out a batch of party dresses about an hour ago," she said. "There's a turquoise one that would be perfect for an upcoming special event."

I gave her a suspicious look. Mia had an uncanny talent for matching her customers with the perfect items that came through her secondhand shop. My friend Frank and I both suspected she was a Belongings Mage, and that she had no idea. Most people in Wisteria didn't know about magic, yet many of them had minor powers they weren't aware of. Mia seemed to know what I'd come in for that day, so did she know about magic?

If I were to cast some spells to find out for sure, then break the news, Mia might appreciate knowing where her talents came from. She might show me even more favoritism as a customer than she already did. Then again, she might go mad from the revelation.

Once a person found out magic was real, they'd also realize that witches like me walked in their midst, along with vampires, shifters, and assorted monsters. Once a person's eyes had been opened, the world became a different place. Mia might not appreciate her mage powers at all if she spent the rest of her days in a state of constant anxiety.

So, instead of casting a spell, I fished for information with a simple question: "How did you know I was in need of a new dress?"

Mia gave me a mischievous smile as she answered, "Your friend Carrot Greyson was here this morning," she said. "I heard all about the wedding."

"That explains everything," I said. Carrot, a local tattooist and mage who used to work with my aunt, was getting married. Her fiance was Archer Caine, the genie who fathered my daughter before disappearing on me seventeen years ago, only to resurface in Wisteria, cause endless trouble, and take a piece of my soul. In spite of all this, he and I were on good terms. *Zara tries to be a good witch. Zara is a forgiving witch.*

Mia said, "Carrot bought a vintage gown that my seamstress is modifying. It should be ready in time for the big day, which is in," she checked the big calendar on the wall, "two days!" She opened a drawer and took out the next year's oversized calendar, which she showed to me. "Time sure flies. I'll be putting this new one up soon enough, but don't worry. I won't put it up early. I wouldn't want to cause any bad luck."

The "new" calendar looked anything but new. It had to be several decades old, with advertisements for tinned foods on the back, and faded, blue-tinted images of sunflower fields on the cover.

"This one hasn't been out in a while," Mia said, patting the calendar. "It's been eleven years since I last used it, because of..." She trailed off, distracted by the sounds of her shop full of lost souls.

"Because of the leap year," I finished for her.

She beamed, pleased that I'd understood what she was talking about. Most people didn't realize that there were only fourteen Gregorian calendars in current use. There would have only been seven—one for each day of the week that January first could fall on—if not for leap days, which created another set of seven, for a total of fourteen. If anyone had been standing next to me, I might have bored them with that piece of trivia. Providing people with unwanted fun facts was a hazard of my trade.

Mia looked anything but bored. "Oh, Zara Riddle! You must be the best librarian who's ever lived. Is there anything you don't know?"

I scoffed loudly. "I'm the owner of a teenager. Check with her for a massive list of all the things I don't know."

We shared a chuckle, and I let Mia get back to her work while I continued my dress-shopping mission.

Carrot and Archer's engagement had been a surprise, sprung on us over the Christmas holidays. The wedding would be a small, informal gathering. Carrot had assured me that even jeans and a T-shirt would be fine, but I hadn't been to many weddings, so I relished the opportunity to dress up.

I warmed up my shopping muscles in the jewelry section. Nothing grabbed me, which was unusual.

I left the jewelry but couldn't get into the dress area due to the hive of activity there.

It had to be the date. It was the thirtieth of December. The other ladies must have been searching for something to wear to their New Year's Eve parties.

I considered leaving, which felt wrong. I rarely left Mia's empty handed.

The last time I'd been there, my friend Frank had bought a gravy boat, and I'd picked up some dinner plates and a dark purple cocktail dress that my mother had made fun of the way she did everything—without mercy. My mother had been invited to Carrot and Archer's wedding, so I needed a different outfit to force her to come up with new material.

Desperate times called for desperate measures.

I cast a few subtle spells to gently shoo the other dress-obsessed ladies to different departments. The sea of people parted, and I breezed up to the dress rack.

My good mood sank as soon as I started checking the price tags.

Why was everything priced so high? Had Mia marked up everything because she knew there would be high demand that week?

I sucked in air between my teeth and exhaled in a long groan.

I checked the next dress, and the next.

They all had obscenely high prices on their tags.

Meanwhile, my spells were dissipating, and the other shoppers started returning.

None of the other lost souls seemed dismayed by the high prices.

I kept going through the rack, determined to find a hidden gem.

Finally, I found the one that Mia must have been talking about. It was the perfect dress for a witch to wear to a New Year's Day wedding between her genie ex-boyfriend and a tattoo mage. It was vintage from the sixties, a dreamy turquoise color, in a tastefully demure cut, with a matching shawl.

I braced myself as I cautiously checked the price tag. Bad news. The number was just as outrageous as the rest. It wasn't like me to complain about prices, but I found myself letting out a not-so-subtle groan.

A petite, dark-haired woman came up beside me, peeked over my shoulder at the tag in my hand, and said, "That's not a bad price for the quality, and that dress would look stunning on you." She reached into her purse and said, "I've got some extra fun money. Why don't you let me buy that for you?"

I was so stunned by the woman's generosity that I was temporarily speechless. Rather than turn and face her, I stared at the tag in my hand, dumbfounded. My gratitude was quickly replaced by a wave of guilt about the spells I'd cast earlier. I really had been misbehaving. *Zara can be a spoiled witch.*

"Thank you so much, but I've got it," I said, pausing to do some quick math in my head. "That's odd. This dress is only a tenth of the amount I usually drop on my visits to Mia's. It's actually a great price. I don't know what got into my head when I started looking at tags. It's like something came over me, and I turned into a penny pincher."

"My husband was a penny pincher," the woman said. "Perry Pressman."

At the sound of that name, a lightning flash of adrenaline shot through me.

The woman was Jasmine Pressman. She'd gone by Carter-Pressman for a while, and even under her maiden name, Carter, but was back to Pressman again. We'd met a few times, but I didn't know her well.

5

"Of course he was," I said. "Perry Pressman. He used to run the Penny Pincher Gazette."

Mrs. Pressman beamed with pride. "As far as penny pinchers go, my husband was the best of the best!"

I knew Perry. Or his ghost, anyway. His spirit had been the second one ever to possess me, back before I'd gotten control over my Spirit Charmed powers. Perry had knocked me unconscious, and then he'd done... well... really nice things for me. He'd wrangled my finances and bills into a better system, and knocked several dollars off my monthly expenses.

I turned to face the woman. She was middle-aged and short, with straight, black hair, neatly parted down the center. She had a pleasant, round face, and a button nose. She had a few wrinkles distributed evenly between frown lines and laugh lines. She must have been a knockout in her youth, and she'd retained that vitality in spite of what she'd been through.

All my memories of Perry Pressman rushed back. I had the eerie feeling I was suddenly at the man's funeral. It didn't help that his widow—was she still a widow if they'd been divorced but she still cared for him?—was dressed in black.

"He was such a nice man," I said to Mrs. Pressman. "I didn't know him when he was alive, but I've heard only good things." This was the kind of situation where a lie was absolutely necessary, so I didn't feel too bad.

She squinted at me briefly. "I know you. Your last name is Riddle. You work at the library."

I looked away out of embarrassment. We had spoken a few times, but our connection ran deeper than she knew. Not only had I been possessed by her late ex-husband, but I'd also been host to her deceased daughter, experiencing the girl's memories as though they were my own. I knew the woman before me much better than she knew me.

The last time we'd seen each other, at the library, she'd noticed I was feeling blue and offered me a very nice hug.

Now here she was again, offering to buy me a dress. What a sweet lady. And she was always so cheerful in spite of what she'd been through, with two devastating losses in less than one year.

"I *do* work at the library," I said, barely managing to keep a normal conversation on track. "And while they don't pay me a queen's allowance, I am compensated fairly. I'm sorry you heard me groaning over the price. I don't know what got into me. Maybe it was a penny-pinching spirit passing through here at random!"

She laughed at that. "Stranger things have happened," she said knowingly.

"I can afford this dress myself, but I do appreciate your generous offer, Mrs. Pressman."

She tipped her head back and laughed again without restraint. "Call me Jasmine," she said, selling me on it with a friendly arm squeeze. "Are you going to try that on?" She pointed at the dress in my hands. "We can be change room buddies." She had a couple of party dresses hanging over her arm.

"Sure," I said. "Let's be change room buddies."

We headed toward the busy change rooms.

It was always a good idea to try on vintage clothes, as the sizing could be unreliable. When Mia's Kit and Kaboodle got busy, customers could jump the line for change rooms by pairing up. It was the same principle as putting more people in your car so you could use the car-pool lane on a busy highway. Jasmine and I did just that.

We made small talk about the after-Christmas clearance sales around town as we wriggled out of our street clothes in the shared room.

Jasmine asked, "So, what's the big event you have coming up? Are you going to a fancy champagne party tomorrow night?"

"I'm staying in for a quiet night, actually. I want to be fresh for the first of January. Some friends of mine are getting married."

"The Caine-Greyson wedding?" Jasmine watched herself in the tall mirror as she turned left and right, checking the fit of a silver dress.

I swallowed hard. "You know them?" It was because of Archer that Jasmine's ex-husband and daughter had been killed. He hadn't harmed them himself—it was all the work of his evil genie sister—but this coincidence still set off alarm bells.

"Not that well," she said lightly. "The bride's great-uncle invited me as his date. We're just friends, so I suppose I shouldn't say I'm his date, but it beats saying I'm a wedding crasher, which is what I feel like. Imagine that! A woman my age, crashing strangers' weddings just for something to do. That would make a wonderful movie, wouldn't it?"

"I suppose it would. What do you mean, *a woman your age*? You're barely forty."

"I'm fifty, sweetheart, but thank you." She patted her midsection, which was bare at the moment, as she was between dresses. "Watch out for fifty," she said with a laugh. "It likes to settle right here, in the middle. That's why they call it middle age."

She really didn't have much in her middle. I was about to compliment her on having a great figure when I noticed the changing room's temperature drop several degrees. That was one sign of a ghost making an appearance. I looked around to see who it would be that time.

My Spirit Charmed skills had really leveled up that year, so even if the ghost was a tough case, I could probably have it dealt with in less than twenty-four hours. They usually showed up after dark, though, and since it was the middle of the day, I wouldn't have been surprised to see nothing in the change room.

The air behind Jasmine shimmered, and suddenly a man was standing there. I knew him. It was her late ex-husband, Perry Pressman. What was he doing there? I'd solved the mystery surrounding his death ages ago. He should have moved on, away from the world of the living, on to the great recycling bin in the sky—or wherever they went.

As if he was anticipating my questions, the semi-transparent ghost man looked right at me and shrugged.

Before I could twist my mouth around the Witch Tongue for an exploratory spell, Jasmine said, in a spooky whisper, "Can you feel that?"

I kept my expression neutral. I had been on edge and feeling suspicious since learning Jasmine was coming to the wedding. Something was going on. Had Jasmine lured me into the privacy of a changing room for an ambush?

"Feel what?" I asked.

"My Perry," she said, still whispering. "He's come back. He's here right now in the changing room. I can feel him standing behind me."

"You can?"

She nodded. "I think he's come for me."

"Are you saying that your ex-husband has come back as a ghost, and he's haunting you?"

She stared up at me with her large brown eyes. With her small button-nose, she resembled an anime character as her eyes grew even larger.

She whispered, "You feel it, right? That chill that goes straight to your bones? He's here with us. I'm not crazy."

"I don't think you're crazy," I said, careful to say it in a flat, perfunctory manner, as though I might be lying even though I wasn't. It was hard to hit the right tone with non-magical people. As a librarian, my calling in life was to connect people with the knowledge they were seeking. It went against my instincts to hold back, but I had to be cautious at all times.

The changing room felt really claustrophobic. Was I already inside a trap? Why had a ghost returned?

I was half in a dress, frozen, and I couldn't recall if I'd been pulling the dress on or taking it off. *Calm down*, I told myself, and shook out my hands to unclench my fists.

Jasmine didn't seem to notice my tension.

She blinked rapidly and smiled. "Maybe I am a wee bit crazy." She held up her hand, indicating a small amount of space between her finger and thumb. "Just a pinch."

My lower back was sweating, and I had tunnel vision. The sounds of the busy store around us seemed to disappear. Was I inside a cramped changing room with a crazy woman? Had I walked right into a trap? Did she have a weapon in her purse?

As a witch, I was spoiled with options for defensive and offensive magic, but there were objects and potions that could disarm me as easily as Kryptonite disarmed Superman. Did Jasmine have a witchbane diffuser with her?

The woman's purse was sitting on the bench behind her. I'd have to go through her to check it.

The ghost still stood nearby, watching silently.

Meanwhile, my would-be ambusher still had one hand at her hip and the other one raised to indicate the "pinch of crazy."

I silently prepared a ball of lightning in the hand that was behind my back. I gave her a smile I hoped was reassuring.

Lightly, I said, "There's nothing wrong with a pinch of crazy, if it helps you get through life."

She suddenly tipped back her head and let out a burst of laughter, as though we had been sharing the most marvelous joke.

Then she pulled on her regular clothes, gathered up the dresses she'd been trying on, and slipped out through the curtain. She poked her head back in and said, "See you at the wedding in two days, sweetheart!"

A moment passed. My vision and hearing gradually widened back to its regular state.

I heard the shop's owner chatting happily on the other side of the curtain. The sound of her helping people find new treasures wasn't as reassuring as it usually was.

There was a murmur and impatient stomping nearby.

People were waiting for the change room.

I tried to hurry myself, but I was only half-dressed and moving slowly.

My reflexes, once activated, took a moment to settle down.

I didn't let the lightning ball in my hand dissipate right away but played with it, rolling it around my knuckles like a magician with a coin.

The ghost of Perry Pressman was gone now, apparently having followed his ex-wife out, but the chill remained on my skin, along with an ominous feeling in my bones.

I had no doubts about what I'd experienced. I'd seen him with my own eyes, plus I'd been overcome with penny pincher feelings at the dress rack. He had been there, in that small room. A problem I'd assumed was taken care of had come back, and that meant trouble for me. And trouble for me usually meant trouble for my friends and family.

Jasmine had said she would see me at the wedding in two days. Was it a threat, or a promise?

CHAPTER 2

The ghost of Perry Pressman didn't return to the changing room.

While I had been rattled by the experience, I did regain my composure.

I finished trying on the vintage dress, changed back into my regular clothes, then let other customers use the room.

I did a quick lap around the store, for security reasons. And also to pick up some cute brass candleholders. And a pair of rainboots. And five mustard-colored tea towels. And one extra party dress, in case the turquoise one didn't meet the approval of my closet, which had a funny way of burying items it deemed unflattering.

The spirit of the penny pincher must have been long gone, because I didn't experience any more bursts of frugality.

At the checkout, I let Mia talk me into buying a pair of costume jewelry earrings to go with the dress. She did not have to try very hard.

I stepped outside, where I paused on the sidewalk to appreciate the snowflakes that were gently fluttering down around me. I wondered what my aunt was doing at that moment, and if she'd be interested in helping me with my reappearing ghost.

My cell phone rang. It was my aunt. She had psychic powers, but they were limited to knowing when someone was about to phone or text.

When I answered, she said, "Now what?" She sounded annoyed, which wasn't unusual or even bad. I much preferred it to her sounding depressed. Whenever she stopped being annoyed with me, that was when I got worried.

"That's not fair," I said. "I didn't even take my phone out of my purse. You can't get mad at me for something I haven't done yet. You're not the Department of PreCrime." I quickly added, "Which is a fictional police department from *Minority Report*. Which is a movie."

She snorted. "I'm familiar with all movies starring Tom Cruise." She shifted seamlessly into her agreeable mode, as she usually did after a brief warm up. "Where are you? I can hear the door chimes on Mia's Kit and Kaboodle. And... the lineup for Lucky's Diner sounds short today. How about you get us a table, and I'll meet you there in fifteen minutes?"

"You are absolutely correct about where I am, and that sounds perfect. I could use some hot soup, and I need to talk to you about—"

"Not over the telephone," she said, cutting me off.

I shook my head. She could be so paranoid sometimes. Did she really think people were listening to our phone calls, or watching us go about our business? Were we really that much more interesting than the other residents of Wisteria?

"I'll get a table," I said.

We ended the call, and I crossed the street to get in line at Lucky's Diner.

I'd just gotten a window booth inside when I saw my aunt walk by briskly.

Zinnia Riddle was fifteen years older than me, but we looked so similar that people mistook us for sisters. Like me, she had thick, wavy red hair, hazel eyes, and a knack for getting in trouble. She claimed to be the more restrained one between the two of us, but at Halloween, she'd accidentally summoned a creature from another dimension who really put a damper on the evening's celebrations.

I'd gotten myself into a number of pickles, but I'd never summoned a demon before.

Luckily for us, and the staff at Castle Wyvern, we did get to the bottom of that particular mystery just in the nick of time, thanks in part to our inventor friend's modified handheld vacuum, which he called a Devil Duster. The real weapon, though, had been solid teamwork between a bunch of witches and supernaturals. If you've ever been to a coven meeting, you know how rare that can be.

Zinnia entered Lucky's Diner, stamping the snow off her feet noisily. She came over to the booth and slipped in across from me, sitting with a loud whoomph. It wasn't like Zinnia to be so noisy, so I raised an eyebrow and waited for an explanation.

It didn't take long.

"My dress doesn't fit," she said grumpily.

"Could you be *less* specific? I do enjoy our guessing games."

She shot me a stinkeye that would have made my resident wyvern jealous.

The waitress came by and suggested we order right away, before the kitchen got slammed. I ordered the daily special, which was soup and a half sandwich. Zinnia ordered the same, plus quiche.

I gave her another eyebrow raise. "That's a lot of food. Will you have room for pie and ice cream?"

"I probably shouldn't," she said. "My dress doesn't fit." She used a napkin to remove her lipstick in preparation for eating, and added, "The bridesmaid dress I'm wearing to Carrot and Archer's wedding. It was perfectly fine at the fitting a few weeks ago, but now it's too small."

I cast a sound bubble spell around our table so I could speak freely.

"Maybe when you got returned to your regular size after the whole Pain-Body Cacodemon thing, we overshot the target," I said. "We could try getting the coven together for an adjustment, but you know how strange this time of year is for scheduling. We probably won't be able to do it before the wedding."

She didn't say anything. She was in a bad mood, all right.

I reached for the canvas tote bag I'd filled up across the street at Mia's, and plopped it on the table between us.

"Lucky for you, I picked up a spare dress today. If Carrot doesn't mind one of her bridesmaids not matching the others, you're welcome to borrow it. If you like it, you can keep it. Consider it a late Christmas present, to make up for the fact that Ribbons ate the one I was going to give you."

Zinnia pulled out the floral dress I'd picked up as a spare. I must have subconsciously been thinking of her, because it was her style.

"This is not your taste at all," she said. "It's so nice."

"You're welcome."

She sighed and gave me a tired look. "You know what I mean," she said softly, with affection. "Honestly, I'm not trying to insult you. Not on purpose. I'm not... *you know who.*" Her eye flash said it all. She was *not* her older sister, Zirconia. Also known as my mother. Also known as the vampire house guest who showed no signs of leaving my home without a formal disinvitation.

"Don't worry about it," I said. "I wasn't offended at all. Plus, after all the shots I've taken at you over those chintz sofa covers you wear, I probably had it coming."

She held the new-to-her dress to her front, checked the fit roughly, and pronounced it perfect.

"If Carrot's seamstress can't let out the bridesmaid gown in time, I'll wear this," Zinnia said. "There's even some orange in the pattern."

"The maid of honor can wear a different dress."

"I'm a bridesmaid," she said. "Carrot insisted. She found out I've never been one before, and she feels that every woman ought to have a chance to be a bridesmaid, no matter the age."

"*I've* never been a bridesmaid," I said, pretending to be hurt about being left out, even though I wasn't hurt. Not much, anyway.

The waitress returned with our hot beverages and a promise our food wouldn't be long.

I heard Zinnia's stomach growl from all the way across the table.

I gave my aunt a third eyebrow raise. "Are you really that hungry, or have you got something scaly hiding in your purse?"

"Enough about me," she said with a hand wave. "How is Zoey?"

"She is the perfect teenaged daughter, as usual. She figured out how to unclog the tub drain all by herself. One day she won't even need me anymore. I'm not sure she needs me now."

"That will be the sign you did a good job. How about Bentley?"

"I haven't seen him much since Christmas day. My mother gives him the heebie jeebies. Plus the baby scorched his favorite wool overcoat."

Zinnia's head jerked. "The baby?"

"Ribbons Junior. We're calling him RJ until we come up with something better."

"Oh, right. The baby wyvern." With a wry smile, she said, "Yet another portend of the coming End of Days."

I pointed across the diner table at her. "This is one of the many reasons I adore you, Aunt Zinnia. People do not say *portend* often enough."

17

Portend of the End of Days or not, the baby wyvern was real. His existence had been discovered shortly before Christmas, but only because my mother and I had launched an investigation. Ribbons had wanted to keep his offspring a secret. It was big news in the supernatural world. The little guy was the first baby wyvern who'd been hatched on Earth in over a thousand years.

My gorgon friend at the Department of Water and Magic had pieced together some of her intel with what I'd learned, and we determined that Ribbons must have mated with a female wyvern during the summer, when a few creatures had been slipping into our world from another dimension. There were no female wyverns around on Earth, which explained the absence of babies. No red wyverns had been spotted locally in several months, so Charlize believed the mother had abandoned the egg.

That tracked with the timeline, as Ribbons moved from a chilly castle into my warm basement around the time the crack between the worlds was mended.

I wished the wyvern would have told me about his single parenthood situation so I could have helped, but he only trusted me as far as he could throw me, which he claimed was about ten feet.

We chatted about wyverns for a few minutes, then Zinnia said, "I heard from Margaret that Ambrosia spotted a ghost roaming around just before dawn a few days ago. Was that the matter you wanted to discuss earlier when you phoned me?"

"You're the one who phoned *me*."

"Please don't correct me unnecessarily. You're as bad as my coworkers at City Hall. Heaven forbid I use green ink on the red stamp pad." She made a my-coworkers-are-cuckoo gesture with one hand. "Now, was there a ghost or not?"

"Yes. It wasn't just any old ghost. It was Perry Pressman."

She frowned. "That's worrying. You ought to catch him and find out what he's up to. Or, at the very least, supervise Ambrosia while she deals with him."

"What about... just leaving him alone? Live and let live? Or live and let... not-quite-live? He's been following his ex-wife around, and she seems to be happy enough about it."

Zinnia flattened her lips in disapproval.

"That poor woman has been through a lot this year," I said. "And none of it was her fault."

My aunt's lips got even thinner.

"She might even enjoy his company more, now that he's dead, and he can't make as much fuss over her credit card statements."

Zinnia said, "Did she tell you that?"

"I'm extrapolating."

Zinnia narrowed her hazel eyes at me. "Did you question her under the influence of spellwork?"

"No. Do you think I should have?"

"Since when do you ask me for advice?"

"I'm getting started early on my New Year's Resolution to think about what I'm going to do before I do it."

She stared at me steadily. "You didn't think about it when you had the chance, did you?"

I looked down at the worn surface of the table. "I made a fireball in one hand because I thought Jasmine might have lured me into the changing room to... I don't know what." I lifted my gaze to meet hers, and raised my chin. "I'm not an OCW. I'm not."

"Relax. I'm not going to tell the others that you're an Overly Cautious Witch. I'm actually proud of you, Zara."

"Sorry. Could you repeat that last part? My mother's been living with me, and some of my mental synapses may be burnt out. It sounded for a moment like you said you were proud of me."

My aunt's face lit up with the loveliest smile. "You silly goose. I *am* proud of you. And so is your mother. Even if she doesn't say it."

"Thanks," I muttered, squirming with discomfort. "Enough about me. Why do you think you've been getting fat? Too many cookies?"

Her smile cracked. "I thought the working hypothesis was that our coven's restoration spellwork was incomplete."

"I was just saying that to make you feel better. Your face is rounder these days. Maybe it's menopause."

She sighed. "Maybe."

"Will that change of life affect your magic at all?"

"One never knows," she said ominously. "It could simply gutter and go out, like the flame on a very old candle."

"You're not that old," I said. "It's probably just perimenopause."

"I'll be forty-nine in two weeks."

"Your birthday's coming up already? I'll have to throw you a surprise party." I grinned. "Forget I said that, or at least promise you'll act surprised."

"No party," she said.

"Why no party? Don't you want to get everyone together for dinner and cake, and party games?"

She forced a big smile. "Thanks to you and Zoey, I feel like I have a party every week."

"You do?"

She sniffed as her eyes welled up. "I do." She dabbed at her eyes with her lipstick-stained napkin, getting lipstick on her fingers. It wasn't unusual for my aunt to get mushy over being included in family events—she'd been living on her own for far too long—but it was strange for her to be so messy about it. Something was definitely going on with her hormones.

Our food arrived, and she dug in immediately, with gusto.

As we ate, we formulated a loose plan to get more information on my returned ghost.

In two days' time, Jasmine Pressman would be at our friends' wedding, so we could use wine, or spells, or both in combination, to find out more about the haunting.

But two days was a long time to wait around doing nothing when a ghost was on the loose.

If Perry had come back from cheapskate heaven—which had to be a great flea market—he was back for a reason. It was possible that, like Jasmine had said, he'd come back for *her*. She'd looked healthy enough to me, which didn't rule out illness but made it seem less likely. Perhaps she was being stalked by someone or something dangerous.

"We need to get some help with this," my aunt said.

"I'll talk to my interns."

"Leave Xavier out of this. The poor boy has no powers to protect himself, and he's still in terrible condition from your last misadventure."

"*My* misadventure? It was *his* cousin who tried to kill both of us."

Zinnia said, "One of your interns should suffice. I suggest you consult Ambrosia, as your specialties are in alignment."

"Hmm." I dipped the triangle end of my half-sandwich in my soup and ate it. "What about your buddy, Margaret Mills? I know she can't see ghosts, but she must be able to do something useful. What did you say her specialty was?"

With a neutral expression, Zinnia said, "I *didn't* say. It's not my place."

"Come on. You can tell me. I'm sure Margaret wouldn't mind."

"If you're so insistent on knowing, go ahead and ask her yourself." Zinnia finished her quiche and licked her lips as she eyed the garnish on the edge of my plate.

"Maybe I will." I handed her the orange wedge.

Zinnia snorted to herself and muttered, "Good luck with that."

"I'll deal with Margaret Mills right after Ambrosia and I wrap up the Pressman haunting for good."

"I'm sure you will," my aunt said with a smile. "In the meantime, I'll talk to Maisy and Fatima about having a meeting, perhaps tonight. It wouldn't hurt to gather one last time this year and wrap up old business so the new year can start with a clean calendar."

A clean calendar. That reminded me of Mia's old calendar, which reminded me of how people tended to repeat the same patterns over and over. My attention drifted out the window while my aunt talked about the "change energy" that was available to all at the start of a new year.

When the waitress came to clear our lunch plates, we ordered pie and ice cream.

Zinnia insisted.

I swear.

After we were done with lunch, I headed out in search of Ambrosia, to find out which ghost she'd seen and where.

CHAPTER 3

When I got home from my shopping and lunch trip, I found the teenaged witch I was looking for right under my nose. Under my nose and underfoot, just like everyone else who felt they had squatters' rights in my house.

She was in my kitchen, making toaster waffles with my daughter. Both of them were yawning, and still wearing pajamas.

Maybe it was a touch of seasonal depression, or maybe my nerves were still jangled from seeing Perry Pressman's ghost, or maybe I was just sick and tired of the crowds of people and pets who were constantly in my house, but seeing those two in their pajamas, eating the food I paid for, was irritating.

It wasn't fair to them, but it was how I felt.

My daughter usually cleaned up after herself, but Ambrosia had gotten lazy as she'd become more comfortable in our house, and she made enough mess for the two of them.

"Good afternoon," I said, trying not to sound as terse as I felt. "It is *after* noon, by the way."

They giggled in response.

Zoey said, "We slept in. It's still morning for us."

"That's not how time works," I said.

I'd picked up some groceries on the way home, and I noted that neither of them were making a move to help put things away. Zoey was a thoughtful kid, and usually noticed when I needed a hand. Ambrosia was rubbing off on her.

I used my levitation magic to send the milk, eggs, and bread to their respective homes, slamming cupboard and fridge doors passive aggressively.

Then, with a flick of my wrist, I sent my purse off to wherever it was my purse liked to hide. My pink leather bag had come into a magical mind of its own lately. It preferred storing itself somewhere I'd never be able to find it without using a spell to call it back to me. I was fine with that. *Zara is an agreeable, accommodating witch.*

I said to Ambrosia, "You might have mentioned the *you-know-what* to me sooner." It came out terse, which, combined with the vagueness, made it downright accusatory. I should have used the word *ghost*, since we were in the privacy of my home, but I'd noticed the window over the sink was open a crack. I used my magic to nudge the window closed. It slammed shut.

Ambrosia whirled around. "Am I in trouble?"

She gave me a wide-eyed look, like a cornered animal, as she fumbled and dropped her steaming waffle. Ambrosia wore thick, black eyeliner, which made her look exactly like a raccoon caught in the trash bins.

Before the waffle could hit the ground, my shifter daughter turned into her fox form, snatched the toasty treat from the air, and ran out of the room. When Zoey was in fox form, she was still herself, but she did exhibit some fox behavior, such as hiding food around the house. The waffle would probably turn up in a few days, behind a couch cushion.

Ambrosia gave me a wary look and shifted so she wasn't in the corner but near an exit. She was even more on edge now that my daughter, her best friend, wasn't there to referee. Not that Ambrosia and I had a combative relationship. The novice witch did some of my grunt work and I let her hang around my house like she paid rent. But she could be jumpy, perhaps worried I was playing the long game to get vengeance for her blasting me unconscious during one of our early interactions.

"Relax," I said. "You're not in trouble. Not unless you did something bad."

"Is this about Margaret and the UFO?"

"I don't think so," I replied uncertainly. This was the first I'd heard about a UFO.

The girl fidgeted with her bangs, which she'd bleached an unnatural shade of blonde, all the better to contrast with her dark eyebrows and even darker eyeliner. A wave of guilt passed over her wide, round, moon-like face.

Ambrosia Abernathy was new to magic, but she was naturally powerful, like me. We looked nothing alike, physically, but the coven teased us both by calling her New Zara.

Since our powers were similar, she'd been getting mentored by yours truly. It would have been hard for me *not to* give her guidance, since she was constantly underfoot inside my house. I did ask that she park her hearse around the corner so that my home, called the Red Witch House by everyone in the neighborhood, didn't become even more notorious.

Unlike the Riddle family, the Abernathys' family tree was not riddled with magic. Ambrosia's parents were, in their daughter's words, "aggressively normal." They did run a funeral home, but other than that, they were as normal as Ambrosia claimed. Zoey absolutely loved spending time at the Abernathy home, which wasn't surprising. Zoey had always fetishized the idea of "normal" people. Weird kid.

I grabbed a bag of freshly ground beans from Dreamland Coffee, and put on a fresh pot.

The kid wasn't volunteering information, so I prompted her directly with a motherly question.

"Did you do something bad, Ambrosia?"

She chewed her lower lip.

I waited. Patience was a virtue when it came to teen confessions.

"I don't know," she finally spat out. "Yes. No. Maybe? I don't know."

She was fighting back tears. She was also rubbing the top of her arm.

"Start at the beginning," I said. "Once upon a time, Ambrosia did a bad thing. She didn't mean to, but..."

Her raccoon eyes widened, and the confession came out in a torrent. "I was just playing with him, honestly! We were playing fetch, and tug of war. Like you do with a puppy. Things got a little rough, but it was all in fun. I was only*pretending* to bite his tail." She squirmed and tugged at the sleeve of her shirt.

Tail? She wasn't talking about Perry Pressman's ghost.

"Show me," I said, pointing at her arm.

She slowly lifted her sleeve, revealing a large white bandage with a visible stain of blood. She peeled up the edge of the bandage to reveal a nasty-looking wound.

My mom instincts kicked in immediately. I jumped into action and applied first aid—the witch kind, with my healing powers.

The "puppy" she'd been teasing must have been RJ, or Ribbons Junior, the youngest member of the household. We'd all been warned by the little one's father that the tyke's bite could be unpleasant, like that of any baby animal, but the wound on Ambrosia's upper arm was much worse than the scratches left by kittens or puppies.

My magic flowed out of me, but it wasn't affecting the wound at all. I tried harder. Still nothing. Was I busted? Had someone dosed my soup at Lucky's Diner with witchbane? They couldn't have. I'd used levitation spells a few minutes earlier.

"Ouch," Ambrosia said as I poked at the wound.

"It's not healing," I said, mystified.

"Don't worry about it." She pulled away from my touch. "I just need a fresh bandage. And time? I've heard that time heals all wounds?" Her voice rose up at the end as it did whenever the teenaged witch got nervous, turning statements into questions.

"I don't like the look of that bite," I said. "Not one bit. We should call Zinnia, and see if she has a salve that can help it heal faster."

I heard my phone, which I'd forgotten to pull out of my purse and was now off hiding, buzzing with an incoming call. It had to be Zinnia and her psychic powers.

Ambrosia was already covering the wound with a fresh bandage. "We don't need to bug your aunt. I'll be okay? It's already looking better than it was last night?" She still sounded uncertain, but I couldn't tell if it was her baseline uncertainty or if she was worried about the wound.

"If you say so," I said, then, louder, "I guess we don't need anything from Zinnia right now."

My phone stopped buzzing.

"I'm sorry," Ambrosia said, her eyes welling with tears.

"You don't have to be sorry. You didn't do anything wrong. You were playing with a baby animal and it bit you. It could happen to anyone."

My words weren't working.

"I'm not mad at you," I said.

She sucked back a sob. Her lower lip was trembling.

"It's okay," I said, softer, and pulled her into a hug. Hugs were the original healing spells, usable by even the least magical of people.

Ambrosia felt tense, like a clothing mannequin in my arms.

I hugged her a little harder, until she softened.

"Nobody's mad at you for getting bitten by a baby monster," I said. "It's not like you did it on purpose."

She sniffed into my shoulder. "But when one witch is weakened, it hurts the whole coven."

My heart broke a little. Ah, to be sixteen, when everything felt like life and death.

"It's just a bite," I said, patting her back. *Zara tries not to gloat, but Zara is so glad she's not sixteen.*

"But it's not just a bite. I... I... I can't do magic."

I released her from the hug. I held her shoulders as I looked into her dark-rimmed eyes. "Are you serious?"

Her cheeks were streaked with black makeup, like a prom queen in a horror movie.

She nodded.

"Your magic is completely gone?" I asked. "How do you know?"

"I can't do anything. I've tried everything I can think of, but I can't cast spells. That's why I dropped the waffle. I mean, that's why it almost hit the floor."

"This is serious," I said. "That waffle was perfectly toasted."

"I can't even access the Witch Tongue." She sucked in a jagged breath. "It's like I'm in one of those nightmares, where you have to take a final exam for a class you didn't know you were taking."

I patted her on the shoulder. "You'll be fine," I lied. "Your powers will bounce right back when the wound heals. It's like how shifters can't get back into human form if they're badly injured. You're just stuck in this state of not having magic. It won't be forever." My lie turned into truth as I became more convinced by my logic. "If getting rid of witch powers were this easy, my mother wouldn't have had to die and come back as a vampire." I didn't know about Ambrosia, but I certainly felt reassured.

Her lower lip trembled. Her chin dimpled with a dozen indentations as she fought to keep control over her emotions. "I might as well be dead without my magic." She was not reassured.

I fought the urge to laugh out loud at her teenaged melodrama.

"Ambrosia, you lived for sixteen years without magic. You can make it another week or two until that nasty bite heals up."

Her chin stopped spasming and smoothed out. "Thanks," she said softly, the way someone does when they don't believe you at all and would rather you stop trying to be reassuring.

There was a tiny cough in the kitchen—a tiny cough that hadn't come from either of us.

We both turned to see Ribbons, our resident full-grown wyvern—perched on the kitchen island. He quietly pushed forward a lidded glass jar that held an ounce or two of something green. It had to be salve, or an ointment. It couldn't have been food, as Ribbons didn't share food. He immediately turned on his scaly heels and flitted out of the room as silently as he'd come in.

I opened the jar and sniffed. It smelled medicinal. I used magic to start applying the salve to Ambrosia's bite. I had no fear of Ribbons tricking me into using something harmful. If he'd wanted me harmed, he could kill me in my sleep whenever he wanted—a fact he mentioned from time to time.

Ambrosia's breathing slowed down as I applied the green cream.

She and I were standing very close together, and I became aware of the scent of her skin. She had a different smell than the rest of my family. Even when she stayed overnight, as she had the night before, sleeping in our sheets and showering in our bathroom with our soaps and shampoos, she still smelled different.

I took my time applying the cream. It had been a few years since I'd had to dress a scrape on my daughter's skin, and, while it had never been good to see my progeny injured, I did enjoy the role of nurturing caretaker.

Once Ambrosia was bandaged up and feeling more calm, she said, "You were saying something about a ghost?"

I'd almost forgotten about Perry Pressman. That morning's adventure in the changing room with his ex-wife felt like a distant memory.

Just then, Zoey entered the room, switching back to her human form as she did.

I told both of the girls about what had happened earlier that day. I used to keep things from Zoey, or at least try to, but she was old enough to handle most of what I dealt with.

After my story, Ambrosia said, "So, the ghost was an older man? That's not the one I saw a few days ago. It was a girl. A woman. Maybe twenty or so." Ambrosia scowled. "I should have done the acquisition spell right away when I was there with her! Now I've got this poisoned bite on my arm, and I can't do anything! I'm so stupid!"

Zoey and I exchanged a look. Ambrosia did overreact, compared to Zoey.

We both assured her that all was not lost, then I asked, "Did the young woman have long, black hair? And was she petite?" I was describing Jasmine and Perry's deceased daughter, Josephine.

"That's exactly how she looked," Ambrosia said. "I saw her at the convenience store, in the magazine section. I didn't know she was a ghost until she walked through some shelves on her way out." She slapped herself on the forehead. "I'm so stupid! I should have known she was a ghost. Duh!"

I pulled Ambrosia's hand away from her forehead. "At least you noticed something. Listen, I was hoping you'd help me cast some tandem spells to summon Perry's ghost for questioning, but I guess you can't, and that's okay. You've actually helped a lot, just by telling me what you saw. That other ghost sounds like his daughter, Josephine.

She was killed up at Castle Wyvern this summer. It was an accident. Someone was trying to assassinate," I gave my daughter an apologetic look before finishing, "Archer Caine."

Zoey gave me a concerned look. "Do you think this has something to do with Mr. Caine?" Mr. Caine was her father, but she had only met him recently and was more comfortable referring to him formally.

"Maybe," I said. "But keep in mind they're just ghosts. What can they really do?"

A moment passed as we all presumably imagined terrible things being done by ghosts, in spite of what I'd said.

Zoey said, "Are you sure the hairdresser is dead?" She was referring to Morganna Faire, former owner of the Beach Hair Shack. Morganna was also the genie Archer referred to as his sister, even though their relationship was much more complicated. The two supernaturals had regenerated endless times throughout history, in various family configurations. You may recognize their names as being similar to a notorious duo in the Arthurian legends. That was no coincidence. Same genies, different era.

"Morganna is gone. I saw her go splat all over the place," I said. "Her energy wasn't destroyed, but the hairdresser body she was in blew up, and there weren't any blanks around. If she's back, it's as a baby."

Zoey raised her eyebrows at me. "A baby wyvern?"

I pointed at her. "I like your out-of-the-box thinking, but I don't believe it works that way."

Ambrosia started to cry. "If I wasn't so stupid, we could get those two ghosts and ask them what they're doing."

"Cheer up," I said. "They might be here for something simple. Maybe Jasmine Pressman is about to have a sudden heart attack and pass over, guided by her family members."

And, on that cheerful thought, I grabbed a mug of coffee and excused myself to go do some research. I ran upstairs and grabbed a book from my nightstand, then headed back downstairs.

Thanks to Ambrosia, I had learned that there were now two returning ghosts in the mix. That had to add up to something, assuming I could find the correct equation.

When I reached the door that led to the basement, I found yet another ghost standing next to it. No surprise there. That ghost was an elderly lady, a former neighbor who'd come to stay with us, along with the budgie—still living—that she'd left to us in her will.

I nodded hello to her, and she responded with a smile as she turned the doorknob and opened the basement door for me.

Now, keep in mind, I was holding a mug of coffee in one hand and a reference book in the other. Since I had my hands full, her opening the door was simply a helpful, thoughtful gesture.

It was so ordinary, I almost didn't catch on to what had happened.

However, I did notice a few seconds later, and it sent a chill of foreboding down my spine.

Ghosts didn't move objects in the regular world.

Well, that's not entirely true. They could do a few creepy things, with extreme effort, such as write messages on steamy bathroom mirrors, but that was the exception to the rule.

My resident friendly ghost had casually opened the basement door for me as though breaking all the laws of physics had required no effort at all.

That was definitely out of the ordinary, even for Wisteria.

Now I had three ghosts who were up to something.

And no intern to do my grunt work.

On the plus side, I hadn't encountered any dead bodies or crime scenes. The ghosts had been harmless so far.

Perhaps the situation was more of an intellectual puzzle than a disaster in the waiting.

I headed down the stairs into the dark basement, where I did all my best research.

I was in a pretty good mood, now that I had a task to focus on.

Earlier, I'd probably been irritated by the girls lounging in their pajamas because, unlike them, I had a hard time relaxing. I preferred being kept busy, and I was still off work for a few more days.

These returning ghosts were a riddle, and I was intrigued by the challenge of solving it.

I settled on the wooden chair at my rough-hewn desk, lit some candles, and opened the first book.

CHAPTER 4

Time flies when you're down in your cozy basement, elbow deep in magical tomes.

One strange thing about my basement—besides the fact that it had magically appeared one day all on its own —was that clocks didn't work down there.

Eventually, I got hungry enough to head back upstairs.

Minerva Pinkman, my resident ghost, was standing at the top of the stairs ready to open the door for me.

"I see you've picked up a new trick," I said to the kindly elderly woman.

She glanced around, avoiding eye contact.

"What's next? Are you going to start talking, too?"

She gave me a startled look, and then faded away to nothing.

"Come back," I said. "I'm not mad at you. I'm just curious."

I was alone at the top of the rickety wooden steps.

"Mrs. Pinkman? Minerva?"

There was a creak behind me, like another door opening.

That was odd.

We didn't have any doors down there. The basement was completely sunk in the ground.

I turned around and headed back downstairs, investigating.

Sure enough, there was another door down there. I swore it was new, but, as with most of the renovations my magical house did, the door had the weathered appearance of having been there for a hundred years.

I grabbed the brass handle and turned it. No lock.

What lay beyond the door? I knew there were secret tunnels underneath the town. Was this one of the access points? Was I about to step into a labyrinth of ancient sewer tunnels? A network of secret underground subway trains? Another world entirely?

The door opened to reveal a wall of red bricks.

There was a creaking of old wood overhead, as though the house was laughing at me.

"Ha ha," I said. "You really had me going."

I poked at the brick wall. It was cool and solid. I knocked on it.

"Hello? Minerva? Did you go through here? Is this a game we're playing?"

She didn't reappear.

The house creaked again. Thick, gray cobwebs and dust rained down on me from the shadows.

"Not funny," I said, coughing as I kicked the brick wall.

This gesture, unsurprisingly, only punished me and my big toe.

I closed the door over the brick wall, doubled back to my desk to grab my empty coffee mug, and ran up the stairs again.

With no ghost to open the door, I had to fling it open myself.

My mother, who must not have heard the door opening or my footsteps on the stairs, let out an undignified shriek when I stepped into the kitchen, cursing and batting away the cobwebs that clung to my face and hair.

"It's just me," I said. "Don't get your broomstick in a knot."

My mother, the vampire, also known as Zirconia Cristata Riddle, clutched her chest and leaned against the kitchen island as though she might faint dead away.

"Zarabella! What are you doing here?"

"I live here."

"I know, but..." She adjusted the top of her dress. She wasn't wearing her usual wardrobe of a white blouse with tan slacks. She was dressed in a French Maid uniform, a black dress with a frilly white apron. I had one just like it in my closet. Or I *had*, until my mother had apparently borrowed it without asking. I'd told her she could borrow anything she needed, but I hadn't expected she'd take me up on it.

"Mother, what are you up to?"

"Cleaning." She waved a feather duster.

"Great." I leaned forward. "Use that thing to get the rest of these cobwebs off me."

She wrinkled her nose. "I don't want to get the feathers dirty."

I figured out what she was up to. It did not take a DWM weapons engineer to figure out what was going on.

"Where *is* Nick?" I asked. "Is he upstairs in the guest bedroom?"

"He's in the living room," she said. "Don't go in there. He's a little... tied up."

I shot her my most disapproving look.

"Oh, Mother," I said.

"I thought you'd gone out for the evening," she said. "Zoey and the other one went to the funeral home to cremate some pizzas."

I didn't bat an eyelash at that. The girls had been joking lately about using the Abernathys' crematorium to fire homemade thin-crust pizzas. They had not actually done so, as far as I knew. I hoped.

My mother hid the feather duster behind her back. "I thought I had the house to myself for the evening, for a change."

"So you decided to make the most of it," I said flatly. "Since normally there are tons of people and pets parading in and out of here like they all pay rent."

"Yes," she said, not picking up at all on my sarcasm. "I wanted to make the most of the peace and quiet. The holidays have been so hectic."

Nick called from the living room, "Hello? Santa Claus is missing his number one elf. This crackling fire is going to waste!"

My mother said, "I'll just clear our things out of the living room and head upstairs. Give me a minute."

"Don't rush on my account," I said. "In fact, don't bother. I'll go to my room, and I'd rather be a full floor away from Santa and his number one elf."

Jingle bells rang in the other room.

"Hang on," I said. "Are you an elf, or a French maid? What's the continuity thread on this roleplaying situation?"

"I'm Santa's cleaning elf," she said.

"I should have known."

Nick called out, "Hello?"

"Go on," I said. "Don't keep Santa waiting. I'll close my eyes when I go past you for the stairs."

"Thank you for being so understanding." She daintily began to brush her feather duster on my shoulders.

I pulled away. "I don't want to know where that duster has been. Just go. Have fun."

She ran out to the living room.

While my mother was preparing to feed on her new blood bag, a buff zookeeper named Nick Lafleur, I threw some Christmas leftovers into the microwave, called for my purse and phone, then reviewed my text messages.

I wanted to send my friend Charlize a cheeky email about my mother getting her bells jingled, but I had a ton of recent messages.

According to the first dozen texts, there were various after-Christmas sales going on around town. These sales were all terribly urgent. Every one of them promised to blow my socks off. I really had to set up better filters.

There was also a message from my aunt. Zinnia had apparently spoken to the other witches about getting together to discuss the reappearing ghosts. The coven was having a meeting that evening. A meeting I was... I checked the time... already twenty minutes late for.

The microwave finished nuking my leftovers and beeped.

I left my turkey-cranberry burrito in the microwave and started to leave. I exited via the back door, so I'd avoid the situation in the living room.

Then I thought better of it, ran back, and grabbed the burrito.

My car, Foxy Pumpkin, didn't approve of people eating messy food inside it, but this was an emergency. I'd never eaten a turkey-cranberry burrito before, and I had to know what it tasted like.

The burrito was excellent.

I used magic to keep it floating in front of my mouth while I kept both hands on the steering wheel.

How did people without telekinesis ever get through the day?

I arrived downtown and turned onto the main street.

The coven meeting was being held in the usual place, the stockroom at the back of Maisy Nix's coffee shop, Dreamland Coffee.

Since the cafe was still open to the public at the front, I parked, slipped into the alley, and entered by the back door, using my magic to twist the locked handle from the inside.

I got the door open easily enough, but the doorway was blocked.

Doorways being blocked was a theme for the evening. First, there'd been the red brick wall in my basement, then the presumably X-rated Christmas tableau in my living room, and now this.

The brick wall in this doorway was Humphrey. Also known as Maisy Nix's komodo dragon.

He was in his human form, as a tall, handsome man, dressed in a red velvet tuxedo paired with a green bowtie. His outfit looked like the costume a person might dress their pet in for the holidays because Humphrey was Maisy's pet. The komodo dragon went for outings as a human whenever his owner, Maisy, needed a date. He was currently doing duty as a doorman.

"Humphrey," I said in a friendly tone, covering my shock. "I see Maisy's let you out of your cage again. Lucky boy."

Humphrey gave me a crooked but handsome smile. "We have met," he said in a deep, friendly voice. "You are the nosy one who keeps all the books. Your name is Zara." He shook my hand. "It is nice to see you again." Humphrey's human breath was as minty and appealing as his komodo dragon breath was putrid. I'd met him as a human for the first time at the town's Christmas tree lighting, during Ribbons Junior's initial reign of terror.

"Nice to see you, too," I said. "Is the, um, *book club meeting* already in progress?" I tried to peer around him but he was doing too good a job as a bouncer.

"Yes. You may enter," he said, stepping aside.

"Good boy," I said. "I'll see that Maisy gives you an extra treat."

"I like pickled herring," he said.

"I'll keep that in mind."

I rounded the corner, and found three witches from my coven sitting at a table. They must have gotten through the initial bickering at record speed. They were conducting some actual magic for a change. They chanted softly while glowing smoke swirled in a vortex above them.

I'd never witnessed a group spell from the outside like that.

Seeing it as an outsider gave me a spooky chill. Two witches were absent, but the three present formed a triad, which made for a strikingly cinematic image. All they needed to complete the scene were pointy hats.

"Hey, gang," I said. "Sorry I'm late, but—"

The magic smoke that had been swirling above the table pulsed into a ball and came at me.

I deflected, working on instinct, but not quite fast enough.

The fireball knocked me flying backward.

CHAPTER 5

Luckily for me, Humphrey was standing between my flying body and the concrete wall. He cushioned the impact. I heard something crack.

"Oof," Humphrey said.

I turned to check on him. "Are you okay? I didn't hit your nose with the back of my head, did I?"

He reached up and touched his nose, which was crooked and already swelling. "Ow." His nose started to bleed. He looked at the blood on his fingers. "Oh, no," he said. "I'm leaking."

I reached up to apply pressure and healing magic to his broken nose.

My hands tingled, as expected. I felt the energy leaving me and mending him. Even though the effort of healing him was draining on my energy, it felt good. After my failure earlier that day to fix Ambrosia's arm, it was a relief to be able to heal someone.

My happiness was dampened by the knowledge that my own stupidity had caused the injury in the first place. I shouldn't have interrupted a spell in progress. What had I been thinking? Nothing. That was the problem. I hadn't been thinking at all. I'd gotten so used to being a witch that I was failing to take basic precautions. Not that I would admit it in front of the coven.

Humphrey's nose bones knitted back together under my touch. The bleeding stopped.

"All better now," I said, pulling my hands away. "As good as new, and just as handsome."

He stared into my eyes. "Handsome?"

I stared back into his eyes. I'd been giving him the compliment as reassurance, but he really was quite attractive. I could see the appeal.

Suddenly, a streak of magic blasted over my shoulder. I ducked, and wheeled around to face my attacker. It was Maisy, of course. No surprise there. But the shot had been aimed at Humphrey.

The shifter komodo-human glowed brightly and then flashed out of existence, replaced by a komodo dragon dressed in a komodo-sized red velvet tuxedo. He flicked his tongue at my boots.

"Hey," I said to Maisy. "You didn't give me a chance to make sure his nose was straight."

"It looked straight enough," Maisy said. "I saw you two gazing into each other's eyes. There was no need for that. The last thing I want is for you to trauma bond with *my* man."

"Your man? You mean *your pet*."

"Whatever." She narrowed her dark eyes at me, like the true frenemy she was.

Maisy Nix and I had a complicated relationship. She'd spent some time at my house over Christmas, and had warmed up to me under my roof, but the cattiness had come right back. We kept having to start at square one, despite making progress time after time.

When it came to me and Maisy, my aunt had a theory that an ancient jinx was in place, cast by our ancestors to keep our family lines from forming too strong a bond. My interactions with her niece, Fatima, weren't quite as catty, but rarely ended well. One time, I'd taken Fatima on a fun excursion to a local watering hole, and she'd practically thrown me out of a moving vehicle.

Maisy was still glaring at me. She snarled, "Stop causing trouble, *Zara.*"

I didn't like the way she hit my name, like it was a dirty word.

I snarled right back. "You're the one who started it when you intentionally blasted me with that group fireball, *Maisy.*"

"No, Zara. You started it when you spoke outside the circle during the incantation."

"No, Maisy. You started it when you failed to remain aware of your surroundings during the incantation."

"No, Zara. You started it when you busted through the security system I set up at the door specifically to keep people out so we didn't have to waste vital energy maintaining awareness of our surroundings while casting the incantation."

"No, Maisy. You started it when—"

The other two witches who were still seated at the table hit both of us with a blast of energy. Not enough to throw us into the wall, but enough to snap us out of our infinite loop.

Maisy and I dropped our metaphorical swords and took seats around the table.

It was a small group, just four of us. Me, my aunt, Zinnia Riddle, plus Dreamland Coffee owner and komodo dragon dater Maisy Nix, plus her niece—who wasn't technically her niece but they were related somehow—Fatima Nix. Two generations from two family lines that may or may not have been jinxed against working together.

Margaret Mills wasn't there because she was off somewhere on a romantic post-Christmas getaway with her inventor boyfriend. I didn't know where she'd gone, but she was unreachable by phone.

Our newest and youngest, Ambrosia, wasn't there either. Since her magic wasn't working, she'd chosen to opt out of the meeting and stay at her house, where she was reportedly enjoying pizza with my daughter, and nursing her wyvern bite.

I turned to the friendliest face, my aunt's, and asked, "What did I miss? Did they figure out how to get you back to your regular size so you're not popping any more buttons?" I pointed to the bust line of her blouse, where she was revealing a colorful bra, thanks to a popped button. "That's cute, by the way. I like purple underwear."

Zinnia made a horrified sound and used a binding spell to close her blouse.

"She's regular size," Fatima said, speaking to me without looking directly at me, as she'd been doing lately.

"Thanks for the update," I said. "How was your Christmas, Fatima? We missed you at caroling night at my place."

Fatima kept staring at the center of my forehead as she dodged my question.

"She's regular height, anyway," Fatima said of Zinnia. "She probably ate too much at Christmas. In January, we see a lot of overweight pets at the vet clinic." Brightly, she added, "Dr. Katz brought in a new line of low-carb pet food. I hear it's very tasty."

I turned to my aunt. "What do you think of that? Do you want to switch over to low-carb pet food? I hear it's very tasty."

Zinnia's lips flattened in disapproval before she replied, "One would not have to ask what one has missed if one showed up on time. If one is to request a special meeting on one's own account, one ought to show more concern for punctuality."

"One was doing research in one's basement," I said formally, then, less formally, "There are no working clocks down there. It's like a casino."

"You need some of these," Maisy said, calling for something with a flick of her wrist. A pair of sand timers floated over and settled on the table. "You can have these, Zara," she said. "A late Christmas present."

"Thanks," I said, almost feeling bad for chewing her out a moment earlier. Almost.

"You didn't miss too much," Maisy said. "We couldn't summon those two ghosts that you and Ambrosia saw."

"That's too bad. But, stop me if I'm being stupid, how would you know whether or not the spell worked? None of you can see ghosts. That's why Zinnia couldn't see the little girl who was—" Zinnia kicked me under the table. Like any normal person, she didn't appreciate being reminded of her errors in judgment.

"Point taken," Maisy said coolly. "Let's try the summoning spell again, now that you're here. Try to focus on the spellwork and not your colorful commentary."

I rolled my eyes as I took her outstretched hand, and Fatima's. Zinnia was across from me, with her pointy-toed boots aimed at my shins. She had a spell for kicking or pinching that she wasn't shy about using, but she used the low-tech method when she could.

I settled my mind and got ready for the spell.

There were already a couple of items connected to the Pressman father and daughter on the table—a hairbrush and a book of sudoku puzzles that had been done in pencil so they could be erased and solved all over again. The puzzles had to belong to Perry, the cheapskate. His daughter had no problem spending money. Her hairbrush looked fancier than anything I'd ever had in my bathroom.

We tried summoning the Pressman ghosts using a spell that Zinnia and I had used on our own a couple of times. It would be stronger but also safer when cast by four.

Unfortunately, even though our spellwork was impeccable, nothing much happened. A couple of cobwebs shook loose from the ceiling, and Zinnia had the sudden urge to rush out and use the washroom, but we couldn't gather up a single ghost, let alone a pair.

Fatima said, "I bet it would have worked if Ambrosia was here."

"*Were* here," Maisy said. "If Ambrosia *were* here."

"Exactly," Fatima said, completely missing the grammar correction. "If she wasn't making pizzas."

I said, "Even if she *were* here, she wouldn't have been much use without her magic. Did she tell you why her magic isn't working?"

"We heard about the bite from *your* pet," Maisy said.

I looked up at the cobwebs that were still drifting down. "Who knew that such an adorable baby wyvern could be so much trouble?"

Maisy snorted. "Only everyone," she said. "Why do you think the females were hunted to extinction or driven off this plane?"

I stayed quiet and let her have her point. There wasn't much to be gained in arguing with Maisy Nix. Or anyone, really. Not that it always stopped me from trying.

Zinnia, who'd just returned from the washroom, said, "Speaking of red wyverns, the elevator at City Hall has been acting up. It's mostly affecting delivery drivers. They've been complaining about the elevator taking twenty minutes to go between floors, even though security footage shows they're only in the elevator a couple of minutes. Some of them are getting suspicious and talking loudly about it to anyone who'll listen."

"They shouldn't be so loud," I said. "Not if they don't want the Men in Black to wipe their minds."

Fatima gasped. "Is the Shadow Man who watches us sleep wiping minds now?"

"It was just a joke," I said.

Fatima let out a breath. "The Shadow Man is no joke."

Zinnia cleared her throat. "As I was saying, delays in the elevator might be nothing, but it could be a sign that the crack between worlds is opening again. The crack goes through both time and space, so irregularities can be varied."

Zinnia had been to the other world through the elevator, but I had not, and I had been intrigued ever since I'd heard about it.

I sat up straighter in my chair. "Really? You mean I might get the chance to see that other world? The one with the tiny people, and the sandworms?"

"Timewyrms," Zinnia said. "And don't be so excited. It's not Cancun. We don't go there for vacations. That world is the only thing insulating us from," she paused and swallowed audibly before finishing, "the Underworld."

Fatima said, "Just say Hell, Zinnia. Everyone knows it's Hell. When you call it the Underworld, you make it sound way too fun."

"That's it!" Maisy said, smacking her open palm on the table and making us all jump. "Those two ghosts have escaped from Hell. That's why they're roaming around."

"I don't think they were bad people," I said, shaking my head. "They were both the victims of violence, not the perpetrators. Sure, one time I witnessed Josephine Pressman leave a library book in an ice cream parlor, but she'd have to commit a lot more library crimes than that to deserve to go to Hell."

Maisy growled. She seemed reluctant to give up on her Hell theory. She jumped up and started gathering supplies from the metal shelving units around us while muttering about casting another spell.

Fatima pouted. "I'm tired, Aunt Maisy. I just want to go home and hear about my cat's day."

"That does sound good," I said in agreement, yawning.

Zinnia muttered about having some ingredients at home that needed drying at a specific time of night.

Not one of us dared get up.

Maisy finished gathering items and laid everything out on the table, then ran us through the syntax.

"We already tried opening a channel," Zinnia said in objection. "It didn't work."

"That one was spectral specific," Maisy said. "This one is different."

Fatima said, "Don't we need a spirit board and planchette?"

"Ouija boards are for kids," Maisy said with a scoff.

"Um." I raised my finger in objection.

Maisy shot me a dirty look. "You know what I mean."

We asked her to walk us through the spell one more time.

This channel-opening spell required eight corners, which was witch lingo for four witches with two hands each. Ironically, it had been a one-armed witch from Ancient Roman times who'd come up with the spell.

We took a short break during which Zinnia ran to the washroom again, then we got down to the spell.

We held hands once again, and cast the incantation that would connect us to any lines of communication that were currently running between parallel worlds. It was similar to picking up a landline telephone inside a house where someone was on a call.

As the spell kicked in, a telephone manifested in the middle of the table. It was a classic piece, a Western Electric model 500 telephone from the 1950s, in black.

The telephone began to ring.

I'd seen and heard a lot of spooky things in the last year, but something about that telephone sent a pang of foreboding right through me.

It rang again, filling the concrete-walled storage and utility room with the sound of a real hammer striking a real bell.

This was no smoke-powered illusion. The phone was real, and it was right there.

Fatima let go of my hand and reached tentatively for the handset.

We other three exchanged glances. Zinnia looked worried. Maisy looked excited. I couldn't see myself, but I felt both of those emotions at the same time.

Nobody stopped Fatima.

She picked up the handset and brought it to her ear.

"Hello?"

She pulled the speaker end of the handset away from her ear a few inches, and beckoned for us to all lean in. We already were, but we got even closer, bumping noses.

Again, Fatima said, "Hello?"

A voice on the other line, female and elderly, said, "Who's this?" I was reminded of Mrs. Krinkle, who'd met her fiery end back in the fall. Was it her? Were all the ghosts of the past year returning?

Fatima didn't state her name but said, "You're the one who called me."

"That's not true."

"My phone was ringing and I picked it up. I swear."

"Okay," the elderly female voice said. "Maybe that's true. Maybe I did call you."

Fatima said, "May I ask who's calling?"

"I'm not supposed to talk to strangers on the phone," the voice said.

Zinnia whispered for Fatima to ask the woman *where* she was.

The receiver must have picked up Zinnia's whisper, as the voice said, "Who was that just now? Who's there with you, young lady?"

"She's a friend," Fatima said. "A nice lady. She helps people."

"That's what they all say," the voice replied.

None of us spoke or moved.

Fatima said, "Are you okay? Do you need help? Is there anyone you'd like to get a message to?"

"How sweet of you to ask," the voice said, practically purring with pleasure. "There is something I'd like to say. Can you ask your friends to lean in nice and close?"

I leaned in even more, but not without making eye contact with Zinnia and flashing my eyes in warning. The voice had said *friends*, plural, not *friend*, singular. Zinnia flashed her eyes right back. She'd noticed as well.

The voice said, "Is everyone listening?"

"Yes," Fatima said. "Are you going to tell us your name?"

"No need," the voice said. "Thank you for inviting me to your secret coven meeting in the back room of Dreamland Coffee. I've always wanted to be included in your exclusive little group. Your coven."

Maisy grabbed the phone from Fatima and spat into the receiver, "Who is this? Answer me now!"

There was a cackle on the other end of the line.

The voice came out of the handset and broke free. It got louder as it filled the room, still laughing. The voice didn't sound like an elderly woman anymore. It didn't even sound human.

Maisy began gathering energy from the air and casting a spell I didn't recognize.

The laughter abruptly stopped, and the voice said, "See you soon! Ta ta, witches!"

Then the voice was gone, the sound replaced by dial tone, then a busy signal.

Maisy let the magic that had been pooling in her free hand drift away.

She made a startled sound and looked down at the handset she'd been holding.

It was turning into black goo. The handset melted and dribbled down between Maisy's fingers, puddling on the table. The cord and the base did the same thing. The black goo oozed outward, covering the entire table like a thick coat of black resin.

Across the room, Humphrey the komodo dragon made a distressed, frightened sound, and scratched at the door of his cage.

CHAPTER 6

Dear friend:

I hope you don't mind me breaking the fourth wall that's normally between us, but I have to make a confession. It's about the words I use.

If you've ever had a lawyer help you with a legal matter, you'll have seen first-hand how words can be used in two very different ways: to reveal the truth, or to obfuscate the truth.

I prefer to use words for good, for revealing the truth. In all of my entertaining and engaging stories thus far, I've endeavored for accuracy. One hundred percent accuracy. I take no pride in being one of those unreliable narrators who flat-out lies. Exaggerates? Maybe. Outright lies? No.

However, I must confess that I may have accidentally lied by omission. I haven't always told you *everything*, as in *every little thing*.

For example, there are some quirky costs to using magic. Specifically, whenever I use my healing powers to fix someone, I suffer a moderate case of constipation over the next few days. I've had to take the witch equivalent of Ex-Lax at least seventeen times in the past six months.

I'm sure that, judging by the *yuck* face you're making right now, you do understand why I've left that particular detail out of my tales.

I've omitted some other things as well.

I'm mentioning this to you now as a fair warning. At some point in the future, for reasons that will become clear after the fact, I *will* be obfuscating the truth about some events. Not right now, but later, probably long after you've forgotten about me giving you this warning. My hope is that you'll remember me mentioning it, and recall me asking for your forgiveness in advance. Please know that I'm only doing what's best for all of us.

Since we're on the topic, I should admit that I've been running sort of a long con this whole time. I've presented to you a much better version of Zara Riddle than the one who exists in reality. Your version of Zara is brave, and strong, and keeps a stiff upper lip, which is code for "doesn't cry in the shower."

This Zara is a glamor, an illusion.

The truth isn't quite as befitting a "strong female heroine."

On December thirtieth, following my meeting with the coven, I went home, locked myself in the bathroom, turned on the shower, slid down to the cold tile floor, curled up into the fetal position, and sobbed pitifully for seventeen minutes.

I might have cried for longer, except Boa was miffed about being locked out of the bathroom, and tried to dig her way in under the door. The sight of her furry white paws grasping around on the tiles, coupled with her plaintive mews on the other side of the door, broke me out of my pity party.

I opened the door and let her in to supervise me while I took a long, scalding-hot shower.

What was I upset about? Was it the fact that two ghosts I'd already dealt with were back in town? Was it the fact that earlier that day I'd nearly fireball-blasted an innocent woman inside a changing room simply because I'd gotten accustomed to being attacked at almost any hour of the day? Was my brain still rattled from when I'd flown backward into poor Humphrey's nose? Or had it been the unsettling sound of the voice over the black telephone, and how it had entered not just the room, but my entire body and mind, shattering the last shred of safety I clung to?

It was all of the above, and more.

Some days, my crazy life made sense. I could find comfort in my routine, my career, my friends and family. On good days, the things I meant to do didn't go as planned but they still generally worked out in the end. More often than not, I had an internal drive that never let up because my goals all seemed worthy of pursuit.

Other days, like those final days of the year, in the limbo between Christmas and the new year, nothing worked. On a bad day like that, one single event could completely throw me for a loop.

The lousy part about the bad days were how they messed with my mind, making me believe that the bad days were the *real* ones, and the good days, where I'd had purpose and motivation, had been an illusion.

On the worst days, I would become certain that the only times I had ever been delusional enough to experience relaxation was when I'd been blissfully ignorant of how truly awful everything was. On the worst days, I believed that the dumb jokes I constantly made were for my own benefit, to perpetually convince myself that I was okay, even when I was very much *not okay*.

Emotions can lie, and so can thoughts, but it's harder for thoughts, because they rely on logic.

My thoughts told me that the only evidence I needed that life was good was the fact that I was still in it. My thoughts reminded me that I had so much to be grateful for. There was my beautiful, resilient daughter. My handsome and brave boyfriend. The incredible house that was my refuge from the world. And my cat. Boa would be upset if I left her out, and the truth was—full disclosure—I really loved that cat. Not as much as my daughter, but, even so, I would really hate to have to choose between them. I would always choose my non-feline kid, of course, but there would be a brief instant of hesitation.

I'll leave it at that.

A good night's sleep was always the best cure for a bad day, so I put myself to bed early.

Even as I drifted off, I was bothered by one idea. That day had been a rough one, to be sure, but I knew that life handed out more than one rough day at a time, and that the worst ones were still to come.

* * *

The next morning, I woke up feeling determined to throw off the gloom of the previous night, even if it killed me.

I sat up, stretched, and forced a big smile onto my face.

I'd slept in, so the winter sun had made it into my room before I'd even opened my eyes. That helped my mood. Boa was snuggled up next to me on my beloved patchwork quilt. I was her second-favorite snuggle buddy, the lucky one only when Zoey was away. I directed my forced smile at the cat. It was better to be second choice than third, and that was something to feel positive about.

The fluffy white cat stretched, made eye contact, and said, "Ham?"

I replied in a perky, upbeat tone, "For breakfast?"

"Ham."

"With eggs?"

"Ham."

"Over easy, or scrambled?"

"Ham."

The cat could speak, thanks to having ingested a magical messenger bird back in October, but she only said one word.

I asked in a very serious tone, "Should I get dressed, or are we doing brunch in casual attire, such as pajamas?"

"Ham."

"Ham does sound good, but what about smoked salmon with bagels and cream cheese? You like salmon. You like it almost as much as..."

"Ham."

Boa and I could go on like this for hours. I won't transcribe every bit of it. You get the idea.

FYI, in case you hadn't noticed, I wasn't feeling nearly as bleak as I'd been the night before. Sure, there were still ghosts and monsters lurking around every corner, but there were also good things, like fluffy cats, rare winter sunshine, lazy mornings, and ham.

I shuffled into a pair of bunny slippers and headed downstairs with Boa hot on my bunny-tail heels.

My mother hadn't emerged from her room yet—she was probably recovering from the previous night's Santa Claus session with Nick—so she wasn't in the kitchen.

The resident wyvern family was either sleeping in late as usual, or keeping a low profile while the Ambrosia-bite thing blew over. It promised to be a quiet morning.

I fed Marzipants, our senior citizen budgie. He seemed happy enough in his cage by the living room window.

I returned to the kitchen and shared a quiet breakfast with Boa.

The budgie's deceased owner, Minerva Pinkman—no relation to the Pressman family, just a similar last name—wasn't around. I hadn't seen her since the previous night, when she'd opened the basement door for me so casually, then attempted to do it a second time before she'd gotten spooked. Where was she? Mrs. Pinkman had been making more daytime appearances lately, and I half expected her to apparate in the kitchen and start moving objects around like a poltergeist, but she didn't.

The quiet was unsettling.

I checked my messages. There was a sweet little note from my detective boyfriend, checking in a few hours earlier. He reported that his night shift was over, and he was hitting the hay over at his place.

I didn't like him working nights. It cut into our time together. But he was a vampire, with vampire needs, so I had to make allowances for what worked for him. He felt more alert and effective at his job during the darkest hours. That made sense to me. Everyone enjoys doing their job the most when they're in the right mood for it.

I wandered around the house and considered what I might do that day. There was a big Christmas tree in the living room that had to be dealt with. I could spend the day packing away all the decorations, including my precious collection of pine-tree-shaped vehicle air fresheners.

What could I do instead, to procrastinate?

I wondered what my aunt was doing.

My phone rang in the other room.

I ran to answer it.

Zinnia didn't even greet me before saying, "I can't find Annette's pen."

I said, "Are you phoning me, or am I phoning you?"

"Is that supposed to be a joke? About last night? If it is a joke, it's not very funny, Zara. I was up half the night with the heebie jeebies over that thing we made contact with."

I sighed. I had not been making a joke, let alone one about the entity we'd phoned, but it was fair enough for my aunt to have made that assumption.

"What pen?" I asked.

"Annette Scholem's pen. We all talked about it at the office, and we agreed to give it to Carrot and Archer as a wedding gift. It's what Annette would have wanted. I'm sure Carrot will make good use of it, given her particular skills. The pen should be with someone who can take care of it, so it doesn't fall into the wrong hands."

She was talking about the pen that her deceased coworker, Annette Scholem, had owned. Annette, whom I'd never met as she'd died before I arrived in town, had accidentally transferred magical energy into the pen. The energy was called animata.

Zinnia had shown me the pen a few months back to demonstrate animata powers, but she hadn't let me use it. If my memory was correct, it was just an ordinary-looking pen, which meant it could have easily been misplaced. The pen would glow under certain spells, though, so it shouldn't have been too hard for my aunt to locate. A glowing object would be easy enough to pluck from a drawer full of pens, but I guessed my aunt had already tried that trick.

"Oh, *that* pen," I said. "How did you lose it?"

"I didn't lose it, Zara. I just... don't know where it is." There was the sound of a refrigerator opening, and glass jars being moved around on a shelf.

"Do you think it's in the fridge?" I asked.

"No, but the ingredients for martinis are in here." There was more clinking, and she muttered to herself, "Are those olives, or green eyeballs?"

"I'll come over to your place and help you find the pen," I said. "Hold off on the martinis until I get there."

"Are you sure you have the time? It's the end of the old year. Energetically speaking, it's the right time to take down the Christmas decorations and give the whole house a good cleaning."

"Since when do I ever do things at the right time?"

She didn't respond.

Judging by the sound of jars clinking, she was still rummaging around in her fridge.

"Floopy doop," she said. "I'm all out of gin. And your gorgon friend drank all my tequila."

"It's too early for booze, Aunt Zinnia. I'll be over in a few minutes with some very strong grapefruit juice."

"Sounds great. Thank you so much for calling me," she said without a trace of sarcasm, and ended the call.

I grabbed the grapefruit juice and headed over to my aunt's house.

Hours later, we had searched my aunt's two-story home from top to bottom, with and without magic, and still hadn't found the pen.

"Floopy doop," she said again.

I picked up one of the non-magical pens we had located. "Why don't we charm another one?"

"It's not possible," she said. "Charms fade a hundred times faster than jinxes, which also fade eventually. Only animata is enduring. The spellcaster must pour some of their soul into the item."

"We can do that. I poured some of my soul into Archer Caine, didn't I? Of course I only did that so my daughter could get to know her father, and so his body wouldn't rot like a hot banana in a paper bag."

My aunt held her fingers to her mouth as she gagged. "Must you be so specific with your descriptions?"

"Yes."

She stared at me a moment, then snapped her fingers and called for her purse and mine.

"The office," she said, her hazel eyes suddenly brighter. "That's where the pen is. I remember now. I sensed that it wanted to be closer to Annette's residual energy, so I brought it to the office and hid it inside Xavier's desk, which used to be Annette's desk."

"I'm glad I could help," I said. "All's well that ends well." I dusted imaginary dirt from my hands. My aunt's house was much cleaner than mine, and dust was scared of settling on her furnishings.

Zinnia didn't speak. She appeared to be deep in thought.

I asked, "Was I supposed to get the couple a wedding gift? They said on the invitations that they didn't want any presents, and I took them at their word. Besides, I've already given them so much, especially Archer, with the daughter thing and the soul thing. Plus I loaned them my roll of packing tape when they moved in together, and they never brought it back."

Zinnia came out of her daze. "You can put your name on the pen along with the rest of the gang from the office," she said. "Come with me to pick it up right now, and you can sign the card." She started leading me toward her front door, holding my purse hostage.

"Why now? I can sign the card at the wedding tomorrow."

"Just come with me."

I held back, wary of her motivations. Zinnia was the kind of witch who, when dining out in a large group, went to the ladies' room by herself. She was extremely independent, and didn't mind doing things alone.

Zinnia frowned at me and stomped one boot impatiently. "Do I need to promise you food, like you're some sort of circus animal?"

"It wouldn't hurt. Why are you so keen to have me go with you to City Hall? Is this about the elevators? Your office is on the bottom floor, Zinnia. Stay away from the elevators if you're so worried about losing a few minutes."

She stared at me.

I stared at her.

Then she said, "Don't say it."

Oh, but I did. "You're being a real OCW." That meant Overly Cautious Witch, and it was usually an invitation to battle.

She huffed, "I am not."

"Are, too."

"You're right." She looked down, defeated. "A witch ought to admit when she's being overly cautious, and that's what I am. As your mentor, I apologize for letting you down."

I said, "A great mentor can admit when she's scared, can't she?"

Zinnia frowned. "I'm cautious, not scared."

I held up both hands. "Easy now."

She looked away and sighed. "Oh, Zara, I don't know what's come over me. Last night at the coven meeting..." Her face went through a bunch of expressions as though trying on emotions and rejecting them all. "That spell... The black telephone..." She lowered her voice to a whisper. "That *thing* on the other end."

"It scared you, too?" At the memory, I got goosebumps all over my arms. "I thought it was just me. When I got home last night, I took a scalding-hot shower, and I still had a chill in my bones."

"Did you dream?"

I shook my head. "Nothing that I remember. How about you?"

"I dreamed about the End of Days."

We stared at each other quietly. I didn't need to ask for specifics to start getting ideas about her dreams. My imagination was all too happy to conjure up images of death and destruction.

Zinnia shrugged it off with a single *tsk*. "One ought not read too much into dreams. We are at the tail end of the year, after all."

"So? What does that mean, besides feeling guilty about not having taken down your Christmas decorations?"

"Zara, sometimes the year itself has a problem accepting that it is over. There can be spasms, or death rattles. It's all to be expected, yet it can be unsettling for those of us who are sensitive."

I agreed, "Plus that phone call last night was freakier than a Stephen King novel."

She held her finger to her lips. "Shh. One ought not speak of entities whose awareness one does not wish to draw."

"Do you mean Stephen King?"

Zinnia scoffed. "Someone else. Someone whose name ought not be invoked."

"I thought that was just a rule for the devil."

She raised her eyebrows. "It is."

"Do you think it was Mr. Pointy Horns himself on the phone last night? Taking a break from poking people with his flaming pitchfork to take a phone call from us gals?"

"I don't know if it was someone quite that powerful on the line, but something *is* happening. I can feel it in every cell of my body. I feel like I'm being changed." She shook her head and laughed self-consciously. "I really am being such an OCW. Listen to me carry on!" She waved a hand. "It's probably just menopause, like you said yesterday."

With a shake of her head, she headed toward the front door.

I joined her, and we stepped out of the house and locked up.

On the porch, I said, in a confidential tone, "From what I've heard, most women would prefer a visit from the devil himself to menopause."

She managed to crack a smile.

We got into my car, since it was still warm, and drove over to City Hall.

We entered the building, which I'd expected to be quiet, only to find the lobby teeming with people and cheer.

CHAPTER 7

City Hall was bustling. The lobby was full of people having a party.

Of all the places to find a busy New Year's Eve party, I would not have guessed the municipal building's entrance would be on the list.

Stranger still, the dress code was extremely casual. I didn't see a single glittering dress or dapper suit.

At the center of the lobby was a gleaming white baby grand piano. A man was playing Christmas songs while people—mostly cleaning staff, judging by the uniforms—gathered around the piano and sang.

Zinnia took my elbow and explained to me, "This is not a planned party, but it does happen every year. The piano is from the mayor's office. It gets brought down at the end of the year to be picked up for annual maintenance. It's in the lobby for a few days, and there's usually a spontaneous party or two. The turnout is much, much higher than we ever get for formally planned events."

"I'm familiar with the phenomenon," I said. "The same thing used to happen at my old apartment building. We even had a piano one year, but not a baby grand."

We turned away from the scene, and nearly ran over a short, dark-haired woman.

It was Jasmine Pressman. Was she there alone, or had she brought her deceased family members?

"Zara," she exclaimed.

"Hello again," I said as I scanned the vicinity for ghosts. None jumped out at me.

Zinnia didn't say anything, but she did squeeze my elbow hard, just in case I hadn't noticed we were talking to the person connected to the returning ghosts.

Jasmine's cheeks were flushed, and her brow was sweaty, as though she'd just experienced something stressful. There were, however, no signs of her ex-husband or daughter with us in the lobby. There were plenty of people celebrating, singing, and drinking eggnog, but no ghosts.

"Busy place," Jasmine said, answering a question I hadn't posed. "I only came down here to drop off some paperwork for a dog permit, on behalf of my neighbor. She's ninety-five, and she doesn't like going outside if there's a chance the sidewalks will be icy. I do a few errands for her. This and that, here and there. I don't mind."

Zinnia said, "The permit department is closed today. Would you like me to take the paperwork for you? I work there, and I'm headed in to pick something up right now." Zinnia held out her hand.

"No need," Jasmine said, clutching both hands to her chest. "I slipped the envelope under the door." She turned away from us, and practically ran for the exit. "See you tomorrow, at the wedding," she called back, barely audible over the Christmas carolers.

After she was gone, my aunt said, "I thought you were going to do something." She sounded disappointed.

"Like use the bluffing spell that I'm not supposed to use unless it's absolutely necessary and a life-or-death emergency? At least according to Fatima, that tattle-tale?

I guess I could have used that on Jasmine, but I was trying to show some restraint."

"Why start now?"

"You're even better at the bluffing spell than I am, and I didn't hear you jumping in."

"Maybe we can try it on her tomorrow, at the wedding," Zinnia said. "Though I can't imagine she has much to tell us that we don't already know." She glanced around. "Can you see either of them?"

"No," I reported.

We left the party, and made our way down the hallway to the Wisteria Permits Department.

We opened the door to the office. There was an envelope on the floor. It was sealed, but I had a spell for that. I opened the envelope with an unlicking spell, and checked inside. It was a permit application for Mrs. Pressman's neighbor.

Then, since I was in a snooping mood, I opened the door to the office supply closet. Oh, how I loved being around tidy stacks of office supplies! I checked out the colored paper clips while Zinnia retrieved the magical pen from inside Xavier's desk.

"Got it," she called over to me, and then, "Oh, dear. Zara, come and take a look at this."

I tore myself away from the colorful office supplies and joined my aunt at her coworker's desk. She was looking at paperwork.

"What am I looking at?" I asked.

"This is a 5C8027 Form," she said, picking up a sheet of paper and shaking it.

"I see," I said, even though I did not see what the relevance was.

"It's for explosives," she said, shaking the page again. "Some construction company is trying to use a 5C8027 Form to import hazardous materials!"

"As opposed to...?"

"As opposed to using a 4Z8028 Form," she said impatiently. "Which would bring it through my department, the Division of Special Buildings, instead of just across Xavier's desk."

"So? Is he not competent enough to handle it? He's a bright young man, and a fast learner. Of course the boy *is* awfully eager to throw his non-magical body into dangerous situations, but I like his spirit."

Zinnia wrinkled her nose and set down the paper with a sigh. "I suppose Xavier Batista can handle this requisition on his own, even if the applicant did use the incorrect form."

Her tone told me she was trying to convince herself more than me.

I replied, "Do you need to get on your computer and do some work? I can kill time in your supply closet. You folks have some no-name sticky notes I'd like to test the application powers of."

Zinnia swayed from side to side before saying, "No. We ought to get going. I do have what we came for." She waved the pen, which didn't give away any signs of being a magical item, then she took another look at the 5C8027 Form. "It is an awful lot of explosives, but I'm sure Xavier will cross-check everything. Plus I can always follow up next week."

"Do you want to write yourself a note?"

She sniffed. "Are you implying there's something wrong with my memory?"

"You're the one who lost your friend's magical pen."

"It wasn't lost at all." She waved the pen at me before tucking it in her purse and pushing me toward the door.

"You mentioned a card," I said.

She frowned and ran back to grab a wedding card from Xavier's desk. I added my name as well as my mother's and Zoey's, then re-sealed the envelope.

We left the office and locked up.

The hallway leading to the fire exit was wet from a recent mopping, so we had to leave via the busy lobby.

On our way through, Zinnia bumped into some more people she knew. They were in a chatty mood, so she introduced me, and we made small talk about the holidays.

A few sugar cookies found their way to us, followed by chocolates and miniature fruits made of marzipan.

As we stood and chatted, even more people greeted Zinnia. A couple of them dragged her over to a makeshift stage, where someone was setting up a karaoke station.

We ended up hanging out in the City Hall lobby, laughing, eating, and singing a mix of classic carols and pop songs from the 1970s.

Midnight came, with its countdown and revelry. Time was flying. So much for my quiet night at home in bed to ring in the new year. This was much better.

After a stressful couple of days, it was exactly the sort of fun and frivolity that the doctor would have called for, if we'd had the good fortune to know a doctor who prescribed spontaneous parties.

As Zinnia took the microphone and prepared to sing a country-western hit song popularized by Dolly Parton, the patron saint of busty witches everywhere, she met my gaze across the crowd and winked at me. Our simple errand had turned into an adventure. The good kind.

I leaned back against the makeshift bar, where a bartender was serving non-alcoholic versions of fancy drinks. We were inside City Hall without a liquor permit, after all. As I leaned there, sipping my Shirley Temple, I felt something magical lighting up my heart.

It was the magical thing that lights up everyone's hearts when they're at a noisy party where everyone's trying to talk at the same time, and nobody cares if anyone's actually listening because they're so happy to just be outside of the house, around other people, somewhere besides work.

It was joy.
That night was about joy.
The pain would come the next day.

CHAPTER 8

New Year's Day

The Wedding of Carrot Greyson and Archer Caine

I slipped on my bunny slippers and attempted to leave my shrunken bedroom.

I didn't get out, because I sleepily walked into the spot where my door used to be.

"Not again," I groaned, and I kicked the baseboard where the door should have been. "What are you up to now, you crazy, plaster-brained monster?"

A new, smaller door appeared in the middle of the wall.

"Is this how it's going to be?" I demanded of the empty room. "Do I need to ask your permission to get a door out of my bedroom? I'm thirty-three. I'm an adult. Sort of."

The door shrank ten percent.

"You're mad at me," I said. "Is this because I kicked that bricked-in basement door yesterday?"

The door shrank another ten percent.

"I'm sorry," I said.

The house could tell I didn't mean it one bit, and it shrank the door another ten percent.

I had to try harder if I wanted to leave my bedroom sometime that year.

"I'm sorry I kicked you," I said. "Twice. It was wrong of me both times. I promise it won't happen again."

The door enlarged, getting just big enough for me to exit without having to get down on my knees.

I gave it a begrudging thank-you as I left my bedroom.

I padded down the hall to the large bedroom that my house had graciously provided for my mother, using space from my room and the linen closet.

The house was gorgeous from the outside, with its dazzling red siding, generous porch, gingerbread details, and triple lancet windows. The pretty exterior hid a magical personality that could be helpful at times, but with a warped sense of humor.

I had tried to house-train my house, so to speak, by limiting its changes, but any resistance on my part led to unwanted consequences, such as doorways being shrunk or removed entirely.

My mother and daughter were both in the large room, getting dressed for the wedding.

"Happy New Year," they said to me in unison.

My daughter would be in the wedding party as a bridesmaid, along with my aunt. I hadn't seen the dresses before, and they really were *something*. Bright orange. Puffy sleeves. Fitted corset. Layers of puffy skirts.

Zoey looked adorable, as always. I stifled a smirk as I imagined Zinnia at her house, getting into the same exuberant outfit.

"Cute," I said to my daughter. "That color sure is something. I guess you and the other bridesmaids will match Carrot's hair."

Zoey beamed. "This orange shouldn't work with my coloring, but I think it does." She leaned in and admired herself in the round mirror above the room's dressing vanity. "This shade highlights my freckles."

My raven-haired mother, who stood behind my daughter, said to me knowingly, "Freckles are trendy right now with the teens. The kids at Zoey's high school are all using filters on their phones to add freckles."

I said to her, "Speaking of which, where are your freckles?" My mother's freckles had never been prominent, but they'd completely disappeared since she'd faked her death and come back as a vampire. She'd also been coloring her red hair black. She was a redhead in denial.

My mother gave me a look as blank as her pale, unfreckled cheeks.

I wasn't ready to let it go, so I said, "If they're so trendy now, maybe you could get your freckles back from wherever they went. Hey, when that elf doctor resurrected you, did you have to pack your bags so fast that you accidentally left your freckles back in Hell?"

She didn't even blink. "Zarabella, you know I'm not one for trends. I prefer a classic, timeless look." She turned and struck a pose. For casual wear, my mother preferred a boring uniform of sleek trousers, tan or brown, paired with plain cream or white blouses, either crisp cotton, with the collars starched to razor-sharp points, or soft, flowing silk. That morning, she had traded her usual bland look for a simple navy-colored dress with cap sleeves. The dress hugged her thin frame, ending at a flattering spot just below her knees.

"You look cute," I said. "Not as cute as you were the other night, in the French maid costume, but cute, all the same."

Zoey said, "What?"

"I'll tell you some other time," I said.

My mother gave me a pained look.

I smiled and said, "But seriously, that blue looks good on you, Mother."

"It's *navy*, dear."

"That's what I said."

"You said blue. This is navy. There's a difference."

I hadn't had a single drop of coffee yet, so I decided to let the blue-navy conversation point be shelved for later. Arguing with my mother was like arguing with my house. Pointless, and liable to backfire.

My mother, satisfied that I'd been set straight on my colors, went back to doing what she'd been occupied with when I'd entered the room, which was fussing over Zoey's hair.

My daughter's thick, red hair was rolled into tight ringlets that would have been horrifying to the style-conscious teen if she'd been wearing anything other than a puffy bridesmaid dress.

I left them to it, went downstairs, had some coffee and breakfast, and then came upstairs to shower and get ready. My closet agreed with my choice, and offered me the vintage turquoise dress I'd picked up at Mia's.

The wedding would be happening soon.

Carrot and Archer were to be wed at a mid-day ceremony at Castle Wyvern, the castle and resort that was one town up the coast. The service would be followed by a luncheon. It was the sort of casual, daytime wedding one would expect for an older couple, perhaps on their second or third marriages. Carrot had only just turned twenty-six, and it was her first marriage, but Archer had been married countless times during his many reincarnations, so it sort of balanced out.

When Archer had reappeared in my life, I'd been attracted to him. I'd even had a fantasy of getting back together with him, for our daughter's benefit, but none of those feelings remained. I was genuinely happy for him that he was getting married to someone else. I hoped things worked out for the new couple. Carrot was interested in having children, so my daughter might get a half-sibling or two out of the deal.

I was working on my makeup, applying my eyeliner extra thick, when the doorbell rang.

My daughter ran down the hallway and stairs, yelling, "Doorbell!"

A moment later, she yelled back up the stairs, "Come quick! We've got a limousine! There's a limousine here to take us to the wedding! A big one!"

My mother ran downstairs and actually joined in the excitement, much to my surprise. I heard her, the woman who boasted about her luxury travels, gushing about the size of the limo, and giggling like a teenager with my daughter.

I smiled at my reflection in the mirror.

Yes, there was a fancy limousine at our front door. I was anything but surprised because I'd arranged for it myself. I'd gotten the idea the night before, at the City Hall lobby party, when one of the elevator repairmen had mentioned he also ran a limo business.

By the sounds of the squealing downstairs, my limo splurge was a huge hit.

I took that as a sign that my new year was off to a great start.

I hoped the mid-day wedding would go just as well.

I finished getting ready.

All three of us climbed into the back of the roomy limousine, and left to pick up my aunt. It smelled strongly of hairspray and perfume in the limo.

We rolled up to my aunt's house. The nice man who was driving us stepped out to go knock on her door.

"I hope she's still coming," Zoey said, chewing the tip of her orange-lacquered thumbnail.

"Why wouldn't she come?" I asked. "Is this about the dress?"

"The seamstress did let it out a little," Zoey said. "But she's just a regular seamstress. No magic."

My mother gleefully rubbed her pale, bony hands together. "Zolandra, is her gown exactly the same as your dress?"

"Exactly the same," Zoey said.

My mother cackled. "Oh, I can't wait to see this."

"If the dress doesn't fit, she can wear the backup one I picked up," I said. "Carrot will understand."

My mother replied, "Where's the fun in that?"

Just then, the door to my aunt's house opened. Zinnia stepped out, wearing a trenchcoat that couldn't hide the orange dress, or her discomfort.

My mother leaned over and whispered to me, "This wedding can't happen soon enough. One more day and my sister would have needed a shoehorn to get into that dress."

"Go easy on her," I said.

"Why?"

"I don't know," I said, genuinely mystified as to why I was always having this conversation with my mother. You'd think a former witch turned vampire would have more awareness of the difference between good and evil. Flummoxed, I said, "Maybe because it's the nice thing to do? Because she's your sister? Your *only* sister?"

"You're right," my mother said. "Thank you for the reminder. I'll talk to my sister about her weight as soon as possible. It's the nicest thing to do."

My daughter said, "Gigi, be nice to Auntie Z."

"I always am," my mother said. "Can I help it if she's always picking fights with me? She had a crush on your grandfather back in the day. Did you know that? She wanted Rhys to herself. I'm so glad he was never interested."

"They'd make a nice couple," Zoey said. "Pawpaw and Auntie Z."

"Pawpaw and Auntie Z," my mother mused. "That sounds like some sort of musical act your generation would listen to." She looked out the window. "Shh. Here she comes."

Zinnia paused outside the limo as she fought to get the top of her bosom settled back down inside the tight-fitting corset. While the dress had been let out somewhat, the seamstress wasn't a miracle worker. There was only so much fabric to go around if one didn't use magic.

At my aunt's age, she really should have been a maid of honor. It was funny but sweet of Carrot to insist that Zinnia play the role of bridesmaid at least once in her life.

The driver opened the door for her, and my aunt slid in.

"Oh, dear," my mother said. "I can hear the strain on those stitches. Have you brought along a mending kit and orange thread?"

"It's fine," Zinnia said, staring straight ahead. "The whole thing has been reinforced with a binding spell." She lifted her chin. "And a double layer of Spanx."

"That doesn't sound comfortable," I said. "Are you sure you don't want me to..."

I trailed off under her gaze. She was giving me the look that said she'd prefer that I change the topic entirely.

"Nice weather for a wedding," I said. "Considering it's winter."

The driver rolled up the glass divider, and the limousine pulled away from Zinnia's house.

As we drove, my mother sniffed loudly. "Stop it, whoever's doing that," she said.

Zoey, Zinnia and I exchanged confused looks.

Zoey said, "Gigi, nobody's doing anything."

"I smell something," my mother said. "Something foul."

We all sniffed. Underneath the hairspray and perfume, there was a faint zoo-like odor inside the limousine.

My daughter, who had the best nose of everyone there, said, "I wasn't going to mention anything, but it seems to be coming from that armrest."

"This one?" My mother flipped up the armrest next to her.

Sitting in the hollow space was a very surprised squirrel.

He was big, gray, and bushy tailed. I wasn't an expert of squirrel identification, but he had a gleam in his eye. It was Petey, the squirrel who regularly made a nuisance of himself in town, mugging outdoor diners for their food.

Petey, who must have been dozing up until that point, suddenly found himself exposed, inside the back of a limousine, trapped with four women of impressive magical powers.

He did the logical thing and dove for cover. In a cave of sorts.

Petey ran straight up my mother's arm, and straight down her cleavage.

Bedlam ensued.

CHAPTER 9

While everyone else in the limousine screamed bloody blue murder, I performed my first ever squirrel-ectomy.

Thanks to some quick thinking and magic, I removed Petey from my mother's navy-blue dress. No squirrels were harmed in the process.

Some harm *was* done to one vampire, a couple of witches, and a fox shifter, but the squirrel scratches healed quickly, thanks to the magic on hand.

My aunt had brought plenty of handy compounds in her purse, which she used to mend the limo upholstery. She then calmly removed squirrel stains from all four dresses.

As for the squirrel, don't worry about him. We pulled the limousine over and left Petey at his favorite tree in town, with a selection of species-appropriate snacks. The snacks were angrily thrown at him by my mother, who had a powerful pitching arm, but Petey chittered happily all the same.

"I've got a bad feeling about today," my aunt said as we climbed back into the limousine.

"It's probably just the double layer of Spanx you're wearing," I said. "Anything that affects the digestive system also affects mood."

"I hope you're right," she said. "My internal organs do feel rather compressed."

"But you look cute," I said. "Like one of those Mandarin oranges you can only get at Christmas. Or a tangerine."

She rolled her eyes as she settled on the bench seat across from me, next to Zoey, where their puffy sleeves and layers of skirt commingled.

"Both of you are downright adorable," I said. "Honestly."

I used my phone to snap a photo of the lovely bridesmaids.

My mother, who was next to me on the other bench, said, "What about me? I'd like to be in a few family photos, for a change."

"Get in there," I said.

We spent the rest of the ride to Castle Wyvern taking silly pictures and having a nice time.

We arrived at the wedding venue right on schedule.

A crowd was milling around the parking area. I saw many of the town's local supernaturals, including several of my aunt's coworkers. They were all good friends with the bride, who used to work with them at City Hall, before she opened her tattoo shop and changed careers.

Dark-haired, stylish Dawna Jones from the Wisteria Permits Department ran up to me, teetering in her spike heels on the hard-packed snow. She held her open can of Diet Coke off to the side as she gave me a friendly hug.

"Ooh, girl, we need to have that coffee date soon," Dawna said. "I'm dying to show you some of my new card tricks."

Dawna was a cartomancer, or card mage. She'd expressed an interest in trying to divine my future using simple playing cards. The future wasn't so secret, she claimed. I'd been avoiding her for exactly that reason. Life was complicated enough without getting vague, ominous hints about my future.

"We'll catch up soon," I said to Dawna, hoping we wouldn't.

I greeted a few more acquaintances while edging toward the entrance. We Riddles had arrived on schedule, but we didn't have endless time to stand around outside in the cold.

Zoey and Zinnia ran off to attend to their bridesmaid duties. From behind, they looked identical.

My mother and I finished making small talk, and entered the castle.

We followed the signs and balloon decorations leading us to the wedding. Everything was bright orange, like Carrot's dyed hair.

I wished Bentley could have been there with me, but he'd been called in to work. He had promised to swing by later for some cake.

As we walked through the stone-walled hallways and ancient arches, my mother said, "Being here takes me back. Do you remember? Right upstairs is where I finally summoned the courage to make contact with you and Zoey again."

"That's not quite how I remember it. I believe *I* was the courageous one who knocked on *your* door. All you did was open it."

"But I knew it was you. I knew your knock. A mother knows."

"You didn't know to duck from my volley of lightning balls."

She scoffed instead of arguing.

We found the venue for the ceremony. It was a beautiful, brightly-lit atrium.

According to the brass sign at the entryway, the glass-walled space was a modern addition to the old castle, which had been brought over from Europe, stone by stone.

The atrium held a number of large potted trees as well as seating—folding wood chairs—for about a hundred people.

The bride's side was already packed full with Carrot Greyson's extended family.

Archer's side wasn't nearly as full. The genie was very, very old, but new to town.

My mother and I chatted with some of the overflow from Carrot's side as they came over to join us on the groom's side.

What a lovely day, and a great start to the new year. I couldn't stop smiling. The whole thing was exactly as lovely as a wedding ought to be.

I finally got to meet Carrot's cousins that I'd heard so much about. Jeremiah and Jebediah looked normal enough, except for the sock puppets they wore on their left hands—sock puppets they offered no explanation for.

The Greyson clan had a long history in the region. There were rumors of them being legendary monster hunters. One of their number, Carrot's older brother, had hunted the wrong beast, and had died tragically the previous summer. Most of the family's exchanges were about how nice it was to be meeting for a wedding and not a funeral.

I scanned the crowd for my neighbor, Arden Greyson. He would be bringing Jasmine Pressman, who might be bringing some ghosts. I didn't see him, but I couldn't see everyone from where I was seated.

My mother's current squeeze, Nick Lafleur, arrived and settled next to her. He had traded in his Santa costume for a tan-colored blazer over a very tight T-shirt that didn't hide his muscles. I'd seen him naked before—at the hospital, not in my living room—and the memories came back to me. I'd been meaning to look up a spell to make myself forget, because I didn't want to picture my mom's boy toy naked, but I hadn't gotten around to it.

My mother said to him, "Thank goodness you're here, Nick. I was attacked by a vicious creature on the way over."

He replied, "Was your daughter being mean to you as usual?"

"It was a squirrel," she said, pouting.

"That little devil! Squirrels have absolutely no respect for the rules," he said angrily. "We try to keep the freeloading vermin out of the zoo, but they can't stay away from the free food."

"The mangy thing tried to hide inside my dress. Right here." She angled forward and pointed to the crack at the top of her neckline.

Nick's anger over squirrels faded fast. "I'd crawl in there, too, if I could." He waggled his eyebrows.

She whispered in his ear.

He murmured something that made her giggle.

I was trying *so hard* not to hear their exchange, but I did catch a few words.

The two of them got to their feet and squeezed past me on their way to somewhere private.

I checked the time. It was still early. I spotted Dawna Jones making her way toward me, so I ducked my head, waited until the coast was clear, then got up and left my seat quickly. I would try again for a different seat closer to the back, where I could keep an eye on everything.

I was trying to be an optimist, but the incident with Petey in the limousine had demonstrated how quickly a celebration could turn to terror.

I worried that Zinnia's fears were a psychic warning that something dramatic might go down at the wedding.

Several agents from the Department of Water and Magic were in attendance as guests, and they were on high alert, eyes watchful and shoulders tense. Judging by the thick jackets several of them were wearing, they were well armed.

I was backing into a dark spot under a potted tree—all the better for surveillance—when I bumped into Charlize Wakeful. I should have known that such a great surveillance spot would already have been taken by another supernatural.

Charlize was a gorgon, and a good friend of mine and Zinnia's. She worked for the Department, but she wasn't a snob about it.

"Nice outfit," I said, looking her over. She was wearing a dress.

The pretty blonde wrinkled her nose. "It's a dress," she said.

"I can see that."

Charlize was a tomboyish computer programmer who usually wore one-piece silver jumpsuits. She'd broken her pattern and worn a pretty pink dress with blue flowers that reminded me of icing on a birthday cake. The dress had probably been borrowed from her sister, who was a baker.

Charlize grinned and whispered, "But don't worry about the dress. I may look defenseless, but I'm packing plenty of heat."

Charlize was referring to her gorgon powers. She could turn the living into stone and back again. She could also produce hot lava.

I asked, "Any juicy intel about local goings-on?"

She smirked. "I heard about your little phone call the other night. Silly witches."

"Who told you?"

"Margaret Mills."

"But she wasn't even there that night."

Charlize grinned. "I know. She's the best kind of snitch."

"Don't take advantage of poor Margaret. She worships you and your sister. It's not fair."

My friend winked at me. "All's fair in love and war."

"What do you know about the entity that was on the phone? Is it anything we should be worried about?"

"If you knew half the things that went on around here, you'd never sleep again."

"Thanks," I said flatly. "I feel very reassured. Hey, did you guys at the department ever consider that maybe there wouldn't be so many catastrophes around here if you didn't have a huge staff of supernaturals working in an underground storage facility holding half the world's magical relics?"

"We're the good guys," she said, then, looking around as she changed the subject to a lighter one, "When I get married, I'll have an open bar, and it will start serving before the ceremony."

"You're getting married? I didn't know you had a boyfriend."

Loudly, so she could be overheard, she said, "I'll marry one of these ushers right now, if one of them could bring me a shot of tequila." She narrowed her powerful blue eyes at a nearby young man. "You," she said, with ancient magic in her voice.

The usher she fixed in her crosshairs blushed and disappeared.

"That's one way of getting a drink," I said.

Charlize grinned. "In life, you have to ask for what you want. You can't stand around like a wallflower."

I took a step back and eyed my gorgon friend warily. It wasn't like her to dispense advice. She couldn't even keep the interior of her car from looking like a garbage dump.

"What about being on guard?" I asked. "You don't have to lie to me. I can tell that your agent buddies are on edge about something."

"Rumor has it something may be afoot."

"I knew it," I said. "Shouldn't you be sober, just in case?"

She shrugged. "Nothing's going to happen. Everyone's probably jumpy because the last time they were all together here at the castle, your aunt's demon tried to eat them. I'm sure this wedding will go off without a hitch."

"I hope you're right," I said. "But back to that voice on the phone. Do you happen to know who it was?"

"There are *many* entities on the other side of the boundaries of this world. I could give you a list, but there's not enough paper in existence. I'll tell you what. I'll make that list, if you go take roll call at the ocean. Ask the water droplets for their names."

"A simple *no* would have sufficed," I said.

The usher arrived with a tumbler of amber liquid.

Charlize said to him, "When do you want to get married?"

He let out a frightened squeak and ran off, leaving her laughing.

Another of her coworkers came over, so I excused myself and left them to their business.

I milled around the atrium, keeping an eye out for Jasmine or the ghosts, but I didn't see any of them.

"Psst," someone said. "Mom!"

It was my daughter, waving me over to a side exit.

I escaped the crowd and went to her. "What's up? Is everything going smoothly behind the scenes? I hope nobody's got cold feet, but if they do, I have warming spells." I rubbed my hands.

"I think something's wrong with Auntie Z. She fainted a few minutes ago. I caught her, and I took her over to a chair, but she could have fallen on the floor and hurt herself."

"It might be delayed shock from the Petey situation," I said. "Combined with that tight dress."

Zoey didn't look convinced. "What if she's going into another one of her dips?"

"Then we'll deal with that if it happens. Should I go back with you to check on her?"

"She wouldn't like that." Zoey looked down and shook her coiled ringlets. "She told me not to tell you. She only let me leave because I have to find a bottle of wine to settle Archer's nerves."

"There's wine? What about *my* nerves? I'll be sitting out here with your grandmother and her boy toy, who's young enough to date you—not that you're allowed to date someone in their twenties, but you know what I mean."

Zoey let my threat fly past her without comment. "I should get back," she said. "I'll tell Mr. Caine I couldn't find any wine."

Just then, an exterior door opened. A delivery man rolling a stack of wood crates entered the hallway. The crates were stamped with logos from a winery.

My daughter and I exchanged a look, and then worked as a team to distract the delivery man and swipe one bottle of wine.

After we'd sent him on his way, I looked down at the bottle in my daughter's hands and said, "Tell your father I'm so happy about this wedding."

A gruff voice behind me said, "Tell me yourself, you gorgeous redheaded vixen."

I turned to find Archer Caine standing behind me, looking more handsome than ever in a tuxedo.

"You clean up good," I said, which was an understatement.

He swiped the bottle from us and began unwrapping the top.

"Being here brings back memories," he said.

I felt my cheeks flush as I looked away. When I'd first met Archer in that body, I'd nearly been overcome with passion for him. I had been channeling a spirit with whom he'd been having a relationship.

"I also remember those memories," I said. "Being here makes it feel like it only happened yesterday."

"Oh, right. That." He looked down at me, his eyes twinkling. "I was speaking about the days when these stones were somewhere else, but I remember that recent time, too. It was nice for me to get to experience that sensual, feminine side of you." He lifted his chin. "But it's too late now. You had your chance, Zara. I'm afraid I'm spoken for." He twisted off the cap of the wine bottle and looked down at it in his palm. "Amazing things, these twist-off caps. What will they think of next?" He offered me the bottle.

"I'll wait," I said.

"Why wait? Life is short." He lifted the bottle to his lips and took a swallow. "Interesting," he said, then he took another swig. "This tastes like..."

He didn't finish the sentence.

He dropped the wine bottle. It crashed to the stone floor and shattered, spraying red wine everywhere.

My first thought was about Zoey's bridesmaid dress. It had survived the limousine ride, only to get soaked at the very last minute with red wine.

My second thought was that Archer's practical joke, in which he pretended to be choking to death, wasn't very funny at all.

My third thought was that red wine didn't normally sizzle when spilled, nor did it let off an acrid, smoky smell like burning electrical wires.

By the time the groom-to-be collapsed to the floor, I'd figured out what was happening.

There had been something toxic in the wine, and Archer was in trouble.

I came toward him, but he used his foot to push me away.

"Don't," he croaked. "You can't save me, Zara."

"Not if you won't let me." I tried to get closer, but he kicked me away again, hard enough to knock me on my butt several feet away.

I watched in shock as he pulled Zoey's ear to his mouth and whispered something to her. She closed her eyes and clenched her jaw as a single tear dripped down her cheek.

By the time I got up again and was close enough to the genie to put my hands on him, he was gone.

Dead.

"Stand back," I said to my daughter.

I unbuttoned his shirt so I could place my hands directly on his chest.

"Mom." She took my arm and tried to pull me back.

"Stand back," I said.

"Mom." She grabbed my arm and yanked me free of him just in time. The poison burst up, through his chest, like a geyser. When it came back down, his whole body collapsed in on itself, as though it had never been anything more than liquid.

The dark fluids trickled out through an empty tuxedo and pooled briefly, mixing with the wine, before seeping away, down between the cracks in the stone floor.

The liquid was gone without a trace.

Zoey's dress was unstained.

A man's tuxedo, clean and freshly pressed, lay on the floor before us. The crime scene was spotless and clean. Even the broken wine bottle was gone.

CHAPTER 10

A magical death doesn't feel like a real death.

It can feel like a trick. The work of a corny stage magician, sawing a beautiful lady in two.

Except Archer Caine wasn't anyone's lovely assistant in fishnet stockings.

And he hadn't been sawn in half.

He'd been... liquified.

And he wasn't coming back.

As the finality of his demise registered in my brain, I said to my daughter, "I'm so sorry."

I apologized, over and over, until she stopped me.

"You couldn't have known," Zoey said. "You couldn't have saved him. He told me it was his time, and that he'd known it would be soon."

I barely heard her.

I picked up one of the cufflinks that lay on the flat, neatly-pressed, empty tuxedo.

Did the cufflink contain his spirit?

If I twisted the gleaming chunk of metal just right, would Archer reappear as a puff of smoke? Genies did that sort of thing.

My daughter asked what I was doing, and I muttered an explanation that sounded crazy, even to my ears.

"He's gone," Zoey said, taking the cufflink from my hand.

I couldn't bear to look at her.

"It was the wine," she said.

"I should have taken a sip when he offered it to me," I said. "Why didn't I test the wine?"

Off in the distance, the old restored bell in the bell tower started to ring.

The bells.

I'd met up with Archer Caine in that bell tower. We had kissed at sunset. I had kissed him with those same lips that had just...

The wine.

Again.

Poisoned.

Like before.

But this time the poison hadn't killed an innocent human. This time, the poison had found its supernatural target.

My daughter said something else, but I didn't hear her.

I couldn't hear much. Even the loud chimes coming from the bell tower faded away.

I wasn't there anymore.

I was inside my own head, like a picture within a picture, within another picture, an infinite recursive image, screaming at myself for not testing the wine.

Why hadn't I at least given it a sniff? Witches had great instincts for detecting poisons. I could have stopped him. I could have saved him.

Why had I made the exact wrong choice?

Wasn't I supposed to be the one who saved people?

How could I be the one who stole a bottle of poisoned wine and then handed it to Archer Caine on his wedding day?

What kind of a person does that?

I don't know how long I spent screaming at myself in my head.

My daughter brought me out of it.

She held my shoulders, looked into my eyes, and said, "I've got to go. Are you going to be okay?"

Nothing made sense to me. Least of all her words.

I asked, "Why? Where are you going? You can't go. Not now."

"I think I should be the one who gives Carrot Greyson the bad news."

Carrot Greyson. The bride. The *widow*. It all started making a bit more sense. My daughter wasn't really leaving me. Not forever. Just for long enough to talk to Carrot. To break the news.

"That's not part of your bridesmaid duties," I said.

"Mom, don't make jokes."

"I'm not," I said. "Sometimes when I'm being specific, I'm just being specific."

We both looked down at the empty tuxedo that was still stretched on the ground.

Archer Caine was gone. He was really gone. Again. There would be a hole in our lives, but not as big as the hole in Carrot Greyson's life.

"Mom, let me be the one to tell her," Zoey said. "She's going to remember this day for the rest of her life, and I think the news should come from someone else who loved him."

"You loved him?" I shook my head and muttered, "Of course you loved him. He was your father, and he cared about you. He loved you, Zoey. I know he did."

Zoey squeezed my arm. "Keep it together. It's going to be okay."

I pulled my arm away guiltily. "I'm the mom here. I should be the one reassuring you, not the other way around. It's not normal."

"Since when do we ever do things the normal way?" She forced a smile that broke my heart. It couldn't light up her sad face no matter how many teeth she showed.

"Normal is just a setting on the dishwasher. That's what you always say."

I fought back the tears that threatened to flood out. I gave her a hug.

"The wine," she said into my ear as we hugged.

"I'll take care of it."

"Mom?" We were still hugging. "I love you."

I squeezed her extra hard before letting her go.

She ran off down the hallway, her orange taffeta gown gathered up in her hands, her hard-soled kitten heels cracking on the stones. She looked like Cinderella fleeing the ball as the clock struck midnight. One of her shoes even fell off. She stopped to take off the other one, and ran away carrying them.

I got to work investigating the wine.

I'd grabbed a bottle at random, so it was possible the entire crate had been poisoned.

I found the kitchen, bluffed my way in as a food safety inspector, and cast some magical tests on the wine.

It was all poisoned.

Every single bottle.

Enough to kill hundreds of people.

A chill rippled through me as I imagined everyone at the wedding raising a glass for a toast at the luncheon, and then drinking poison. It would have been a blood bath.

There was a rustling of taffeta. Zinnia was by my side.

"I've alerted the authorities," she said in a hushed tone. "It helps that most of them were already here."

"Good job," I said.

"Margaret and Dawna are taking care of the phone tree as we speak."

"Great thinking," I said. "I didn't think to do that. My brain isn't working right. You'd think I'd never been in a horrible situation like this before, and yet it keeps happening. Why does this keep happening?"

She put a comforting arm over my shoulder. "You're doing the best you can."

"That doesn't change the fact I'm always a day late and a dollar short. How could I have let this happen? I'm the one who gave him the wine, Zinnia. I practically poured it down his throat. Did Zoey tell you he offered me the bottle first? Why didn't I take a sip? I could have—"

"You could have left that turquoise dress empty on the floor. You could have left behind your daughter. You could have left me, right when I need you the most."

I jerked my chin up and met her gaze. There was more worry in her hazel eyes than usual.

I stammered, "Y-you need me?"

"Riddle women are tougher than we look, but we are stronger together." She cleared her throat, glanced away, and said, "The guests are being notified as we speak. The Department will be holding everyone here so they can interview the staff and guests."

"Just like last time," I said.

She gave me a confused look. "Last time? This is nothing like the Halloween ball. That was so awful, and all my fault. I can't believe I was so stupid. I put so many people in danger." She held her breath and closed her eyes, as though that might help dispel the guilt she still felt.

I'd been referring to a different incident. My aunt hadn't been at Castle Wyvern for the last wine poisoning. She knew of the event, but it likely wasn't fresh in her mind, as she'd stayed with my daughter during the time I was locked in at the castle. I took a few minutes to refresh her on the details.

"I see. This current situation does bear some resemblance," she said, rubbing her thumb the way she did when she was feeling shaken. "It's almost as though someone is being framed. I wonder..."

She trailed off, staring into the distance.

The castle kitchen's head chef, whom I'd introduced myself to already, came over with two shot glasses containing amber liquid.

"Samples of our premium tequila, as requested," the chef said.

I gave Zinnia a please-forgive-me look. "It's probably safer than the wine," I said. "Plus I knew you'd come help me in the kitchen, and I thought it might settle our nerves."

"Perhaps I ought to join you," she said. "A shot of something to reduce my executive function has been on my mind lately. Perhaps it's what I need."

We double-checked the tequila for poison, then I tossed mine back. It was a high-quality variety, suitable for slow sipping, but I had work to do.

My aunt didn't drink hers. She paused with the glass against her lips, her brow furrowed, as though something had just occurred to her.

She handed me her glass and said, "I trust you won't let this go to waste."

I did not.

I shot back the tequila, licked my lips, and stared at my aunt as several puzzle pieces fell into place.

The task at hand, with the poisoned wine, took a back seat to another pressing matter.

What was going on with Zinnia?

First, there was her weight gain and increased appetite.

Second, she'd been scatterbrained, unaware of who had called whom on the phone, and even losing track of her friend's irreplaceable magic pen.

Third, she'd been physically nauseated by my use of a metaphor involving rotting fruit.

Fourth, she'd fainted on Zoey.

Fifth, she had just declined a perfectly reasonable medicinal shot of tequila.

There was one logical explanation.

"Aunt Zinnia," I said. "You're pregnant."

Her eyelashes fluttered. "What?"

"It's not menopause," I said. "You're pregnant."

As I spoke those magical words, the suffocating sense of doom I'd been feeling started to lift. Was there a little one on the way? This could be the ray of hope we all needed.

My aunt cast a sound bubble spell around us.

I'd already cast one, but it seemed my aunt was about to tell me something very, very secret.

CHAPTER 11

The bubble of privacy had been double cast.

I bounced on my toes impatiently as I waited for Zinnia to tell me whether or not she was pregnant.

I wanted her to hurry up, but I also wanted to stretch out the moment forever. Unlike some of the other events of the day, this might be good news.

"Well?" I bounced some more. "Are you preggers with a little floopy doop or not?"

"I suppose it is *possible*," Zinnia said.

"Ooh," I said. "Nice. I like how you're drawing it out. This is a nice moment between us."

"I'm not drawing it out."

"Yes. You are. You're pretending it's all a big mystery."

"It is," she said.

I put my hands on my hips. "Like you don't already know."

"Zara, I don't know."

I rolled my eyes. "Come on. How do you not know? You're a witch. I'm pretty sure the very first spell created by the very first witch ever was to find out whether or not she was pregnant. When it comes to females throughout all of human history, I can't think of anything that could be more important than knowing *that*."

"There are certain detection spells, but I never learned them. Did you happen to pick some up?"

I let out a sharp laugh. "I don't need to. I've got the spells to *prevent* such things, and I stay away from wine coolers, so I don't *have to* know the spells for pregnancy detection." I paused and gasped as another piece of the puzzle fell into place. "Zinnia, when you say *it's possible*, that must mean you and some guy... Uh... Did you have...?" I couldn't say the word. Not to Zinnia.

She shot me a dark look. "That is generally how it happens."

I staggered backward, barely staying inside our sound bubble. "With whom?"

"It doesn't matter," she said. "Because I'm probably *not* pregnant. All of my symptoms can be explained by menopause." She waved her hands. "Or maybe it has something to do with," more hand waving, "what appears to be a nefarious plot to kill off the majority of the supernaturals in this town."

I gave her a skeptical look. "You think Phase One of this diabolical plan was to make you, Zinnia Riddle, too fat for your bridesmaid dress?"

She pressed her hands to her stomach. "It was that pie you made me eat at Lucky's Diner."

"Sure, it was," I said with an eye roll. "You're pregnant. What kind of floopy doop have you got in there? Is it a little shifter? Or did it happen when that guy came to see you after Halloween? Your ex from New York. What's-his-name. Mike Harrison!"

"Mitchell Harrington," Zinnia said, pressing her lips flat.

"Wow," I said. "That's going to be awkward. Do you think he'll leave New York and come here?"

"It's not him," she said.

"How do you know? The timing matches up."

She raised her eyebrows. "Mitchell Harrington stayed in a hotel."

"Sure, he did," I said, winking. "I bet you two ordered room service, didn't you?"

"Let's not get ahead of ourselves," she said. "We don't know yet that it isn't simply pie and ice cream."

"That's true. You have been eating more. Plus you are super old."

Her eyes flashed. "I'm only forty-eight!"

"For a few more days, then you'll be forty-nine, which is practically fifty. All the older celebrities who are having babies get pregnant using a team of doctors. Speaking of which, did that necromancer of your sister's do something to you?"

Zinnia scoffed. "It's not commonly known, but fertility can spike during the late forties."

"I have heard of that," I said. "The ovaries throw a big going-out-of-business sale."

"You *could* say that," she said, and then, "Of course *you* would say that." She tugged at the too-tight corset of her bridesmaid dress and heaved her growing bosom for a sigh. "Let's get to work so I can go home and change out of this thing and..." Sadness crossed her face. *And grieve for the loss of our friend*, I finished for her in my head.

I wasn't ready to deal with death and poison just yet.

"Aunt Zinnia, if you need more clothes, I have some of my old maternity wear in my closet. I didn't get big until the last month with Zoey, but I still have some jeans with an elastic panel in the front that I practically lived in back then."

"Work," she said sternly.

We got to work.

Our first task was getting rid of the poisoned wine.

Zinnia took a sample from a bottle for further testing, and then we poured the remainder down the drain. When it came to poisons that could destroy supernaturals as powerful as genies, the usual rules for maintaining a crime scene went out the window. Some things were too dangerous to be left lying around.

Both of us knew we'd get in trouble for discarding evidence, but, when it came to dealing with the Department of Water and Magic, we were the sort of witches who begged forgiveness rather than ask permission.

After taking care of the wine, Zinnia went to check on Carrot, and I returned to the atrium.

It wasn't a pretty sight.

The Greyson family, who'd been so happy to be attending a wedding instead of a funeral, were now a somber bunch. Few of them had gotten to know the groom-to-be during the couple's whirlwind romance, but all were saddened.

While DWM agents questioned the guests one by one, I worked my way through the crowd, chatting with people, using my bluffing magic to peel away any lies.

One of the people I'd been keeping an eye out for appeared across the crowd. Jasmine Pressman. The petite, older woman was holding onto Arden Greyson's arm—clinging to him, really—and both of them looked devastated by the news.

The official cover story for the non-magical attendees was that Archer Caine had suffered a heart attack, and had passed away before he could be taken to the hospital.

People were buying the story, though rumors were circulating that he'd been mixed up with drugs and might have overdosed by accident. It was a reasonable enough rumor, given how young and healthy Archer had appeared to be.

My aunt disappeared at one point, and returned later with flushed cheeks.

"Well?" I stared at her expectantly. "Did you take a test?"

"It's positive," she said.

"Congratulations!"

She shook her head. "Not that sort of test. I haven't been to the drugstore yet. Margaret is here, and we did a materials analysis on the wine sample. It tested positive for red wyvern venom."

"Oh, no," I said. "I'll talk to Ribbons right away. If that girlfriend of his is involved, I... I don't know what I'll do."

"This is exactly why there aren't any of them to be found in this world. I wouldn't be so quick to blame Ribbons. He has shown his loyalty, and I'd be shocked if he or his family was involved. The main way their venom gets over to this side is through illegal imports."

"Illegal imports," I said. There was one person in town who had a reputation for building deadly devices and importing poison. He was a repugnant little man, and not just because he was a gnome—I had nothing against gnomes.

My aunt and I stared into each other's hazel eyes, then said, together, "Griebel Gorman."

CHAPTER 12

Griebel Gorman had not been in attendance at the wedding.

But even if he had been there, and had raised a glass of poisoned wine during the toast, he would have been a person of interest.

The diminutive gnome was the person who'd supplied the red wyvern venom the last time someone had gotten killed at the castle by drinking poisoned wine.

After a short discussion with my aunt, I did the smart thing, and passed his name along to the DWM agents in charge of the investigation.

The agents were Rob and Knox, a pair of bird shifters who balanced out each other's strengths. Rob was the brains and Knox was the brawn.

Rob greeted me with a warm, "If it isn't Miss Snap Crackle Pop!"

"Ha ha," I said, as one must when being mocked by a friend.

The grin on Rob's face slid off. His heavy-lidded eyes looked sad. "Things sure took a turn today, huh?" He nodded at the huddled groups of people inside the atrium. "Not quite the event folks were expecting. I get the willies thinking about it. If all that wine had been served to the guests..."

His brawny coworker, Knox, said, "Someone would have noticed. Lots of people here have good noses." Knox had a deep baritone voice that enhanced the reassurance in his words.

"But not everyone," Rob said. "Not me. I blame my small nostrils. Plus I'm not patient at all when it comes to toasts. I would have taken a sip and been dead before the first speech."

"Like a canary," Knox said.

Rob's face twisted up. "What did you just call me?"

Knox, who didn't pick up on some subtleties, repeated himself plainly, "A canary."

"How dare you," Rob said, and he wasn't joking.

They were both bird shifters, so I guessed that Rob was taking Knox's comment about being a canary in the worst way possible. I'd never seen the two best friends have a true argument. This day was not going well. So much for the best start to a new year.

I had to put a stop to the misunderstanding. "Rob, Knox means you'd have been the canary in the coalmine. The proverbial first warning. Canaries are sensitive to gasses, so coal miners used them to detect dangerous conditions."

"Oh," Rob said. "That does sound familiar. I probably knew it at some point, before pop song lyrics pushed it out of my brain."

I got to my point. "Does the Department have Griebel Gorman in custody for questioning?"

"I'm not sure," Rob said. "Why?"

"He supplied the red wyvern venom the last time someone got poisoned here. Seems pretty obvious to me that he might be involved again."

Rob swished his mouth from side to side. "Maybe *too* obvious, if you know what I mean."

Knox said, "I like obvious."

"When you pick him up for questioning, be careful," I said. "He's got those spikes in his clothes, plus he teleports."

Rob said, "Nothing's ever simple in this town, is it?" He ran his hand through his shiny black hair. "I went to school for animation. Did you know that, Zara? I wanted to work for Pixar. In another life, I could have been sitting at a desk, drawing fantastical monsters instead of..."

"No," Knox said simply. "I could not do this without you."

Rob pulled out of his emotional sinkhole. "Exactly. Which is why I have no regrets."

"Good," I said.

He puffed up his slim chest. "As for the gnome, we'll follow up on every lead, but I don't know when we'll be able to get to Gorman." He rubbed the back of his head. "Wait. Is he the gnome with the tight pants? The one who works in permits?"

"That's his nephew, Gavin Gorman," I said. "Griebel is the uncle. Small guy with small hands, big nose. He's a Little Person."

Knox said, "Oh, no. Not Griebel. I like him. I always like Little People."

Rob elbowed his partner. "Everyone is a Little Person to you, big guy."

"That is true," Knox said.

I interrupted with, "If you guys are going to be tied up here at the castle, maybe I could check on Mr. Gorman." I rubbed my fingers together. "I haven't fireballed anyone in ages, which is surprising, considering my mother has been staying at my house since before Christmas."

Rob pulled a shiny weapon from his holster. "Do you want to borrow my cocoon gun? We've worked out most of the kinks."

I didn't dare touch the cocoon gun, cool as it was. "Magic and tech don't play nice," I said. "You guys keep your sci-fi gizmos, and I'll stick to the witcher-i-doo."

"Be careful," Rob said gravely.

"Yes," Knox said, equally grave. "Don't question him alone. He is cute, but he has tricks."

"I'll bring my aunt," I said. "She's an old friend of his."

The agents didn't look reassured.

I told them to focus on their interviews at the castle, and left them to it.

Next, I located Zoey. She was with my mother, and both were consoling Carrot.

Carrot's vintage wedding gown was stunning, which only made the scene more heartbreaking.

I pushed the feelings down. Grief would have to wait.

I called my mother aside, and relayed my plans to question the small gnome, if I could find him. My mother said I could go ahead and leave the castle ahead of them, and that she and my daughter would get a ride back to town with Nick.

I asked her, "How's Zoey doing?"

"She'll be fine," my mother replied curtly. "She has all of us. If there's one thing we've learned in the Riddle family, it's that men can't be counted on, but Riddle women stick together."

"That's not fair," I said. "Your family chased off my father. That's the only reason he wasn't around. And, as for Archer, he got killed seventeen years ago. He only got that body recently. He's been in Zoey's life as much as he could be."

She sniffed. "He could have tried harder."

"What about your new guy, the tasty zookeeper? Is he also no good, due to being a man?"

She said nothing.

"I know you're upset," I said gently. "We're all upset. Let's not make it worse by singling out an entire group of people to blame." I rubbed my forearms and glanced around at the castle interior's old, stone walls. The place gave me the creeps. "Speaking of the blame game, do you think that might be exactly what someone intended?

Poison a bunch of people, then set up someone or something to take the fall?"

She raised her skinny, black eyebrows. "Political intrigue."

"Maybe a false flag," I said.

"You think the gnomes are behind this?" She wrinkled her nose. "Dirty old gnomes."

"I feel like you're not hearing what I'm saying."

"I bet it was the gnomes."

"Has someone cast a hex on me and inverted everything I'm saying so that you hear the exact opposite?"

"Gnomes are greedy creatures," she said. "They're always lurking around, snooping for opportunities. They're drawn to money, you know. Or anything of value."

"I don't want to get into this stuff right now," I said, which was partly true. I didn't want to get into it *ever*. Yes, the stereotypes about some supernaturals were based on reality. Yes, it was amusing to poke fun at others for their quirks. Yes, sometimes it went too far and wasn't fair. But I wasn't going to waste my time trying to educate my mother. Besides, I had a feeling she only made those sweeping statements to get a rise out of me.

"I should get going," I said.

"Be careful out there," she said. "Do you want a fresh vial of my blood to take with you? Just in case?"

"That's generous of you, but I'm good." I gave her a kiss on the cheek, and let her get back to consoling Carrot and my daughter.

With that taken care of, I rounded up my aunt, and we left the castle.

The limousine and driver were still there, waiting for us in the parking lot. I'd paid for a full day.

The driver greeted us solemnly. "Sorry to hear about your friend."

I was sure the uniformed man had already been questioned by the DWM agents, but just to be careful, I cast a bluffing spell and questioned him. He admitted to having cheated on his taxes by fudging his expense receipts, but was guilty of nothing worse than that.

My aunt gave him the address for Griebel's appliance repair shop, and we both got in the limo.

My aunt slid in across from me and stretched out on the long bench seat. We had ample room now that it was only the two of us. She checked the armrest for squirrels. There were none.

I felt like I should say something, but I got hit with a wave of exhaustion. I really would have preferred being in my own car, or a regular taxi. Anything but a limousine. It felt so wrong.

My aunt said, "It was a lovely idea for you to rent this limo today."

"It doesn't feel so lovely right about now," I said. "It feels awful."

"I know," Zinnia said. "That's why I said what I said." She leaned across the space and patted my knee. "How are you doing?"

"I can't complain. I mean, I feel wretched, but imagine how Zoey feels. She barely got to know her father, and now he's gone. And poor Carrot."

"They're not *you*," Zinnia said, revealing the compassionate side that I appreciated so much. "How are *you*, Zara?"

"Not good."

She squeezed my knee. "Action is the best response to anxiety. It will feel good to do something." A dark look crossed her face. "It will feel good to use Trinada's Confession Hex on Griebel Gorman."

"But that's only for... Oh, right. The usual bluffing spells don't work on goblins." Goblins didn't have very many powers, but they could detect mind control. They weren't immune to bluffing spells—my aunt had used her powers on the gnome who worked in her office with some success—but Griebel was particularly wily. Getting the name of his client—assuming there was one and he hadn't tried to murder a hundred people for his own amusement —wouldn't be easy.

Zinnia gritted her teeth and practically growled, "I'd like to be the one who holds him upside down while we force the confession."

"Zinnia! I thought he was your little buddy who could do no wrong! Even when he threw the spike grenade that went through my hands, you acted like it was just some quirky habit of his."

"He was my friend, until he went too far." She looked out the window as the limousine left the parking lot.

I didn't hate the idea of torturing Gorman, but there was one flaw in my aunt's plan. That sort of magic required more witchpower.

"We need a third tongue and set of hands for Trinada's Confession Hex," I said. "We don't want to accidentally invert the whole thing." When spells went wrong, they tended to go very wrong.

"I shall incapacitate Griebel until Margaret or one of the others can join us." There was a menacing edge in her voice. "The key is to keep the little gnome levitated so he can't stomp his foot on the floor."

"Zinnia, don't take this the wrong way, but I've never heard you sound so bloodthirsty."

"He could have killed us all with that poisoned wine. And for what? Payback for not being on the guest list? Did he intend to wipe out everyone in power just so that he could ascend to the top?" She scowled at the passing trees. "That's exactly how it works with the power-hungry, isn't it?"

A couple of key facts linked together in my head.

Griebel was an old friend of my aunt's, and he hadn't always been on her bad side, plus he was male. Was he connected to my aunt's personal predicament? That might explain her sudden ire.

I told myself to keep my mouth shut. *Zara tries to be a good witch. Zara doesn't poke the bear.*

"Aunt Zinnia, did you sleep with Griebel?"

I never had excelled at listening to myself.

"What?" She gave me a look of genuine disbelief. "Are you asking what I think you're asking, or are my ears broken?"

"If it wasn't Mitchell Harrington who knocked you up, who was it?"

"It was *not* Griebel Gorman, I assure you. Have you lost your mind?"

I held my hands out. "Don't zap me. I had to ask!"

She turned to the window again, muttering under her breath.

She muttered the whole way back into town, cursing me without actually cursing me, as well as practicing a few combat spells that I hoped were not intended for me.

The limousine pulled up in front of our suspect's business.

It was an appliance repair shop. Given how cheap appliances had become, and how most people bought replacements rather than cough up the money for labor-intense repairs, the shop should have aroused more suspicion than it did.

The store was sometimes closed for months at a time, typically whenever Griebel Gorman had done something awful and was trying to keep a low profile. He had other side gigs, such as working as a groundskeeper at Castle Wyvern. It had been wise of him to have quit that job and reopened his repair shop so he wasn't on-site at the castle for that day's events.

Zinnia and I got out of the luxurious vehicle, I settled with the limo driver, and we were on our own again. Just a couple of witches in fancy dresses—one teal and one orange—at noon on New Year's Day.

All the shops were closed for the holiday, and the streets were quiet. Most residents were still at their homes, nursing hangovers, and breaking their first resolutions.

The appliance repair shop had a handwritten sign taped to the glass door: *Closed for vacation. Hold all deliveries.*

My aunt twisted the door's lock from the inside using magic, and entered without hesitation.

"Careful," I said. "Knowing him, this place is booby trapped to the rafters."

CHAPTER 13

My aunt and I entered Griebel Gorman's dark appliance repair shop.

I cast a threat detection spell while scanning the dusty shelves for suspicious items. There were waffle irons, coffee makers, boxy old TV sets, record players, video game controllers, and a big stack of clock radios.

Everything looked normal enough, but so had a certain toaster that had tried to kill me. It had been an appliance that Griebel Gorman had modified to be a death trap.

I might have appreciated the gnome's mechanical genius more if his contraptions weren't always trying to kill me.

"He's not here," Zinnia said.

There was a squeak overhead. Long nails in old wood.

She whispered, "Did you hear that?"

We both looked up at the ceiling.

I whispered, "That's his apartment, right?" There was another squeak. "He's definitely up there."

Zinnia cracked her knuckles, sending pink sparks flying through the dimly-lit repair shop.

"That's new," I said of the sparks.

"Oh, it's very old," she said with a knowing look. "Follow me. There's a stairwell at the back of the building that goes up to the apartment. Stay behind me, and don't try to lighten my mood. I like my mood exactly how it is, thank you."

I did as told, distracting my sarcasm tongue by twisting it with the language of Witch Tongue.

I also cast a sound bubble spell to quiet our shoes on the rickety old wooden steps.

We got to the small hallway at the top, and stopped at the door to the apartment. The door was ajar by a few inches.

"Someone's in there," Zinnia whispered.

"Should we wait for backup?"

"Margaret is currently a block away, telling Barry how to parallel park." My aunt and her best friend shared a psychic link. The readings usually ran from Zinnia to Margaret, but it went the other way sometimes. Margaret Mills wasn't my top choice for backup, but she was better than nothing.

On the other side of the door, something fell to the floor with a crash.

Zinnia gave me the signal—the signal that we were not waiting for Margaret after all—and kicked the door open.

"Close your eyes," she said.

There was another crack of her knuckles and pink sparks.

I clenched my eyes shut.

She cast the old magic, filling the apartment with a flash of bright, pink light that was uncomfortable even through my eyelids.

Someone in the apartment screamed, someone else swore, and more items clattered to the floor.

She told me to open my eyes, and we stepped inside. My aunt swept the door shut behind us, sealing us in with whoever else was in there.

I didn't see Griebel Gorman, but there were two people there that I knew. They were bumping into each other inside the apartment's kitchen.

One was Dawna Jones, the card mage I'd been avoiding at the wedding.

The other was her on-again-off-again boyfriend who also worked at City Hall, Gavin Gorman. Gavin was Griebel's nephew, and also a gnome. Gavin was, unlike his uncle, regular height.

Gavin held his hands over his eyes and demanded, "Who did that? Uncle Griebel, are you here? Was that one of your traps?"

Dawna, also holding her hands over her eyes, said, "It's the witches. I saw a bit of red hair right before the flash went off. Do you believe me now, Gavin? I told you something big was going to happen today." She couldn't see her boyfriend, yet she managed to kick him in the shin successfully. "Why didn't you listen to me? You never listen to me."

Gavin groaned. "Dawna, you and your cards. I'd listen to your prophecies more if you weren't wrong most of the time."

"I'm not wrong all the time. I'm right about lots of stuff. Remember the train, and the big storm? I saved us a long detour."

"So what? If you take enough guesses, you're bound to get lucky now and then. Even a stopped clock is right twice a day. That doesn't make it accurate."

"You're the worst," she said. "We're breaking up for good. It's over."

"Fine. Couldn't be happier. Good riddance to you and your cards." He lifted his foot and stomped a single time. Two more stomps and he'd teleport out of there, back to his home base.

Dawna, who still had her eyes closed, said, "What was that? Did you stomp your foot? Don't you dare stomp your foot when we're in the middle of a discussion. If I hear another stomp, that's it. One more stomp, and we're over."

Gavin laughed. "You already broke up with me. You can't use the threat of breaking up with me after it's already done."

Dawna also laughed. "I guess not. Maybe we'd better get back together, so you'll actually listen to me on occasion."

"If you insist," he said, reaching for her blindly, his eyes still squeezed shut. "Where are you?"

"I'm right here," she cooed, also blindly reaching for him.

They started kissing as though they were alone.

My aunt wasn't saying anything, so I did.

I cleared my throat and said, "Stop contaminating a potential crime scene."

The two pulled apart and turned to us, opening their eyes a crack at a time.

Gavin said, "Zinnia Riddle and Zara Riddle. Conducting your own investigation, outside of the established protocols, I see."

"I'm checking up on an old friend," Zinnia said. "There's nothing wrong with that."

"And I'm checking up on my uncle," Gavin said. "There's nothing wrong with that."

"Then why do you look so guilty?"

He retorted, "Why do *you* look so guilty?"

I checked my aunt's face. She did look a little guilty.

"You're the guilty one," she said. "Did you even bother telling anyone you were coming here? No, of course not."

"I didn't have to tell anyone. I have a spare key. I'm allowed to be here. At least I didn't break and enter, unlike you two."

"We broke nothing," Zinnia said, holding her hands up. "Nothing."

"The laws still apply to witches," Gavin said.

While those two squared off, Dawna turned to me and said, "We just came by to see if Gavin's uncle was okay.

He has a reputation in this town for getting the sort of poison that might have been in the wine."

I played it cool. "There was poison in the wine? Whatever do you mean?"

"The wine that Archer Caine drank before he melted through the floor."

I nodded slowly. "So, you two didn't buy the cover story about the heart attack."

Dawna gave me a sheepish smile. "This isn't my first rodeo." She looked down at her stylish stiletto heels. "I just wish someone had taken my card reading more seriously." She smacked her chest. "*I* should have taken it more seriously. I should have insisted on more security at the wedding when I notified the DWM about the threat."

"You gave them intel? That's why they had so many agents there."

Dawna nodded. "I do what I can, but they get frustrated when I pass along threats that don't actually happen. I keep telling them that the only reason the threats don't happen is because we know about them, and we do something. That's the whole point of prognosticating the future, isn't it? If you get a reading, and you try to stop something, but then it happens anyway, or if the act of you trying to stop it is what ironically makes it happen, that would be..." She frowned and trailed off.

"It would be a self-fulfilling prophecy," I said. "Like in the legend of Oedipus. Or Romulus and Remus. Or The Tale of Attaf."

Dawna frowned. "Wasn't it Shakespeare who came up with that?"

"The self-fulfilling prophecy is as old as humanity. Maybe older. I'm a fan of The Devil with the Three Golden Hairs. An oldie but a goodie."

While Dawna and I had been chatting, Gavin and my aunt had either resolved or given up on their arguing.

Gavin, fully recovered from the blast of pink light, went back to what he must have been doing when we'd entered—rummaging through stacks of mail and paperwork.

Gavin muttered to his companion, "What am I even looking for?"

"Evidence," Dawna said.

He gave her an irritated look. "Do you actually think I'm going to find a purchase order for a vat of red wyvern poison?"

"You never know until you look," Dawna said.

My aunt interjected, "Gavin, was your uncle already gone when you arrived?"

"It sure seemed that way," Gavin said. "The shop was locked up with that sign on the door. When Dawna and I came upstairs, all the lights were out. My uncle usually has that old radio on whenever he's home," he pointed to a wood-cased radio from the 1920s, "but it was turned off and stone cold."

All four of us were quiet for a moment.

I asked the group, "Is it possible he's just on vacation?"

"My uncle doesn't take vacations," Gavin said. "He's a homebody, like most of us gnomes. Gnomes love their homes."

"Then the sign on the door might be a clue," I said. "He knew people would come looking for him."

My aunt clenched her jaw. "That's clearly evidence he is involved with whatever's going on." She clenched her hands into fists. "When I get my hands on him..."

"Dawna," I said. "You were saying that you knew there would be an attack today? You knew someone would kill," my voice hitched in my throat, "Archer Caine?"

Her dark-brown eyes glistened. "Oh, Zara, I didn't know what was going to happen, I swear. The cards told me there was going to be a shift in power, starting today. I didn't know what it meant." One tear slipped down her cheek. "What use are my stupid powers if I can't do anything?"

Gavin put his arm around her. "It's not our job to stand in the way of fate. What's meant to be will be. The point of all those old stories about prophecies is that you can't escape your fate. There's an end in store for all of us."

"Easy for you to say," Dawna said, fighting back more tears. "You can stomp your foot three times and you're home. It's going to be hard for fate to make something really bad happen to you."

"That doesn't keep me out of danger," Gavin said. "Not that I can even do such a thing. Haha. How funny that is, that people believe gnomes can stomp their foot three times and teleport. The imaginations of some people!"

None of us said anything. An essential part of being a gnome was denying gnome powers.

Gavin said to his currently on-again girlfriend, "Don't act like I have it so easy. You're the one who can walk into any gas station and leave with a winning scratch-off ticket. It must be nice to have unlimited access to fun money."

"Unlimited access?" Her jaw dropped. "It's just like you to assume that I have unlimited access. You have no idea what I've been through in my life. No idea!"

"Hey," I said. "Can we focus on the problem at hand for a minute?"

They continued arguing.

I cast the spell to bite them in the butts.

That got their attention.

"Dawna," I said. "If the cards told you anything at all about what's going on, you should tell us."

Before she could answer, we were all startled by a noise.

Behind the closed door, there was a trampling sound on the stairwell. It sounded like an army was coming to back us up.

The door shot off its hinges in a blast of magic.

In came Margaret Mills, stampeding in like a rhino. There was a single gray curl sticking up from her forehead like a horn. She nearly shot us all with her green fireballs.

Wide eyed, she said, "What did I miss? Are we going to torture the gnome now? I'm here, so let's get this thing underway! Who's got the combustibles? We should all be wearing pointed hats to access the higher source without flowback. Why do we never have hats when we need them? Zara, dig up some black scarabyce blood. I happen to know Griebel keeps it with the dishwashing liquid."

It was just like Margaret to bust in late and start barking orders.

When she paused for a breath, I broke in with a plea for her to calm down.

Margaret gave me a stunned look. "I'm one hundred percent calm. Where is he?"

"He's gone," Zinnia said. "We would have told you as much if you'd stopped for a second." Zinnia squinted and pressed her lips together, as though she was fighting to refrain from saying something else.

"Don't you *dare* call me that," Margaret said with indignation. "I do not! I am not!" She paused. "You might be what? Really? But how? But with whom?"

"Get out of my head," Zinnia said. "Get out and stay out."

Margaret, who had a knack for reading my aunt's mind without permission, said, "What do you mean you don't know for sure? You haven't taken a test?"

Zinnia waved one hand in a subtle gesture.

Margaret shrieked, and then scowled at her best friend as she rubbed her bottom.

I turned to see if my aunt's coworkers had picked up on Margaret's blabbing about Zinnia's possible pregnancy. Judging by their round eyes, they had heard and understood everything.

When Zinnia didn't volunteer more information, I changed the subject. "Margaret, what you missed is that Dawna was telling us about her prognostications. She's been getting warnings in her card readings. There was something about a balance in power shifting today."

"The cards!" Margaret pointed at Dawna, jabbing her finger excitedly, as though she'd come up with the idea of cartomancy herself. "Dawna, your cards can tell us where Griebel went!"

Dawna tilted her head to the side. "I don't know about that. It's hard for me to get specifics, particularly about locations."

"I'm sure you can do it with the right supplies," Margaret said. "I've got some items back at my place." She paused and looked around the apartment. "I haven't been here in ages. I forgot how pleasant it was up here. Griebel's place is a lot nicer than you'd expect."

Gavin said, "What's that supposed to mean?"

Margaret shrugged. "Everyone knows gnomes like homely homes."

Gavin frowned. "Homey homes."

"That's what I said. Homely homes."

"Homey homes," he stated. "Without the L. Homey, not homely."

"Gnomes like *homely* homes," Margaret insisted, and she began singing a song about it.

The two continued arguing, caught in an infinite loop of correcting each other. They might have gone until sundown if my aunt hadn't blasted both of them with another bite in the buttocks. There had been a lot of bottom biting in the apartment. It was almost as though we were all turning against each other, exactly the way some evil third party wanted us to.

Once the arguing settled, Dawna said, "I'd be happy to do some readings with you, Margaret, if you think it will help."

Everyone looked at Zinnia, the senior member of the group.

Zinnia said, "We ought to do everything we can."

"Yay!" Margaret waved her hands. "This is going to be fun! Everyone's coming to *my* place for a change!" She stuck out her tongue at Zinnia.

Zinnia said to the shorter, frizzy-haired witch, "How about you pick up the supplies and meet us at my house? I haven't felt comfortable at your house since the snakes started breeding in the furnace ducts."

"Hah!" Margaret gave her best friend a triumphant look. "I'm in the UFO this week. No furnace ducts, no kids, and no snake farm."

The rest of us exchanged a worried look. The UFO?

CHAPTER 14

We left Griebel Gorman's apartment and repair shop, locking up after ourselves.

I'd already dismissed our limousine, so Zinnia and I got a ride to Margaret's place in Dawna's car.

My aunt and I rode in the back together, while Gavin sat up front.

"He should have offered you the front seat," I grumbled to my aunt.

"I'm perfectly fine back here," she said, struggling to pull on her seat belt.

"Of course you are," I said, helping her with the buckle.

She took in a big, noisy breath.

"Careful," I said, one eye on her bosom. "If one of your sweater puppies breaks free, I don't want to get it in the eye."

"For heaven's sakes," she said, sounding a couple of generations older than she actually was. Sometimes my aunt seemed to be 48 going on 100.

The car started moving.

As we rode along, I couldn't help but notice how uncomfortable she was.

I leaned over and said, "We could ask Dawna to swing by your place so we can get you out of those Spanx."

"No need."

"A few more hours, and you'll need a can opener."

"I will not!"

"You'll be like one of those tubes of dough you get in the refrigerator section at the grocery store. Whatever you do, don't let the zipper down. You'll never get it up."

"You're enjoying this. You're enjoying my suffering."

"I'm *savoring* it," I said. "This is a special time. One day, after the baby comes, we'll look back on this and laugh."

"I doubt that."

"Trust me. You will. How about we get you out of that thing? At least loosen the corset. You can wear my jacket. I don't really need it." I tried to give her my jacket but she wouldn't take it.

She stubbornly stuck her nose in the air. "I've never been a bridesmaid before. Carrot wanted me to enjoy one full day in a puffy taffeta gown, and that's exactly what I'm going to do. For Carrot."

"You do enjoy being a martyr, don't you? I thought it was just my mother, but it may be a Riddle family trait."

She said nothing.

We arrived at the place that was Margaret's home away from home.

It was the Windsong Mobile Home Park, just up the hill from the Windsong Marina.

Dawna drove slowly along the paved path linking the recreational vehicles, complaining about how the numbers on the addresses were too small.

"There it is," Gavin said. "You can't miss it."

Dawna said, "I can't believe it. Margaret Mills has a UFO."

We parked the car, and all jumped out to gawk.

There really was a UFO.

Margaret Mills and her ex-husband were currently taking turns living in the family home to take care of their four children. Keeping the kids in the same house helped the children have more stability during a difficult period.

Margaret's ex had an apartment for when he wasn't at the family house, but when Margaret was off rotation, she made her home in a shiny silver trailer. It wasn't an Airstream, but a no-brand-name model that looked even more like a shiny silver UFO.

Margaret was already at the circular door, opening it and waving everyone in.

Zinnia, Dawna, and Gavin stepped inside. The trailer rocked.

Margaret's boyfriend, Barry Blackstone, stood with me at the entrance.

"Give them a minute," he said. "It's a tight floorplan. It works better if you bring people in a few at a time."

"I've been in a camper van before," I said. "I'll wait until they're seated." I stepped back and looked over the impressive metal trailer.

The winter sun was low on the horizon, but hadn't set yet. It was reflecting off the silver surfaces, yet it wasn't glaring or causing spots on my eyes.

"The reflective surface has dampeners," I said.

"You noticed," Barry said with pride.

"This must be one of your creations," I said.

Barry Blackstone was an inventor and genius.

He tried to act nonchalant. "Oh, this ol' thing is just a project I've been working on for a while. Margaret and I have taken her down two hundred feet a couple of times. She shakes a little, but she's sturdy."

I said, "Are you telling me this trailer is also a submarine? You take it diving? In the ocean?"

"Oh, no." He winked. "Of course not. Diving into the open ocean with an unlicensed submarine? That would be rather dangerous." He gave me two more winks, one with each eye, or one wink from each of the brothers who shared the body.

"So that's why you're parked at the mobile home park that's next to the marina. For easy access."

"Access is easier than you'd think." Another wink.

"Barry, I'm just glad you're on our side." I shook my head in amazement. The UFO explained why Margaret was sometimes unreachable by cell phone. She must have been underwater during our last coven meeting.

"Margaret always dreamed of living in a luxury penthouse on the thirteenth floor of a building," Barry said. "I gave her the exact opposite, and she loves it."

"Funny how life works out that way."

"Funny," he agreed, proudly patting the side of the vessel. "She's a good UFO."

"Does it fly? Like a real UFO?"

He chuckled. "UFO stands for Underwater Floating Oasis. If I'd wanted it to fly, the shape would be much different."

"Of course," I said. "Any plans for building one of those?"

His eyes twinkled. "Oh, who can say?" He kept patting the shiny side. "She spends most of her time on dry land, for easier commuting, but you can imagine how peaceful it is underwater. It's a genuine oasis."

"I'm sure it is," I said. "I'd love to go for a dip sometime."

"And you shall. How's Foxy Pumpkin?"

"Probably mad at me for renting that limousine today, but what can you do?"

"She's a good car," he said solemnly. "She'll get over it."

We stood in silence, out of conversation.

Neither of us spoke of the metaphorical elephant.

At that time, on that day, we both should have been at the wedding luncheon, toasting the newlyweds, not standing in a mobile home park in formalwear.

"Okay then," Barry said.

"Okay then," I agreed.

"I'll leave you folks to your book club meeting," he said. "If it's all the same to you, I'll head back to my shop to look at some of these items I, uh, *borrowed* from Mr. Gorman." He picked up the canvas tote bag that he'd filled up back at the appliance shop. He'd darted around in a frenzy, grabbing dusty old appliances like a bargain shopper at a five-for-one sale.

I bid him a good day, and stepped into the UFO to join the others.

The interior looked exactly like the inside of an updated Airstream trailer. The upholstery was all cheerful shades of yellow.

The others—Zinnia, Margaret, Dawna, and Gavin— were already seated at a cozy booth with square cushions that presumably converted into a bed.

I squeezed in, and sat quietly as Margaret lit some special magic candles and laid out a few of Griebel Gorman's personal items. There was a pair of tweezers, heavy-duty toenail clippers, and something for trimming nostril hairs. Of all the things to swipe from the gnome's home, why those?

Margaret explained, without my having asked, "Grooming items are the most personal of personal items. Better even than jewelry."

I shot my aunt a look. Was Margaret reading my mind now, too?

Margaret stuck her nose in the air and said, "Yes, Zara, you've gotten on my wavelength lately, and it's extremely annoying, with all of your constant jokes." She shook her frizzy gray curls, and went back to cutting special grooves into the sides of the candles.

Across the table, my aunt gave me a helpless but sympathetic look.

Margaret Mills was in our heads now, whether we liked it or not. I wondered if that was somehow connected to her specialty—the one she refused to name or talk about.

"Never mind about that," Margaret said.

"Brrr," Gavin said. "Being around so many of you witches is truly unsettling."

"I like it," Dawna said to him. "Why are you still here, anyway? You don't have anything to offer. You're not even a minor mage."

Gavin scoffed. "Women!" He tried to get up and leave, but he was blocked in, trapped in the corner of the cozy booth by the rest of us.

Margaret said, "Were you going somewhere? If you're doing a run to the store to get Dawna some Diet Coke, I'll have root beer."

He crossed his arms. "Anyone else have an order for the errands boy?"

"Coffee would be great," I said.

Margaret said, "Change my root beer to coffee, too."

He waved at the UFO's small kitchenette. "Don't you have a coffee maker here?"

Margaret pouted. "It only makes one little cup at a time. You could stop by Maisy's."

Zinnia said, "You can't. Dreamland is closed today, along with all the other coffee shops. It's New Year's Day. Everything's closed."

"Coffee would be nice, though," I said. "My tequila wore off an hour ago. Stupid adrenaline."

"Fine," Gavin said. "I'll just zip over to my apartment, get my personal coffee maker, pick up my car, and drive all the way back over here so I can make everyone a nice, hot coffee."

He'd been saying it sarcastically, but everyone treated him as though he'd been sincere.

"Gavin, you're so sweet," I said along with the others.

"Close your eyes," he said with a groan.

None of us did. Nor did we make any movements to slide out of the booth so he could escape that way.

With a grumble, he reluctantly stomped his foot three times.

He disappeared without so much as a puff. Gnome powers.

"Cool," I said.

"He hates doing it in front of people," Dawna said, giggling.

The rest of us burst into laughter as well, the way only a group of women could.

It felt good to laugh after the day we'd had.

I looked over at Zinnia and wondered if she was thinking the same thing I was—that Dawna should be invited to our coven meetings, despite being only a minor mage and not a full witch.

Margaret said, "That's a good idea."

"Stop it," Zinnia said. "Stop reading our minds, Margaret Mills, you show off."

Margaret looked up from her modified candle, wide eyed. "Was I doing it again? I swear I don't mean to. Honestly, Zinnia and Zara. Do you really think I want to hear what people think? I make my hair gray specifically so that most people ignore me, and don't think about me at all. It's naturally brown." Her eyes glistened. "Zinnia, I didn't go gray prematurely. It's a spell. I have to make it this color, using magic."

I was stunned. I'd always known there was something funny about Margaret's hair, the way it seemed to have a mind of its own, but I'd never imagined she'd been dying it gray.

Zinnia made a sympathetic sound.

Dawna reached out and patted Margaret's arm. "I totally understand. I don't want to have this compulsion to lay out cards and see glimpses of the future. People say it's a gift, but they also say it's good luck when a seagull poops on your shoulder. People lie." She looked directly at me. "We all pretend it's good that we have these powers, but it's a curse, isn't it?"

I didn't have an answer. After seeing my daughter's father melt away in a puddle, I had been having a difficult time summoning optimism.

Margaret said, "Every coin has two sides."

Zinnia said, "We must be brave and do what needs to be done."

It felt like I should say something, so I did. "Pitter patter, let's get at 'er."

The others nodded in agreement.

Margaret lit the candles, we all held hands, and turned to Dawna.

It was time to witness the cartomancer in action.

CHAPTER 15

Excitement flowed through me, along with magic, as I waited in anticipation of what the card mage was about to reveal.

Dawna said, "This is really nice, holding hands with you ladies, but I actually need my hands free to shuffle the cards."

The two sitting next to Dawna moved their hands to her shoulders.

Dawna began shuffling the cards.

She was excellent at shuffling, like a dealer in a casino, or a close-up magician.

She laid out the cards in a pattern that made no sense to me.

"It's working," Dawna said excitedly.

My aunt squeezed my left hand. An extra pulse of magic flowed through me.

"Easy now," Dawna said. "Don't juice it to the max and blow my head off."

Margaret, Zinnia, and I reduced the flow.

Dawna resumed the cartomancy.

Margaret muttered, "This would be better with pointy hats."

The energy in the circuit changed. It was happening.

"He is gone," Dawna said in a deeper, more dramatic version of her usual voice. "The gnome left his home. He left his home to roam."

The three of us witches exchanged looks. Was she serious with the rhyming?

"He left home alone," Dawna said. "He went to the phone. He left home because of the phone, the phone."

She must have meant the phone that we'd summoned at our last coven meeting. The phone we'd picked up, only to hear that strange, otherworldly voice taunting us.

There was an intense crackle in my hands. A prickling. The energy flowing in the group was changing. There was fear in the blend. I got goosebumps between my shoulder blades.

"No," Dawna said. "Oh, no." She started gathering the cards in her hands. "No, no, no."

Zinnia said, "We can't stop now."

Dawna twisted, trying to pull her shoulders out of Zinnia's and Margaret's hands, but she was unable to break free. The flowing magic was locking us together.

Dawna clenched her jaw, shuffled the cards, and bravely laid them out once more.

"Two moons," she said. "Shifting sands. Flowing lava. Deep waters. Giant worms beneath the surface. The gnome left his home for the land of two moons."

Zinnia said, "Who was the poison for? Why did he do it?"

Dawna laid out another card. It was the Queen of Hearts.

"The poison was for all of us," Dawna said gravely. "Every last one of us."

Zinnia said, "But why?"

Dawna tried once more to shrug the hands off her shoulders but couldn't do it. She was shaking now, her whole body trembling from the effort.

"I don't know," she said, her voice shaking. "It doesn't say. It only says—" She cut herself off and pressed her lips together.

We would have all leaned in closer, but there was no more space. Our heads were practically touching.

I suddenly realized the purpose of pointy hats. It was to prevent witches from hitting their heads against each other during situations exactly like this. I kept the observation to myself, but not from Margaret, who squeezed my hand in acknowledgement.

Zinnia kept prompting Dawna for more. "What else does it say?"

"One for each moon," Dawna said. "One witch for each moon. Two moons, two witches." She chewed her lip and looked into my aunt's eyes. "Two witches of red. Two witches of riddles. One who knows all."

The other three ladies looked at me. Was I the one who knew all? I could be a know-it-all, but I never claimed to know all.

Zinnia whispered, "That's us."

The others murmured what felt like condolences.

"This is good news," I said. "Honestly, I didn't think we were going to get anywhere with Dawna's card reading."

Dawna gave me a hurt look.

"No offense intended," I said. "You're doing the best you can. It's magic that has a mind of its own."

"Griebel has fled to the other world, and we must go after him," Zinnia said. "It's not *good* news."

"But it's not bad," I said. "At least now we have a game plan. Griebel went to that other world that you guys went to without me, and now we have to go there and track him down."

Zinnia didn't look excited.

"Cheer up," I said to my aunt. "You can still hold him upside down until he tells us who tried to poison us all."

"You make it sound so easy," Dawna said.

Margaret said, "The other world is anything but easy, Zara. Your magic won't work. Plus that world is full of crazy people who turn you into a statue for no reason whatsoever."

"Okay, it won't be easy," I said. "But we can make a plan. And it might be fun. I had to do a stakeout with my mom before Christmas, and we ended up having a nice time together. We reconnected. Come on, Zinnia, where's your adventurous spirit?"

Dryly, she said, "My adventurous spirit checked out after it got me in trouble."

Dawna leaned over and whispered to me, "Is she really pregnant?"

"We're not sure," I whispered back.

Zinnia said, "I can hear you both."

I shrugged. "Would you rather we talk about you behind your back?"

"Yes."

"So, about our upcoming road trip," I said. "We need to get a copy of the elevator key to get there, right?"

Margaret nodded. Zinnia's head appeared to be stuck.

I continued, "So, we'll get the key, take the magic elevator at City Hall to the hidden floor that goes to the other world, get in there, torture the gnome, get the job done, pick up a few postcards, and come back with some cool stories."

The others didn't look so certain.

I turned to Dawna and said, "We're successful in our mission, right? If the cards said we were heading over there to get killed, it would say so, right?"

She looked down, rearranged the cards, then looked up again. "Two witches go over, and two witches return. Both witches of red, which I think means redheads. Both witches of riddles. Both stars of the show."

My aunt said, "Do the witches return with everything they went over with?"

Dawna frowned at the cards. "There are two suns in the sky, but also two sons as in children. Or one son. Or one and a half. Or one who is and one who will be." She swished her lips from side to side. "One who is and one who will be? That could be interpreted a few ways, but there is a son," she said. "A riddle within a riddle."

I looked at Zinnia and said, "Congratulations. You're having a boy."

Margaret said, "It's true. You're pregnant, with a boy. Congratulations. It's not pie and ice cream."

Zinnia looked more terrified than I'd ever seen her. "It's not pie and ice cream?"

Margaret said, "I ran the test as soon as Zara clued me in. I've known since we were back at Griebel's apartment."

Zinnia looked at her friend in shock. "You did?"

"It's a very old, very simple spell," Margaret said. "Take it from the witch who has four kids. It's a spell that's well worth knowing."

We were all still linked by hands and shoulders. The energy flowing through us pulsed with our emotions, commingling. I was feeling my emotions, as well as the others'. I had rarely felt so messy and mixed up on the inside. The last time I'd felt that exact blend of emotions had been when I'd found out I was pregnant with my daughter.

Dawna said, "Zinnia, you should still pick up one of those plastic sticks from the drugstore. You witches are impressive and all, but not everything has to be done with magic."

"I'll get a stick," Zinnia said.

The energy flowing through us changed again.

Dawna had stopped trembling. "I've got a good feeling about this," she said. "I know things might seem bad right now, and Archer Caine is really gone, but it could have been so much worse."

We silently acknowledged that she was right.

Margaret said, "I have the kids tomorrow. I can't go with you to the other world unless I can get a babysitter. Maybe I could borrow Humphrey from Maisy so I can tag along."

Dawna let out a sudden, blood-curdling shriek.

It was such a shock, it broke the circle. Margaret's and Zinnia's hands flew off her shoulders.

"Sorry about that," Dawna said. "It reshuffled in my mind, and it wasn't good." She shook her head. "Margaret can't go with you. It only works if it's just two witches."

"And so it shall be," Zinnia said, lifting her chin. "Two witches of riddles shall travel to the land of two moons."

"With the son who is and will be," I added.

Zinnia nodded. "We'll need to prepare a few things. We can leave in the morning." She asked Dawna, "Does that work?" She tugged at the bodice of her tight-fitting orange bridesmaid dress. "Can we take a minute to breathe and get changed, then go first thing tomorrow, or does that throw everything off?"

Dawna gathered the cards, shuffled them and laid them out again.

We started to witchpool our magic but Dawna said it wouldn't be necessary, as she had a clear reading on this particular query.

"Leave at dawn," she said. "Get the elevator key from..." She trailed off and cocked her head at Margaret. "You've got a key?"

Margaret gave us an embarrassed look. "Barry may have made one, using the chameleon potion. For research purposes."

Zinnia shook her head. "You got turned into a statue the last time you went over there. Don't tell me you were planning to take a trip over."

Margaret slumped in her seat, looking guilty and chastised.

Dawna said, shaking her head, "Margaret, you can't go over there again. I'm sorry, girl, but you've got that big ol' mouth of yours, and there are too many powerful entities over there."

Margaret snorted. "Oh, I can't go, but Zara can? Please. What do you think is going to happen when *she* goes over there?"

"It should be okay," Dawna said, rubbing one eye with her pinkie finger. "The cards say so. It seems it would work out if any two Riddles went over. Zara, it could be your mom and your daughter."

"Zoey's not a witch," I said. "And neither is my mother. Plus she dyes her hair black now, so she doesn't even fit the description. Also, neither of them is pregnant with a son. That I know of."

Margaret said, "Zoey's not pregnant."

We all stared at the gray-haired witch.

She shrugged. "I ran the spell on her and the other teenagers at Castle Wyvern today. I smelled pregnancy hormones in the air, and I thought it might be one of them. I had no idea it was coming from this old bird." She grinned at Zinnia.

Zinnia pressed her lips together.

"You shouldn't have tested my daughter," I said to Margaret. "But I must admit the test has put my mind at ease. Zoey is a careful girl, but she is just a teenager, and she does have her hands full navigating life as a shifter."

Dawna said, "Zoey is much more than a shifter."

We all turned to look at the card mage.

Dawna rubbed her eyes and squirmed in her seat. "The cards are always talking about her."

"They are?"

Dawna gathered the cards and began shuffling. "She's always popping up," the card mage said. "Probably because of the big prophecy."

My stomach churned. I tried not to think of that ancient scroll, or the prophecy that named my daughter.

This was *exactly* why I'd been avoiding Dawna and her cards.

Zinnia asked Dawna, "Was the poison in the wine intended for Zoey?"

"It was intended for all of us, including her," Dawna said, setting the cards down to rub her eyes. She was getting worn out.

I'd been noticing her eye rubbing in particular because they made me nervous. Dawna had very long, elaborately decorated fingernails. They were deep red, decorated with green sprigs of holly and golden jingle bells. Several of the nails had chips in them.

It wasn't like Dawna to let her nails be chipped or out of date. She must have been distracted lately by her readings. Ordinarily she would have changed her nails between Christmas and the wedding to match the wedding theme. Her long nails should have been orange.

"There's also something about a third party," Dawna said, returning her attention to the cards. "Not Zinnia's baby, but another male. He's like a son, but not a son." She looked at me. "Do you have any other kids besides Zoey?"

"Not that I know of," I said, as I always did. Ha ha.

Margaret yawned.

Dawna said, "We can try a few more readings, but I'm tapped out at the moment. I'm worried you ladies might stop my heart if you put any more of that magic through me. Do you want to play a hand of Canasta while I recharge?"

Without waiting for an answer, she began shuffling and dealing out cards for four-player Canasta.

There was a tap on the door of the mobile UFO.

All four of us yelled, "Come in!"

Gavin entered with the espresso machine he'd brought from his place.

He got it set up in the small kitchen, and made us the most wonderful coffee while we played Canasta, then hashed out the details of a trip to the other world.

I was nervous about going, but also excited.

I didn't love the reason for the mission, but I couldn't wait to set foot in another world. It would be so interesting to walk on the red desert sands under a sky filled with two large moons.

Dawna eventually recharged and did one more reading.

She rubbed the corner of her eye with one long, chipped nail, and said, "That's odd. You're supposed to bring someone else with you for good luck, and it's the last person I would have expected."

"Bentley," I guessed.

"Too obvious," she said. "It's someone else."

CHAPTER 16

The sun had long since set when we finally left Margaret's cozy UFO.

Gavin Gorman had his car there, so he left on his own while my aunt and I got a ride back to our houses with Dawna.

Dawna was yawning as we left the mobile home park.

"Ooh, I'm going to dream long and hard tonight," she said. "I don't know how you witches find the energy to do all the things you do."

"Some extra energy comes with our magic," my aunt said.

Zinnia was in the front seat, and I was in the back, half listening as I checked messages on my phone.

Zinnia asked our driver, "Any more clues about that third person who's joining us on the trip tomorrow?"

"I'd rather not say," Dawna said.

"That's not fair," Zinnia said. "You can't bring it up and then not tell us."

"I know, I know," the card mage said with a sigh. "But you have to trust me. I need to sleep on it. Everything becomes clear in my dreams. I'll know for sure in the morning, and I'll bring your third party to the top floor hallway at City Hall to meet you."

"Is it Karl?" Karl Kormac was a manager in the permits department, and a sprite.

"No."

"Is it Gavin?"

"No."

"Is it someone from City Hall? From the DWM?"

"I'll tell you what," Dawna said. "I'll give you a name now, before I've slept on it to be sure, if you tell me the name of *your* guy."

"What guy?"

"The one who got lucky with you."

My ears pricked up. I put down my phone and gave them my full attention.

"I'd rather not say," Zinnia said.

"Why? Is he married?"

"No."

"Is he a shifter? I know witches and shifters aren't supposed to get together, but that didn't stop you with Jesse."

"Please don't mention that horrible man's name. Let the dead rest. Especially him."

"Margaret told me you have a chunk of him," Dawna said. "A cremated chunk."

Zinnia replied icily, "Margaret Mills likes to tell salacious stories about others to deflect from her own personal failings."

"Who doesn't?" Dawna cranked up the car's heaters. "Come on, Zinnia. Tell me. Who's your babydaddy?"

My aunt made a sound of disgust. "That's such an ugly term."

"If you don't like it, change it. Get a ring on that finger, girl."

"Get married? Why?"

"Your son needs a father in his life."

"A father," my aunt said softly, then, sounding dazed, "*My son.*"

"Is this really news for you, Zinnia? You really didn't have a feeling something was up before Margaret told you the news?"

"It's all entirely new," she said. "I haven't even been out of this orange dress since the idea first crossed my mind. Oh, Dawna, it's so humiliating."

"I hear you," Dawna said with kindness.

I got the feeling my aunt had forgotten I was in the backseat, and I was witnessing the intimacy between two long-term coworkers when they thought they were alone.

"Knocked up out of wedlock," my aunt said with a wry laugh.

"At your age," Dawna teased.

"At my age," Zinnia agreed.

"And in that dress. What was Carrot thinking? You look like an overfilled Creamsicle."

"I really do," Zinnia said, not sounding annoyed at all. She really had a strong bond with Dawna Jones. If I'd made the Creamsicle comment, she wouldn't have taken it nearly so well. I felt a pang of jealousy about their relationship.

Dawna said, "We'll have to throw you a baby shower. We can do it at the office if you don't want everyone from work invading your house."

"What about your place? I'd love to see for myself how many cats you actually own."

"No can do," Dawna said. "Karl will insist on coming, and that man cannot be in my home. I have a lot of antique chairs that won't hold him up. You've seen how many office chairs he's broken."

"He's not even that big," Zinnia said.

"I know, but he sits hard. He's a hard sitter."

"That he is."

The two of them gossiped about their workmates the rest of the way to my house.

Zinnia seemed confused about why we were on Beacon Street.

"This is my stop," I said, speaking up for the first time on the ride.

My aunt said, "Floopy doop! You scared me Zara. How long have you been lurking in the dark back there?"

"Since we left the trailer park," I said. "Is that dress cutting off the circulation to your brain? You're not exactly firing on all cylinders. How did you think I got in the back of Dawna's car? Do you think I flew by broomstick, cast a permeability spell on the window, and slipped in a block ago?"

Dawna said, "You witches can do that?"

"It's possible," Zinnia said.

Dawna shuddered. "Note to self. Always check the back seat for witches."

I got out of the warm car, careful not to slip on the cold, icy sidewalk. I was wearing hard-soled, high heel shoes that matched my turquoise dress rather than sensible winter boots. What a day. It felt like a year ago that I'd put them on.

"Thanks for the ride," I said to Dawna, who'd lowered her window to say goodbye. "I hope those dreams work out for you tonight. Let us know if anything else changes, and we'll see you in the morning with our surprise travel companion."

"I'll do what I can," Dawna said. "And remember, you don't have to go." She chewed her lower lip. "Except it would be a lot better if you did." Her gaze flitted around nervously. The relaxation she'd been feeling at the start of the drive was gone. She was tired, but also wired.

"I'll bite," I said. "What happens if we don't go?"

"Just the end of the world," she said. "No pressure."

That was the first I'd heard about the world ending. She'd left that out during our chatty games of Canasta back in Margaret's mobile submarine home.

"No pressure," I said.

Zinnia said goodbye, gave me the usual warnings about being careful, and they were on their way.

"Be careful," I muttered to myself as I walked up to my house, casting grit on the ground ahead of me so I didn't slip on the ice. "I'll be careful," I said.

I pulled my phone out and saw a text message from Rob.

I wrote back to him: *I'd like to take you up on your offer after all.*

Rob wrote back immediately: *I'll swing by your house in a bit. Will you be awake at midnight?*

I replied: *I can be. See you then.*

I slipped my phone back into my purse, but didn't enter my house right away.

I stood on the porch, enjoying the quiet.

Once I stepped inside, there would be the chaos of family members, human and pet, all demanding my attention and needing to use the washroom while I was taking a bath, even though there was a perfectly good powder room on the lower floor.

For a moment, I relished the silence, the stillness, and the coolness of a winter night.

The back of my neck tingled.

I wasn't alone.

"I know you're there," I said.

"You did not," came a husky voice at my ear. "You were guessing."

"You've been standing there for... sixty-eight seconds."

"Nice try. I was already here before Dawna's car pulled up. I saw you throwing grit on the sidewalk as you walked up."

I didn't turn my head. "You should know better than to lurk around in the shadows and then sneak up on someone like me. What if I'd fireballed you?"

"What if I'd bit you on your exposed neck?" His lips grazed my skin suggestively.

I turned to my vampire boyfriend and kissed him.

After a moment, Bentley pried me off him, looked down, and said, "That's a new dress."

147

"It's vintage. Why are you staring at me like that? Don't tell me you're picturing my dress on the floor."

"I'm not," Bentley said, almost smiling in that cool way of his. "I would not disrespect your wardrobe by discarding it on the floor. I always throw your things on the chair beside the bed."

"Are you staying over?"

"Only if I'm invited."

"I invite you to stay overnight tonight."

"I accept."

"Good. Because I'm leaving in the morning for the world with two moons, and I might not see you for a while."

He raised one dark eyebrow over his gleaming, silver-gray eyes.

"Let's go inside," I said. "I'll tell you all about it."

We went into the house.

The place felt absolutely enormous inside, thanks to my having spent the last several hours inside Margaret's tiny submarine home. I was able to spread both arms out at my sides and not touch any walls.

My family had gotten home before me.

My mother greeted Bentley with air kisses on each cheek, as was her custom with him. The two had been romantically linked at one point, but they hadn't been intimate. What really happened was that my mother used the magic of an amber pendant to hypnotize him and keep him under her thrall even in her absence.

Bentley had believed he was dating her at the time, and that she was his "little blueberry muffin." But she'd just been stringing him along platonically so she could prepare him to be my guardian and protector—not that I needed one. Except for the couple of times I *had* needed a guardian and protector, and he'd saved my life. But I'd saved his a few times, too, so we were even.

My daughter was in the living room, playing with Marzipants, the budgie. The two had once been enemies, back in our old life. Things were so different now.

After checking on her, I ran upstairs to change out of the turquoise party dress into something more comfortable. My closet had something waiting for me—an oversized rock band T-shirt and a thick pair of sweatpants. Not the thin, clingy variety of sportswear that was tailored for yoga classes, but warm, fuzzy-lined, old-fashioned sweatpants like I'd worn in high school gym class as a kid. I pulled on some equally warm socks and ran back downstairs to join the others.

The four of us gathered in the living room, and caught each other up on everything that had happened in the hours following the tragedy at the wedding.

Zoey shared that she'd cried even more than she had over her first boyfriend, but that perhaps that experience had prepared her for this one. She would get through it.

Zirconia shared that the castle had dumped out all of the wine, even the bottles without poison, and that the service of their waiters had really dropped a few stars since her last stay, so she would be adjusting her online review.

When it was Bentley's turn, he cast his silver-gray eyes downward and said, "This will hurt the entire town."

I said, "That's nice of you to say, but you don't have to lie on our account. I know Archer made you uncomfortable, and that you'll be happier with him out of the picture."

"It's already hurting the town," he said. "Things are getting ugly. People are turning against each other."

My mother made a tsk-tsk sound. "People are supposed to stick together through difficult times. This is exactly what I told those waiters when they refused to let me order off the luncheon menu, just because they were ten minutes into the dinner service."

I shot her a dark look. "You had dinner at the castle?"

"Only because I couldn't have lunch."

"You ate a meal there?"

"I had to, Zarabella. My beautiful granddaughter—your daughter—had to replenish her tears," said the black-haired vampire. "She had three orders of soup, extra salty."

"I did," Zoey said.

We went quiet and turned back to Bentley. The man had gotten used to us cutting him off mid-story. He had a supernatural level of patience.

"You were saying," I said to him.

"That's all I have to say," he replied. "People are turning against each other."

"What do you mean? Were there arguments at the castle?"

"Yes," he said. "And someone burned down Vincent Wick's residence."

Sounds of surprise rang up from all three Riddles present, along with a loud squawk from Marzipants, who liked to participate from his cage.

I asked, "The place by the dump? I mean, the exchange station, or whatever it's called? Where they do the composting?"

He nodded.

I said, "The place where Vincent Wick has that creepy underground room with all the surveillance equipment he uses to spy on people all over town?"

"That's the one," Bentley said.

"Why?"

"People thought he might have been involved in the poisoning. His sister, Tansy Wick, used to be the main supplier in town for hard-to-get items."

"But not red wyvern venom," I said. "Not anything like that. She was a sweet old woman who loved her greenhouse plants and her beloved dogs. She had a special garden for left-handed snails."

Bentley kept his gaze down, as if embarrassed on her behalf. "She also bred carnivorous plants."

"True," I said. "But why would people burn down her brother's place? Is it just because he took over her greenhouse operation after she passed away?" As I asked the question, I realized that must have been exactly what had happened. "Who did it? Who burned down Wick's place?"

"Persephone Rose is working on the case," Bentley said. Persephone was my half-sister and the other detective in town. "The chief has everyone working to keep the whole town from blowing up."

To keep the whole town from blowing up.

I shuddered as a bad feeling crept along my spine.

My mother abruptly stood. "We have rice pudding in the fridge."

She disappeared to the kitchen and returned with a bottle of wine and glasses. No rice pudding.

Zoey and I exchanged a look. We'd never had rice pudding in the fridge since we'd moved there. We ate the fresh cardamom rice pudding—no raisins—at Vijay's buffet, but never at home. In spite of that, my mother had referenced imaginary rice pudding at least three times in the last week as a pretense for getting wine.

She handed me the bottle. I cast a spell to detect poison. It likely wasn't necessary, given the many protective charms we had on the house, but it was just another sign that things were changing. There had been our life before the wedding, and there was our life now. We were living in the *now*, which meant checking wine for poison.

"You may have a glass, if you'd like," I said to Zoey. "A small glass. France rules." We all knew she'd had alcohol before. She and Ambrosia had gotten into trouble a few times, as all teens did, though sometimes they used inebriation spells instead of booze.

"No, thanks." She got to her feet. "I'll just hit the hay early, if it's okay with everyone." It was, so she shifted into her fox form and ran off to bed. Being in animal form gave her comfort during times of stress. There was something about the wiring in the animal brain that simplified things. She'd reported feeling more present that way, less concerned about the past or future.

The three of us finished the bottle of wine, as well as its friend. With our constitutions, the three of us could have had two bottles each and been fine, but we stopped before the third.

As my mother returned to her previous complaint about the dinner service at Castle Wyvern, I looked over at my handsome boyfriend. He didn't feel comfortable around my mother, and usually avoided her, but that night he seemed almost relieved to be in her presence. She was his maker, technically, so I imagined that gave him some reassurance during what promised to be a tumultuous time in the town's history.

He reached over and squeezed my hand.

At midnight, I excused myself and met Agent Rob on the porch. He loaned me something, which I thanked him for. I invited him in, offering to rustle up a third bottle of wine, but he declined.

I returned to snuggling on the couch with my boyfriend, who was listening to my mother talk about the obscenely wealthy rock stars she hung out with in Venice.

Bentley said, "I would buy that album, if they did reunite."

"That'll be the day," she said with a laugh. "Maybe when Hell freezes over, those two can be in the same room together."

"You never know," Bentley said. He patted my knee. "Who was at the door?"

"My other boyfriend," I teased.

He dropped the subject, understanding that I didn't want to discuss the matter in front of my mother.

My mother pointed to my T-shirt, and said, "I know half the members of that band. The dead half. Did I ever tell you how I met them?"

She had, the last time I'd worn the T-shirt, but Bentley hadn't been there for that one, so I let her spin her yarn.

All three of us were tired, but we were in no rush to leave the living room. As soon as we closed our eyes, it would be morning again, and I would be leaving for another world.

But not yet.

For now, it was nice to sit next to Bentley on the couch, sip wine, and listen to Marzipants squawking in response as my mother told the least believable version of her story yet.

When she wasn't looking, I removed the DWM cocoon gun from the back of my sweatpants, and slipped it under a couch pillow for safekeeping.

CHAPTER 17

Monday, January 2nd

My aunt and I entered City Hall an hour before dawn.

The lobby was eerily empty compared to the last time I'd been there. Gone was the beautiful grand piano and the cheerful crowd that had been singing Christmas carols only two nights before.

Zinnia was struggling with her suitcase. The wheels kept locking up.

"Give me that," I said, taking the handle from her. The suitcase rolled just fine once I had it in my hand. "You must have been jinxing it," I said.

She snapped, "I did no such thing!"

"Zinnia, I heard you cursing it back at your house, when you couldn't fit everything inside. You can't do that, not even as a joke. You probably hurt its feelings." I paused to give the suitcase a tender pat. "There, there. Your master is just feeling cranky because she peed on a stick and found out exactly what everyone else already knew."

She had taken the simple drugstore test three times, and it had come back positive each time. There was still no word from her about the father, let alone her plans for the future. That morning on the drive over, she'd dropped a comment about staying in the other world forever. Given how much she'd stuffed into her suitcase, it didn't seem like an empty threat.

The mistreated suitcase rolled along smoothly at my side, even more obedient than my own bag.

The thing about inanimate objects was they all had energy, to some degree. An item in a witch's possession could easily become hexed if the witch didn't show it respect. As with human beings, a little thank-you now and then went a long way.

As I sent gentle thoughts toward both suitcases, I felt a pang of guilt about my treatment of my house. That morning, my bedroom door had been in a different spot yet again, and I'd taken a wrong turn on the way to the washroom and stumbled into a surprise linen closet. I'd had a few choice words for my house, and none of them had been positive.

As I'd walked out with my suitcase, I had felt the house sulking.

On some level, I'd been glad about hurting my house's feelings. Respect had to run in both directions. My house hadn't shown me much courtesy lately.

I hoped my trip to the other world kept me away for a few days.

I hoped my house would get jealous, and wonder if I'd ever come back.

That would serve it right.

My aunt walked ahead of me, leading the way through the fire doors and into a stairwell.

We would be taking the stairs up to the top floor, where, according to Barry Blackstone's research, we had the best probability of catching the elevator that would take us to another world. He'd explained it to us in great detail—detail I won't bore you with, but it did involve layers of paradox as well as the mayor.

As my aunt climbed the stairs, she asked over her shoulder, "Do you have the key?"

"I have *you*," I said. "And you have the key."

"I do?"

"Check the gold chain that's around your neck. That white pendant that looks like ivory but isn't ivory is the key."

"Oh. Right. Did Barry say it was a copy, or the original?"

"The copy *is* the original," I said. "Remember the whole thing with the paradox? People keep making copies, but then they become the originals, due to time travel."

"Oh. I knew about that. Margaret and I made a copy. Is this the same one?"

"Yes and no," I said. "Paradox, remember?"

"I'm glad *you* were paying attention." She held onto the handrail and kept climbing as she looked at the little white doohickey on her chain. "It's funny. Margaret and I made that copy, but I can't for the life of me remember quite how we did it, or what material we used."

"You've got that Pregnancy Brain thing. I had it with Zoey. The thoughts would just fall right out of my head, mid-thought."

Zinnia continued climbing stairs without comment. We were halfway up.

I said gently, "Are you sure you're up for this? Charlize said they can send some agents to track down Griebel, once they work out the protocols. I'm sure Dawna was exaggerating about the end of the world."

"No. We're going. We must be brave and do what ought to be done."

"But what if someone else will do it? I know that sounds like a cowardly thing to say, and that sort of response leads to nobody doing anything, but is that really the case here? The DWM didn't set up shop in this town for no good reason."

She stopped climbing stairs and turned to look at me. Her cheeks were flushed, and her face was different. Her cheeks were fuller, and her lips were ruby red. The pregnancy was changing her. She looked absolutely lovely. I'd been a teenager when I'd had my daughter, so I hadn't noticed the changes on my own face, the way my body had invigorated itself for the task.

"You don't have to go," she said. "There's no guarantee Griebel will talk to us, even if we can locate him. This could be a wild goose chase. Why don't you go back to your family? To Zoey? I can do this on my own."

"Dawna said it had to be two Riddles. What's the point in having a card mage run a probability spell on your mission's outcome if you ignore her findings?"

My aunt stared at me, her cheeks growing even more pink.

"Besides," I said. "I've never been to the other world, and I'm overdue for a vacation. Long overdue."

She grabbed her suitcase handle from me, leaned over and said to the inanimate object, "You are a wonderful suitcase. I love your color, and your sleek shape, and the organizer pockets inside. Good suitcase. *Very* good suitcase."

She turned and started up the stairs again. The suitcase hopped up obediently.

I patted my suitcase and thanked it as well.

We were only planning to be in the other world for a day trip, but it didn't hurt to be prepared. Our magic wouldn't work in the other world, so we'd packed everything from extra socks to first aid kits.

Plus I had something extra my aunt didn't know about. The cocoon gun I'd borrowed from Agent Rob. I didn't trust myself to use it in the regular world, where my magic might jinx it, but using it in a different world where I didn't have magic was a whole 'nother thing.

We reached the top floor hallway just as the door to the office of the mayor was closing.

I called out, "Hello? Mayor Paladini?"

There was no response. The glass panels next to the door remained dark, the office unlit.

Zinnia said, "If the mayor had wanted to see us off personally, she would be here."

"Does she know we're going? Does she know what we're doing?"

"The mayor knows everything," Zinnia said. "She's a Time Paladin. She comes from a long line of paladins, who valiantly keep order—"

"I know what she is," I said, cutting my aunt off. "She's basically Dr. Who, without the phone booth."

Zinnia pressed her lips together a moment in thought, then said, "Yes. Like Dr. Who, but not an alien. That we know of. Margaret has her theories."

"Margaret also believes that Mayor Paladini hunts Dalmation dogs for sport."

Zinnia raised one eyebrow. "Have you seen many Dalmations around this town?"

I didn't have a response for that.

Zinnia pressed the button for the elevator. It was already on the top floor, and opened immediately.

I said to my aunt, "Here we go. Do you need to go pee? I mean one last time in the regular world, with flush toilets. That wasn't a joke about taking another pregnancy test. Speaking of which, did you bring anything with you for childbirth? What if being in this other world makes your baby grow rapidly, and you have to give birth right away, biting a stick and holding onto a tree, like this?" I put my hands on either side of the elevator doorway and partly squatted. "This is how they used to do it," I said. "Back in the old days."

She strode past me, into the elevator. "There's no need to be nervous." She beckoned me in.

"I'm not nervous."

"You are. You always blather like that when you're nervous. It's your tell."

Her words stung. It was embarrassing to have someone else understand my inner workings better than I did.

I stepped into the elevator and slung one back at her. "Yeah? Well, you always rub your thumb when you're anxious. The thing about my delightful patter is that it happens when I'm happy, too. You don't ever rub your thumb when you're happy, which makes *your* tell an even bigger tell."

We both looked down at her hand. She was rubbing her thumb.

"Well," I said.

"Well," she said.

"I guess we're both nervous."

"I guess we are."

She pressed the button to keep the elevator doors open.

We were waiting for Dawna to arrive with our mystery companion.

"They're late," my aunt said.

"Only thirty seconds," I said.

She released the button. "It's bad luck to leave late."

The doors started to close.

There was the sound of a door opening, and someone running in the hallway.

Dawna yelled, "Hold the elevator!"

I stopped the doors with my boot, and gave my aunt a told-you-so look.

She pressed the button to keep the doors open without them banging into my foot.

Standing in the hallway were Dawna Jones, the cartomancer who'd promised us a successful mission, and her Wisteria Permits coworker, Xavier Batista.

I'd gotten to know Xavier lately, and not just from Friday bowling night. He didn't have any powers of his own, but he had a keen interest in magic, so he'd been helping me with a few things as an unpaid intern. Mostly he'd been cleaning my car and almost getting us both killed.

Breathless, Dawna said, "You need to take Xavier with you. I did some more readings, and it's for the best. Please don't report me to the top ladies in charge for being sexist, but you two won't have any powers over there, and there might be dangers. You'd be better off with a man, even if it's just Xavier."

"Hey," Xavier said, giving Dawna a hurt look.

"Sure," Zinnia said. "We'll take him."

"Why not," I said.

"Oh," Xavier said. He looked disappointed that he hadn't needed to argue with us to be included.

I waved him in. "I guess being my intern is sort of like being a son. That must be what the cards meant."

He stepped into the elevator and gave us a bashful look. "I didn't pack anything. Dawna didn't give me any time."

Zinnia said, "Don't worry. I packed extra."

Dawna was giving me a funny look. "Zara, why are you dressed like a ninja?"

"This?" I patted my layers of clothing. Every item on my body was a near-black, midnight blue. "My closet picked it out." I stuck my hands in my pockets. "Once I located the darn thing, anyway. My stupid insulation-brained house shuffled my closet to the back door. Nearly half of my footwear turned into rubber boots. And I don't mean half of my pairs. I mean half of each pair. The left shoe is fine but the right shoe is a rubber boot. Can you believe the nerve of that?"

Dawna pulled her head back. "Ooh, girl, you are not selling me on this witchcraft stuff."

"I think she looks nice," Xavier said. "Navy blue looks good on redheads. Zara, your mother looked very attractive at the wedding."

"Down, boy," I said.

He said, "What I mean is, she looked attractive for a much, much older woman."

I nodded in approval. "Welcome to our adventure party," I said.

Dawna was wringing her hands nervously. Her long nails were even more chipped, as though she'd been using them to put an antique finish on new furniture.

Zinnia asked Dawna, "Did your dreams bring you any news or refinements, besides the addition of Xavier?"

Dawna rubbed her eyes. She must have had a hard night. There wasn't a single fingernail on her hands that didn't have big chips in the Christmas-themed nail art.

Zinnia said, "Well?"

"Xavier has to bring something back," Dawna said. "Something secret."

"Good for you," I told the young man as I gave him a pat on the shoulder. "Get yourself a cool souvenir. I'll be looking for postcards, myself. I hear this place has tiny people you could put in your pocket. It's probably better if you leave them where they are."

"Duh," Xavier said, looking horrified at the idea.

The three of us said goodbye to Dawna, who took a step back and watched us from the hallway, nervously picking at her nails.

My aunt unfastened the chain from her neck, leaned forward, and used the chunky white pendant—the paradoxical elevator key—to twist a circular component within the elevator's panel.

The doors closed. The elevator lurched into motion.

We plummeted downward so rapidly that gravity lost its grip on us.

I floated up, kicking my feet uselessly.

My aunt and Xavier floated up as well.

We were like three astronauts, inside a spaceship the size and shape of an elevator.

Before I could ask the obvious question, my aunt said, "This didn't happen last time."

Xavier said, "We were taking the elevator from a different floor, going in the other direction."

We bobbed around the elevator, gently bumping into each other and our suitcases, ricocheting gently off the mirrored walls.

"Question," I said. "This other world we're traveling to, it's the one that separates us from the underworld, right? The bad place? The one commonly known as Hell?"

Zinnia said, "That is my understanding."

Xavier said, "This other world may not be Hell, but it's not exactly paradise if you get swallowed by a timewyrm and taken to their den for... entertainment." He shuddered. Xavier and another girl from my aunt's office had not had the best of times in the other world.

I said to both of them as we floated around, "Would you two say this other world, with the timewyrms, is like the delicious filling inside a sandwich, and that Earth and Hell are the slices of bread?"

Xavier was too busy trying new flexing poses in the mirrors while floating to reply.

My aunt said, "I wouldn't put it that way, personally, but I suppose one *could* describe it that way." She bumped into my face with her butt. "Sorry," she said.

I pushed against a mirrored wall, curled up, and did a midair roll before coming to a stop in the starfish position. Xavier kept posing, and my aunt continued bobbing around with her hands at her chest, as though she didn't want to get dirty fingerprints on the clean mirrors and upset the custodial staff.

I said, "So, what happens to a sandwich when the filling disappears?"

She was perplexed by this question. Or happy. She was upside down, relative to me, and I couldn't tell.

She said tentatively, "In this scenario of yours, whatever would have happened to the filling of the sandwich?"

"Something ate it."

"A layer of swiss cheese, bacon, and lettuce, maybe," she said. "But nothing would eat a whole world."

"You wouldn't say that if you took a peek into the mind of Chessa Wakeful, like I did." Chessa was the descendent of a powerful entity who'd immigrated to Earth from the other world we were traveling to. She was the most powerful of three triplets. Her sisters were gorgons, and they were plenty fearsome, but Chessa had the powers of a goddess. I'd seen into her consciousness. The precious veil of my sanity had lifted, and I'd seen things. Horrible things. Monsters devouring worlds.

Zinnia had no response.

Xavier was still admiring himself as he posed like a superhero in flight.

The panel lit up for the first time with a floor number.

It read: 10.

Gravity returned slowly. We all linked hands and returned to standing positions.

9.

My body felt like its regular weight again. The suitcases stopped rolling around on their wheels.

8.

My body felt heavier than usual.

7.

Standing was uncomfortable. We were so heavy now.

6.

My aunt took a seat on her suitcase. Xavier dropped and sat cross-legged on the floor.

5.

I also took a seat on my suitcase. "Are we going up again? Why?"

4.

My aunt looked up at the top of the elevator car. "If we stop suddenly, we'll hit the ceiling hard."

3.

I said, "We should lie down on our stomachs, so we hit the ceiling butter side up. Or down. Either way, the buttocks are nature's safety foam."

2.

Xavier said, "I'll do whatever you tell me to do," and he got onto his stomach on the floor.

1.

My aunt and I both slid off our suitcases and onto the floor, on our stomachs.

There was a creaking sound. It was the suitcases next to our heads, groaning under the pressure.

My eyes were still open, so I saw the number on the elevator panel change. It turned from 1 to what I first thought was a sideways number 8, but was actually the infinity symbol.

The weight that was bearing down eased up. The air returned to my compressed lungs. My pulse surged, pounding in my ears.

We'd stopped moving, and at a reasonable rate.

"Ride's over," Xavier said. "Please return your trays to the upright position."

My aunt let out the most pleasant sigh I'd heard in a long time.

Xavier bounced up to his feet, and tried to help my aunt up. She refused to take any assistance. No surprise there.

Xavier got between us and the elevator doors. He took a fighter's stance, fists raised.

Zinnia smirked at me. *Our hero.*

The young man clenched his jaw and said through gritted teeth, "Watch out for the timewyrms. Their weakness is their lack of aim. With mouths that size, they didn't have to evolve to be precise."

Zinnia said, "Evolve? I'm not sure evolution was involved. Not in this particular world."

I took a similar posture to Xavier, with one fist raised in defense and the other hand on the DWM's cocoon gun, which I had strapped in a holster under my navy wool jacket.

My aunt looked at both of us and shook her head as she stepped to the back corner of the elevator.

There was the familiar BING of the elevator, and the doors opened.

That was when the water rushed in.

CHAPTER 18

I didn't know about Xavier, but if there had been a written list of all the things my aunt and I had prepared ourselves for, a flood of water would have been about halfway down the list. Flooding by water was not ideal, yet it came below flooding by hot lava, which came below a whole bunch of horrible things.

The rushing water sent us all crashing into the back corners of the elevator. I heard a mirrored wall behind me crack as my suitcase slammed into it.

Zinnia and I grabbed our suitcases to our chests, and floated up with the rising water. The flood was moving at a slower than expected rate, probably due to some magical forces inside the elevator in this version of City Hall.

"It's going to stop," Zinnia said calmly. "Don't be in a rush to exit."

Xavier gave her a horrified look. "Don't be in a rush to exit the flooded elevator? I don't know about you, Zinnia, but this body didn't come with gills."

"Wait," she said. "It should only fill to the top of the doors. There's a channel of air above us."

"If you say so," Xavier said.

All three of us floated upward with the water line.

It did stop filling when it reached the top of the doors.

All three of us were head and shoulders above the water line, breathing the air bubble trapped at the top of the elevator.

"There we go," Zinnia said calmly. "No need to panic. City Hall takes care of its own, in any dimension."

Xavier said, "I don't feel very taken care of." He grabbed onto the metal channels at the top of the elevator —the ones that held the acoustic tiles—and eyed the water below him warily. "Did you see something moving down there? One of those timewyrms?"

"The timewyrms are like the mayor," Zinnia said. "They don't care for water."

Xavier didn't look convinced.

"At least it's not a bad temperature," I said. "We won't freeze to death before the air runs out. Speaking of which, we should probably get out of here sooner than later."

"The air may not ever run out," Zinnia said. "We have no idea how far the sealed channel above us runs, or what the gas exchange barrier with our regular world is like."

Xavier said, "If we're heading out, I'll dive down and grab the elevator key."

"I already got it." Zinnia showed us the key, which was back on her necklace.

"Great," I said. "Should we use it to close the elevator doors and head back? Should we try again another day, with scuba gear? I did take those scuba lessons last summer. They say everything in life happens for a reason."

"No." Zinnia shook her head and nonchalantly swatted a glowing yellow octopus away from her face. "We aren't turning back now. Dawna didn't say anything about us all coming over with scuba gear and oxygen tanks."

"Dawna's not very good at cartomancy," I said, which made Xavier guffaw.

"That's not fair," Zinnia said. "I could be highly critical of *your* coworkers, Zara, but I hold my tongue. Dawna Jones is doing the best she can."

"You sound like Bentley," I said. "Am I really that hard on other people?"

My aunt replied, "Your daughter is the ideal teenager for a reason."

"What's that supposed to mean?"

"Hang on." She swatted the octopus toward me, then dipped her head below the water.

I had to hand it to her. Dipping into mysterious water was a great way to change the conversation.

She resurfaced. "I can see plenty of bright light through the water, coming in by the doors. We aren't far from the surface. Do you suppose this is a river, or ocean?"

Xavier, who was cupping the octopus in one hand, said, "There aren't usually octopi in the rivers in our world."

I licked the water on my lips. "Ocean," I said. "Unless the rivers in this world are salty."

"Ocean it is," Zinnia said. "Shall we?"

"Um," Xavier said.

We both looked at him.

"Never mind," he said. "I'll figure it out."

Zinnia patted him on the shoulder, took a breath, and submerged once more.

Xavier said to me, "Zinnia's pretty tough, huh?"

"Not tougher than me," I said. "Right?"

"I don't know." He took a gulp of air and went down.

I took a breath, and followed them.

The water was bright blue, which was a good sign.

Our suitcases were probably leaking, but mine was still buoyant enough to help me rise through the water.

As I floated up, I recalled the time Chessa Wakefield's spirit had been inside me. The woman had many powers, including the ability to stay underwater for hours. I had enjoyed those borrowed powers, and my time at the bottom of the sea. Barry Blackstone was right about it being peaceful down there, like an oasis.

This time, however, I didn't have Chessa's magical gills, so I was extremely relieved when I finally surfaced.

"Oh, good," my aunt was saying. "Breathable oxygen."

"That is good." I took a big breath. "You never know how much you appreciate oxygen until you don't have it."

Xavier cheered. He sunk into the water, flailed awkwardly, and gasped as he resurfaced.

"First time swimming?" I asked.

"Yes," he said, struggling to keep his nose above the water line.

Zinnia said, "Xavier Batista, you grew up next to an ocean. Are you telling me you've never learned how to swim?"

"Our ocean is always cold," he said, burbling as he fought to keep his mouth above water. "Got it," he said. "I got it. I'm not sinking."

He was treading water. Not very well, but not bad for his first time.

I treaded water as I took in our surroundings. I was relieved to see something besides the open ocean. In one direction, there was a sandy shore backing onto a forest.

"Xavier, you've mastered treading water, so it's time for your first swimming lesson," I said. "We're only about a mile from shore. I recommend the backstroke."

Zinnia said, "I recommend we take that boat."

Xavier and I both said, "What boat?"

CHAPTER 19

"*That* boat," my aunt said. "The one that's tied to something over there."

Still treading water, I turned myself around to follow her gaze.

Sure enough, there was a small wooden boat bobbing about twenty feet from us. It was tied to something that looked an awful lot like a dock. Why was it out there, a mile from the shore?

My aunt said, "That must be..."

"City Hall," I said. "The roof, anyway."

"Yes. I didn't place it right away. The elevator was in the side of a mountain the last time I was here."

"Maybe we're in a different world this time."

"I don't believe so. Barry has been researching the connection, and he was certain."

"I'm glad that man is on our side."

She and I began swimming toward the roof. Xavier flailed and splashed in his own unique style.

All three of us grabbed the concrete edge, and flopped onto the solid surface as though we'd been swimming for days. I could tread water just fine, especially in the salty ocean where I was more buoyant, but watching Xavier struggle had been exhausting.

I cast a spell to dry our wet clothes.

Nothing happened.

My aunt noticed my null spell and said, "Your magic won't work over here."

"I know that," I snapped back. "I was just double checking."

She said nothing, but I could feel her thinking it, in a non-psychic way.

"Sorry," I said. "This is going to be hard, having my magic taken away. I probably snapped at you because it reminds me of that time you dosed me with witchbane."

"I did that for your own good," she said.

"Sure."

She removed her warm winter jacket and wrung it out manually. I did the same with mine. Xavier took off his jacket and T-shirt. I noted that he had been working out. The tall, slim, dark-haired young man wasn't as scrawny as he'd once been. I also noted that he took his time putting his T-shirt back on, as though hoping other people were taking such notice.

"At least it's a nice day to get soaked," Xavier said.

He was right. Although it was January and freezing back in Wisteria, down here—or *up* here, or *over* here, or *in* here—it was a pleasant summer day.

I unbuckled my wet suitcase and checked its contents. The case hadn't completely filled with water, but everything was damp. My aunt's case was the same. Note to self: get waterproof suitcases for offworld travel.

Xavier said, "What were you two saying about this dock? I couldn't hear you over... trying not to drown." He kicked at the surface. It was a layer of rocks, over black tar.

"That's pea gravel," my aunt said. "We're standing on the roof of City Hall. Not *our* City Hall, but a different version of it that's also, paradoxically, the same version."

Xavier hopped a couple times. "Do you think the mayor can hear us walking around up here?"

"Perhaps," Zinnia answered.

Our male companion knelt down and scratched at the roof with his fingertips. "Hey, what would happen if we used an ax to break through this material?"

"You'd let out all the air," my aunt said flatly. "Then we wouldn't be able to return home via the elevator."

Xavier straightened up and stuffed his hands in his pockets. "So, are you saying you *don't* want to try?"

In unison, Zinnia and I said, "No."

"Okay," he said. "You're probably right. I guess this is why we all had to come together. It's like that saying. Three heads are better than one."

"It's two heads," I said. "Two heads are better than one."

"Then three heads must be even better," Xavier said. "If we have to vote on something over here, it's an uneven number, which is great." He puffed out his chest. "It's a good thing I came with you ladies."

My aunt forced a smile. "We certainly are glad to have you." Without the benefit of a bluffing spell, she wasn't convincing.

"I'll get better at swimming," he said. "Once you find a weakness, only then can you eradicate it." He swished his hands through the air in karate chops. "That's my resolution for this year. I'm going to forget about magic powers, and focus on eradicating my weaknesses. Yesterday, I threw out all my comic books. No more daydreaming about superpowers for me. I'm all about the here and now. What is." He thumped his chest. "What's in here."

"Good for you," Zinnia said. "I look forward to seeing you transform further into the fine young man I know you to be."

"I asked Knox to be my personal trainer. He said he might get me a pass to work out in the gym at the DWM. Wouldn't that be something?"

"I'm not sure I like the idea of you going all the way down there," she said.

He grumbled that the other gyms in town were for wimps.

While the two of them talked about Xavier's plans to be all he could be, I went to see about the boat.

It was a small, beat-up, sun-weathered dinghy that someone had tied to a non-functioning security lamp fixture. The rope was frayed, holding on by a few threads.

As I examined the rope, I thought about what Xavier had said about three heads being better than two. When it came to rope, each individual fiber was weak on its own, but twisted together, many fibers became a strong rope. Rope was a good metaphor for a community.

I did a safety check of the vessel—not that we beggars could afford to be choosers—and began loading our suitcases into it.

Xavier and my aunt came over and climbed in, and we began making our way over to the shoreline.

The old dinghy had one oar and one paddle, so we had a lively discussion about whether we were rowing or paddling. Xavier was elated to put his muscles to use.

"This is just like the rowing machine at the gym," he said.

We reached the sandy shore of the beach without incident. My aunt had warned us of the ambush by tiny people she'd faced on her previous visit. I had to admit I was slightly disappointed that nobody jumped out of the bushes with nets. We had brought net-cutting pocket knives for exactly that reason, and it was always a shame when supplies didn't get used.

We dragged the boat up to a tree, tied it for extra security, and then hid the oar and paddle in a different location, for even more security.

As I took one last look at the boat, I said, "This feels familiar."

Xavier said, "Like you've been here before? I've been here before, and this isn't even familiar to me. It was all sand and mountains last time."

"It's not familiar in that way," I said. "You know how all the old legends and fairy tales have common elements, even across different cultures? Lots of those stories have a ferryman. He takes you across a river, for a price. For example, Charon, the Greek ferryman of the dead, asks for a coin to ferry dead souls across the River Styx. The ones who can't pay are doomed to wander forever."

Xavier's eyes widened. "Did you bring any money? I've only got a few bucks until payday."

"Don't worry about it," I said. "If we see a ferryman on the way back, at least I've got credit cards. They take VISA everywhere."

Nobody laughed, which was a shame.

My aunt started toward the forest, dragging her suitcase through the sand and onto a hard-packed dirt trail.

I asked Xavier, "Is that the way to the village? Or the castle?"

"It's the way to *somewhere*," he said. "Everything has changed a lot since we came here last time."

My aunt paused and called to us, "Come along. We can't stay on the beach forever." She shielded her eyes from the sun and looked out across the sea. "Even though it is rather lovely."

"We can relax next time," I said as I dragged my suitcase over to join her on the trail. "We have a great book about vacations at the library. It says the first time is for scouting, and the second time will be for relaxing."

"I've never been on vacation," Xavier said. "Not a real one, without my parents."

Zinnia said, "A vacation would be nice."

I looked down at her stomach. The pregnancy was on my mind. There wouldn't be any vacations in her future, once the baby arrived. She would be lucky to get a shower twice a week.

We all started down the path.

Xavier made a few remarks about running into a Tin Man and a Scarecrow.

After an hour of walking through the forest, we had exhausted the topic of the Wizard of Oz.

I needed something to ponder besides the unpleasant sensation of wet socks in wet shoes.

"Enjoy your personal time now, while you can," I said to Zinnia. "You have no idea how few hours there are in a day until you have a baby."

She replied with her nose in the air, "You were little more than a child yourself when you had yours. I'm sure it's much different for an adult."

"I don't think so."

"It will be fine."

"You'll need help," I said.

"I'll allow you to help me. You may babysit from time to time."

"You'll need more help than that," I said.

"There's always Margaret."

"Not that kind of help."

"Margaret Mills has four children," Zinnia said with exasperation. "They're all alive and healthy. Are you telling me you don't think I can handle just one?"

Xavier wisely continued to stay quiet. His eyes were wide, and he looked like he had questions, but he kept them to himself.

"No one is saying you can't handle it," I said. "I'm just telling you that, if I had to do it all over again, and I had the option of having a supporting partner involved, I would do what I could to make it work with that person."

She stopped in her tracks and stared at me. "What are you implying?"

"Did you even tell the guy?"

"You mean, did I phone Mitchell Harrington and beg him to buy me a ring so he can make an honest woman of me?"

So, it *was* him! I played it cool and shrugged. "You don't *need* a ring, but it can't hurt."

She gave me a hurt look. "Of all the people, I thought *you*, Zara, would understand."

"Oh, I understand," I said. "I understand very, very much. You want to keep your independence. You don't want to have to count on anyone else. You don't want judgment, or advice, or help in any form. But what was that thing we talked about back on the roof? Something about two or three heads being better than one? A single thread can break, but if you pair it with more, it becomes rope."

Zinnia's eyes widened and widened, as though she was trying really hard to cast a painful spell on me. She wouldn't succeed, due to us being in a no-witching zone.

Then she tilted her head, looked over my shoulder, and said pleasantly, "Well, hello there."

A tiny voice behind me in the forest replied, "Hello to you, Zinnia Riddle!"

I turned to find a tiny person standing on a tree branch. The person was a woman, smaller than a Barbie doll, with similar dimensions.

Zinnia said to her, "Tippi, right?"

The tiny, busty woman clapped her hands. "You remember me! I'm so honored that you remembered!"

Zinnia said, "You and your people ambushed my group with nets the last time we visited. It's hard to forget something like that."

Tippi waved her small hand as if to say ambushing people with nets was as normal in her world as shaking hands.

Then Tippi continued to gush excitedly. "The others are going to be so envious that I got to see you in person again, along with the famous Zara Riddle and the handsome Xavier Batista! Are you three here from Earth on a tour to promote your new show?" She had a high, squeaky voice, but what it lacked in volume it made up for in enthusiasm.

My aunt looked confused. "My new show?"

Xavier watched the exchange quietly, frowning.

"The one we watch on the lightboxes," Tippi said. "About the adventures of the Riddles and friends on Earth! Oh, we watch all of your stories. My favorite episode was when the Goblin Hordes invaded the library!" She turned to me. "Zara, what is it like to work with Kathy? We don't have very many trolls over here, thank goodness. I mean *sprites*, because that's what you call trolls. That tongue of hers really scares me!"

The three of us exchanged confused looks. Tippi watched stories about us on her lightbox? Did she mean a TV? Or a laptop? What stories?

A little yellow door in the tree trunk opened, and the tiny woman was joined by an equally tiny man with a black goatee. He wore coveralls over his round belly, and a tiny red knitted cap that didn't quite cover his bald head.

He grumbled, rubbing his eyes, "What's all this noise about? I was trying to sleep."

Tippi said, "Riollobo, I'm talking to Zinnia and Zara Riddle out here, you cantankerous old fart!"

"I'm not a cantank—" Riollobo did a double take when he saw us. His tiny jaw dropped.

Tippi elbowed him.

He removed his knitted cap and bowed.

"It is an honor to meet the one who invented *hooking up*," he said.

Tippi curtsied. "Such an honor," she said.

Zinnia blushed. "I did not invent hooking up. I only told you about it, or the term, anyway." She explained to us, "I unwisely used that phrase to describe what Xavier and Liza Gilbert had been doing on the third floor at City Hall."

Xavier shrugged. "It's nice to be known for something instead of for nothing."

Another tiny person, male, emerged from the door in the tree.

He took one look at us and fell to his knees, shrieking.

Zinnia leaned toward me and Xavier and said, "This is not the reception I was expecting. Something very strange is going on."

"This isn't bad," Xavier said. "Compared to my last visit. By which I mean being swallowed up and spat up by the timewyrms to serve as their playthings while the rest of my coworkers partied in the lap of luxury at the castle."

The tiny people squealed excitedly to each other.

Xavier said to me in a hushed tone, "Whatever you do, don't ask if these small ones are people. They are definitely people, as is anyone, of any color of shape, who vaguely resembles a person. If you see something, always assume it's a person. I made a couple of stupid remarks the last time we were here, and I still wake up in the middle of the night cringing at the memory."

I said to our group in an equally hushed tone, "We've got bigger fish to fry than interworldly etiquette. It seems our reputation has preceded us. How do they know about Kathy and the Goblin Hordes? That was an in-joke at the library. It wasn't public knowledge."

Zinnia said, "I'm as mystified as you."

"At least they remember me as more than the guy the timewyrms spat up," Xavier said, beaming with pride.

We waited for the tiny people to settle their shrieking friend.

Once the newcomer had settled down, he was introduced to us as Tottotho.

Zinnia said, "It's lovely to see you all again." She explained to us that she had met all three of the small people at the castle during her last trip. They hadn't exchanged names and niceties during the initial ambush and capture by net plus ogre, but had later enjoyed a sumptuous feast of roasted giant raven plus ice cream cake.

Zinnia said to Tippi, "It's been over half a year for me. How about you?"

"It's been about that long for us, too," said Tippi, the apparent spokesperson of the trio.

"But everything is so different now," Zinnia said. "There's an ocean where there used to be a mountain."

"The king didn't like how things were," Tippi said. "After Queen Beth left us, we got a whole new king." She mimed blowing a trumpet, and said, "Long live the new king! Long may he rule!"

Riobollo said, "I don't know why new kings and queens always have to change things around." He crossed his arms with a harumph. "Queen Beth put a stop to the death matches, which seemed like a good idea at the time, but we have become soft as a people. Our civilization has been on the decline ever since. Now we have this new king who's softer than ever. This one has declared the ravens an endangered species, and has stopped the hunts. It's going to be the end of us all."

I shot a look at Zinnia and whispered, "Any chance the new king is your old pal Griebel?"

Zinnia said to the tiny people, "Tell me about this new king of yours. Is he, by any chance, from my world?" She held one hand at chest height. "About this tall? Big nose?"

"He's not from your world," Tippi said. "The new king is one of the blue ones. He has spikes in his face. I believe your people compared him to a puffer fish. You met him yourself when you were here."

Zinnia frowned. "Do you mean the waiter? Was he wearing a tuxedo?"

Gravely, Tippi said, "In our world, even a waiter can become king. Especially if he pushes the old volcano king into a black hole."

Zinnia said, "Good for him. Long live the new king. We aren't here about him, but about a different man. He's not your size, but he's not my size, either. His full name is Griebel Gorman. He's a gnome from our world. We're looking for him because we're... dear old friends."

The three tiny people conferred in hushed voices, then Riobollo said, "I don't like gnomes."

Tippi said, "Someone like that lives over in Lollipop Lane."

Zinnia said, "Can we get directions?"

The three conferred again, and Tippi said, "I will draw you a map. Give me a moment." She disappeared inside the tree.

The male who'd been shrieking also darted into the trunk. He came out a moment later with a pad of paper and a pencil.

Meekly, he asked, "Can I get your autograph, Mr. Batista?"

Xavier jumped forward like he'd been waiting his whole life to be asked that question.

Zinnia and I signed the paper as well. It took a while to figure out a way to hold the tiny pencil with our enormous hands. It reminded me of people getting their names written on grains of rice. Using a miniature pencil would have been much, much easier with magic.

Xavier asked the small folks, "How do you know about us, anyway? Have people from our world been coming over here and telling stories in whatever you guys have for pubs around here?"

"We see your stories on the boxes of light," Tippi said.

Riobollo, who still had his arms crossed, made a loud harumph. "Boxes of light," he said with another harumph. "It's an idiot box. A boob tube. It's making everyone around here stupid."

My aunt and I exchanged a look. They had television here? She shrugged. Why not?

Xavier peppered the tiny people with more questions, and the full story came out.

The citizens of this world did have television now. They used what they called lightboxes to watch programs that were filmed in their own version of Hollywood, as well as "imports" from our world. The most popular import program was The Regal Riddles, which featured me and my family.

"No way," I said. "I've got to see this."

The shy, star-struck fellow wheeled his television to the doorway so we could see it for ourselves.

The Regal Riddles was an hour-long dramedy that aired weekly. From what I saw, it was a mixture of recreations, acted out by locals, interspersed with actual footage, taken from what appeared to be every single security camera in Wisteria, plus undercover footage shot on cell phones by people who were going to be in big trouble once I figured out who they were. According to the show, we had a mole at the library. I was grateful, at least, not to see the interior of my house on the program.

"This isn't real," I said to the tiny people. "I don't fly all over town on a broomstick, like this actress playing me."

The three looked disappointed.

Tippi said, "You don't? Why not? If I could fly, I would fly everywhere."

"We have to keep our powers secret," I said. "But don't let the truth stand in the way of a good story."

Tippi said, "But some of it is true, right? You are dating a dark, mysterious vampire?"

"Yes, but it's not like what it looks like on your show. My goodness. I don't think I could bend that way if I tried."

Xavier said, "Wow. That actress..."

He had his eyes glued to the screen.

My aunt was unimpressed. Probably because the actress playing her did her voice in a British accent, for no reason.

Zinnia said to me, "I'll have a talk with Vincent Wick as soon as we return home. He'll put a stop to all of this nonsense."

I replied, "Unless he's the one supplying the material. Think about it."

My aunt glowered. "No. He wouldn't."

"First Griebel. Now Vincent Wick. Your dear old pals aren't the most ethical, are they?"

She said nothing.

Xavier, who was still glued to the screen, said, "It doesn't bother me one bit. I think it's cool. I don't know what you two are getting worked up about. It's just entertainment. What's the harm?"

"The harm," Zinnia said with wafer-thin patience, "is that we are exposed. In light of recent events at the wedding yesterday, we ought to be extremely concerned about security breaches such as this."

Xavier wisely shut up.

The program cut to commercial break, which had a volume twice as loud as the show. Riobollo turned the lightbox off with a loud harumph. He reminded me of Zinnia's boss at the WPD, Karl Kormac.

"Here's your map," Tippi said. "I made it as big as I could."

The map was bigger than the autograph paper we'd signed, consisting of many small pieces of paper taped and glued together, but it was still quite small.

We thanked the residents of the tree, and set out for Lollipop Lane.

It was only an hour away, by human foot, but we had to stop several times to provide autographs for more of our adoring fans.

Xavier loved every minute of his stardom.

I teased him, "Don't get too comfortable here. It'll be hard to go home again."

He joked back, "Why would I ever go home?"

We kept going.

Tippi's map, though small, worked well enough.

After a couple of wrong turns which brought us through a stinky bog, a very concentrated snowstorm, and a region with way too many dragonflies for anyone's comfort level, we arrived at Lollipop Lane.

As you might imagine by the adorable name, it was a village of colorful cottages. The homes were small, but, unlike the tiny people's homes in tree trunks, these ones were scaled for humans.

One surprising aspect of Lollipop Lane was that the homes were all on wheels. Apparently the Tiny Home movement that had been catching on back in our world had also captivated people in this world.

Tippi hadn't known which cottage belonged to Griebel Gorman, but my aunt knew as soon as she saw it.

"That one." She led us right up to a giant clock on wheels, with working gears all over the surface.

I stepped up to the door and prepared to knock.

"Careful," Zinnia said.

I took a step back and waved for her to go ahead and do the honors. The gnome was her old friend, after all.

Zinnia stepped up and knocked. "Griebel it's me, Zinnia. I just want to talk."

CHAPTER 20

Xavier and I waited at a safe distance while my aunt banged on the door of Griebel Gorman's fancy clockwork house.

The door didn't open. The gears all over the home continued to turn at the same pace.

"I don't see the point of all that clockwork," Xavier said. "It doesn't even tell the time. That clock face has a bunch of weird symbols where the numbers should be, and there aren't even twelve of them."

"Time must be different here," I said.

"I'll say. The minute hand goes forward and then back."

A tall, red man walking by us casually said, "That's an art piece. If you're looking for the actual time, check the cupcake tower."

"Thanks," I said.

The red man paused. "You folks aren't from around here." He squinted. "You look just like those people who are always getting into improbable situations on the boob tube."

"We get that a lot," I said.

Xavier grinned.

While my aunt continued thumping on the cottage door, I asked the man, "Does Griebel Gorman live in that clockwork house?"

He frowned, making his all-red face look particularly angry. "Not everyone in a small town knows everyone else. It's a dumb stereotype. We're not all hicks who play fiddlesticks." With a snort, he turned and walked away.

Xavier laughed. "I like this place."

"They could be friendlier," I said.

He shrugged. "You get what you get, and you don't get upset."

I waved in the direction the red man had gone. "But he started it. You and I were talking to each other about the clocks, and he butted in."

"Maybe it's a cultural thing."

"This place is weird. It's hot, and it's not as much fun as I thought it would be."

"I like it," Xavier said.

Meanwhile, my aunt had picked up a rock, and was using it to bang on the door even harder. "Open up right now. I've come a long way, and I'm in no mood to be kept waiting."

There were still no signs of human or goblin life from inside the clockwork house.

The red man was gone, but a few of the other residents of the other houses gave us curious looks. They were all full-sized people, like us, except they were not like us. They all had crayon-colored skin tones, unusual head shapes, and equally wild hair. I tried not to stare, but it was hard to keep from gawking.

Xavier asked me quietly, "What races are these people? Are they all the same, or are they different species?" Before I could answer, he said, "Some of the girls are cute. Those are girls, right? I mean, they have girls here, don't they?"

"Calm down," I said. "And keep it in your pants."

He sputtered, "I wasn't thinking about *that*!"

I gave my young male companion a raised eyebrow.

He stuffed his hands into his jean pockets and looked away.

Zinnia was breathing heavily, taking a break from battering the door.

I said to my aunt, "Maybe he's gone fishing. We could canvas the neighborhood."

Canvas was a new term I'd picked up from Bentley. He was always canvassing. It used to be that the word canvas made me think of waterproof book bags. Now it made me think of crime, and how there was always plenty of information available if one was patient and asked around. The key to solving a crime wasn't guns and cars, but hours of time. Also, having a badge didn't hurt.

Zinnia huffed and puffed angrily, her cheeks red. "I know he's in there. I saw movement through the peephole. Not in a pattern, like the clockwork. The gnome is home."

I joined her on the step and glared at the door handle. "This wouldn't be an issue back home." For a witch, there was no such thing as a locked door.

Xavier said, "Step aside, ladies."

We stepped aside.

Our brave hero backed up a few paces, then ran at the door and launched himself into it, wisely using his boot instead of his shoulder. Bashing into hard doors with soft shoulders was a newbie mistake that only led to injuries. A good kick was the right tactic, if a battering ram wasn't available.

The door flew open.

The gnome, Griebel Gorman, who'd been hiding on the other side of the door, let out a surprised cry and stomped his foot once.

If he managed to stomp his foot two more times, he would be gone without so much as a puff of smoke.

My aunt was the closest to our suspect, but she hadn't made any moves to tackle him. His foot was raised. We didn't have much time.

I reached for the special toy I'd brought over, courtesy of Rob at the DWM.

The gnome stomped a second time.

Unlike us witches, his magic reportedly worked in that world. He was already in his home, so the triple stomp that normally brought him home would surely teleport him somewhere else.

The gnome raised his knee for the third stomp.

Before his boot could hit the floor, two things happened. He was simultaneously tackled by Xavier, and shot by me.

The cocoon left my weapon with a powerful kick that made me stumble backward.

The sticky web coated its target like magic, even though it wasn't magic at all.

My aim had been true, and the cocoon worked as advertised.

The gnome was incapacitated. He was also tightly wrapped to Xavier Batista. They were like two mismatched potatoes, shrink-wrapped together.

Both of them tipped over and fell to the ground, wriggling.

My aunt stared at me in disbelief. "Zara, what was that?"

I pretended to blow the smoke off my cocoon gun—there was none—then holstered it again.

"Introducing the new and improved DWM Cocoon Gun," I said. "Don't leave home without it."

Meanwhile, the writhing mass of Xavier and Griebel started making horrible noises.

They were suffocating.

I ran into the cottage, yelling, "Air holes! Quick, Zinnia, we need something sharp or they'll suffocate!"

The new and improved cocoon gun did come with air holes, but the alignment wasn't perfect, and it definitely didn't have two air holes for a double capture.

Zinnia and I used the pocket knives we'd brought along, and quickly cut breathing holes through the strong material.

Xavier, who couldn't see from inside the shroud, proudly said, "I got him!"

"You sure did," I said.

Griebel Gorman sputtered angrily, using every curse word I knew and a few I didn't.

My aunt knelt next to the smaller side of the cocoon lump and said, "You know why I'm here, don't you, old friend?"

He replied, "I didn't do it!"

She used her thumb and middle finger to thwack him on his forehead.

He howled as though she'd kicked him in the stomach.

She thwacked him again. "Talk."

"I had to do it," he said. "I had no choice, Zinnia. You've got to believe me."

"There's always a choice," she said. "You could have come to me."

He squirmed against the cocoon, which only made it draw tighter.

On the other side, Xavier let out an *oof* sound. "Hey, Spider-Woman, can we speed this up before your web kills me?"

Zinnia caught my eye. "Does the cocoon kill detainees?" She winked. I caught on that we were going to use old-fashioned bluffing, without magic.

"It's unclear," I said. "The department has had a few casualties, but they assumed it was from the lack of air holes. However, the web *is* made of a resin that's a known cytotoxin."

Xavier said, "Uh, ladies? I can't feel my face. Is that normal?"

Griebel squealed, "Let me out of here!"

Xavier sounded equally panicked. "I can't feel my tongue!"

Griebel shrieked in a panic.

Zinnia thwacked him on the forehead again. "Third time, old friend. Who hired you?"

All at once, the fight went out of him. He stopped struggling.

With a sigh, he said, "It was Morganna Faire. She didn't fully reincarnate after Archer killed her at the castle. She came over here to this world, and lately she's been using the new phone system to make contact in our world."

Zinnia said, "That's a relief."

I said, "It is?"

She said to me, "Compared to the entities that might have been on that phone call, this is relatively good news. At least we know who we're dealing with."

Griebel whimpered. "Let me out of here, please. Don't leave me like this. I'm not a terrible person, I swear. She wanted the whole batch of wine poisoned, and I had to do it or she was going to kill me, but I added a compound so it wouldn't kill anyone but the genie. I swear to you I'm telling the truth. My word is my bond."

"We'll see about that," Zinnia said, and she used the knife to cut his whole face free.

She stepped outside of the tiny clock house, got something from her suitcase, and returned.

"You'll have to drink this," she said, holding a small vial of red liquid over his mouth. "It's a sample of the wine from the wedding. If what you're claiming is true, and it's not deadly to anyone but genies, you should be fine."

"I'll drink it," he said. "Can you let me out of this thing? I promise I won't run. My word is my bond. I won't run."

"It's not the running I worry about," Zinnia said. "I can outrun you in high heels, old friend."

"I won't stomp," he said, and he swore the oath again.

My aunt used her knife and began freeing them, starting with Xavier.

Xavier squirmed out of his side of the cocoon. "Hey, isn't Zoey Riddle half genie? Wouldn't the poison have killed her?"

Griebel's nostrils flared. "I don't know," he admitted, avoiding eye contact with me as he pulled the sticky web off himself.

Xavier was right. My daughter was half genie.

Griebel could have killed my daughter?

It was one thing to poison all the supernaturals in town, but to callously allow one specific innocent to die—my daughter—it was more than I could handle.

I saw red.

I threw myself at the gnome.

Xavier managed to get fully out of the cocoon just in time to hold me back.

I struggled against the young man, but he was strong. Not supernaturally strong, just a man. Much stronger than me without my powers.

I spat curses at the gnome. If Xavier hadn't been holding my fists, I didn't know what I would have done.

"That's enough," my aunt said to me. "Zara, I'm as angry as you are. Believe me. But punching this gnome won't make you feel any better."

"I'd like to at least try," I said.

"He's liable to spit in your eye," she said. "Their saliva can be rather caustic. I don't recommend getting into a brawl with one of his kind."

I'd all but forgotten about the acidic saliva. I'd read about it in the book I called the Monster Manual. It was a special enzyme that came from a gland under the tongue. Not something a person wanted to catch in the eye, especially in a world where a witch's healing powers didn't work.

I settled, relaxing my arms in Xavier's grasp.

"Now drink," my aunt said, holding the vial to the gnome's lips.

Griebel had his hands free now, but he kept them at his sides as he opened his mouth and allowed her to pour in the poisoned wine.

We waited. Xavier kept his hold on my arms, as though aware that my red wave of rage had not fully ebbed. The young man got himself into plenty of fistfights, so he probably had a good intuition about such things.

A minute passed.

The gnome didn't melt.

Another minute went by.

The clockwork mechanisms all over the house created a pink noise that muffled the sound of people outside. I could hear them going about their business but none of the details.

My core temperature seemed to be cooling. It wasn't, since core temperatures didn't change much, but it felt like it had gone from boiling to just simmering.

Xavier finally released his grip on my arms.

I gave him a sheepish look as a thank you.

He nodded and gave me a casual chin lift that said *no problem, friend.* Xavier could be a cool guy.

Five minutes later, Griebel was still alive, proving that he'd done what he could to mitigate Morganna Faire's plans.

The gnome's stomach made unpleasant noises, like he'd eaten a bad taco, but he hadn't dropped dead. Darn.

"See? I'm not a bad guy," he said.

Zinnia said, "Nobody is going to thank you for *not* poisoning half the supernaturals in town, least of all me."

Griebel wiped sweat from his brow and rubbed his large, bulbous nose. "Are you saying I shouldn't expect any parades in my honor when I come back?"

"It might be best if you don't come back at all," Zinnia said.

"Aww," he said. "You'd miss me."

"Let's give it a try, and I'll let you know."

His stomach burbled aggressively.

"There are some side effects," he said, wincing and holding his midsection. "I'll need the bathroom soon." His large nose turned a deep shade of red.

"Is there anything that can be done?" Zinnia asked, showing a smidge of compassion. A smidge that I would not have shown the man. I'd have made him drink the last droplets from the bottle and lick the rim.

"I could use something to settle my stomach," the gnome said. "Did you bring any Pepto Bismol with you? The generic brand they sell here isn't nearly as effective."

"I don't have that," Zinnia said. "I do have peppermint oil."

His stomach burbled even louder. "Peppermint oil won't work," he said.

Xavier nudged me. "Zara, didn't you have Pepto in your suitcase? I saw it when we were on the roof."

I gave him a dirty look. All his credit for being a cool guy evaporated.

"Hang on," I said with a groan. I retrieved the bottle from my damp suitcase, and gave it to the gnome.

He cracked the plastic seal and drank the whole thing, straight from the bottle.

"We'll need to deal with Morganna," Zinnia said to all of us. "She made one attempt on our lives, so we ought to assume she'll make another. What can we do?" She looked at the gnome. "Would shutting down the phone lines stop her from meddling in our world?"

"Maybe," Griebel said. "I don't know. Cutting the phone lines won't do anything if she's gotten out."

The doorway to the tiny home darkened.

Adrenaline made me reach for my gun again.

A man stood in the doorway.

"Don't move," I said to the shadowy man. "I have a gun pointed at you." I tilted the cocoon shooter so it caught the light.

I hoped the shadow didn't make me use the gun. It was out of the main ammunition—it only carried a single cocoon. There was a second function, but it was much, much deadlier.

CHAPTER 21

The shadow raised his hands. "It's just me," he said.

It had taken me a minute, but I recognized the voice. It was either Chet Moore, or Archer Caine, and one of them was reportedly alive and well in London.

"Archer?"

"It is me, Zara," he said. "How is Zoey?"

I relaxed and dropped the weapon to my side.

"She misses you," I said. "But at least she didn't get poisoned along with you."

"I am grateful for that," Archer said. "How is Carrot?"

"I don't know," I said, feeling bad that I hadn't made time to connect with her personally. Everything had happened so quickly after the wedding.

"She is grieving," my aunt said, sounding cross. "Archer Caine, you didn't even give her the dignity of becoming a widow. There's no word for what she is."

The back of my neck twitched. My aunt sounded angrier at Archer than I would have expected, considering he was the only real victim of the poisoning.

"I am so sorry." The genie leaned against the doorway as though physically weakened by his sadness. "I am deeply sorry about everything. If I had known how much trouble I would bring to your world in that body, I wouldn't have stayed."

That body? His face was in the shadows, but I could tell he was still wearing Chet Moore's borrowed face. I wondered, did he even have a body or a face that was his own? I could never remember what he'd looked like the first time we met. Even his name evaded my memory. The man was like a mirage.

Archer continued. "I knew it was dangerous for me to stick around, but I foolishly thought I would be able to protect the ones I love."

His words were tinged with heartbreak. I had no magic to help me ascertain the truth, but I felt his emotions resonate in my body. He had regrets.

Zinnia didn't say anything.

Xavier was quietly examining the clockwork parts of the house, allowing us our moment.

Griebel was quiet, except for his stomach.

"Zara, I am sorry," Archer said.

"Don't be sorry," I said, unable to take more of his pain. "It was your sister, or *your companion*, or whatever Morganna is to you. She's the one who did this. She pitted us against each other, and for what? What on Earth was she trying to get out of it, anyway? Is she trying to take over the town? The world?"

"My sister can be vengeful," Archer said. "She wants... to hurt me."

"That's it? I hate to break it to you, Archer, but not everything is about you."

"With Morganna, it is always about me," he said. "I try to love her, Zara. Through every time and every incarnation. I try to love her so that she doesn't hurt others the way she does, but there is always something that plants a seed of evil in that heart of hers. I try, time after time, but I am just one djinn, and I can never give her enough to stop this pattern from repeating itself, over and over."

A minute of silence passed.

Nobody else was saying it, so I did. "Archer, maybe she wants more from you than just a sibling relationship, if you know what I mean."

He let out a hollow laugh. "We have been lovers many times."

"Oh," I squeaked out. There went that theory.

"We have ruled great lands as king and queen," Archer said. "She has been my mother, my daughter, my priestess, my best friend, and my lover more times than I can count. I have given her everything, and it is never enough."

"Yup," Xavier said.

We all turned to him.

Xavier shrugged. "Liza Gilbert," he said as an explanation. "The more I give her, the worse she treats me. Sometimes I think she doesn't care about me at all. Like she was put on Earth to torture me." He rubbed his cheek.

I asked him, "How's your face? Is it still numb?"

"A little bit."

"The cocoon wasn't toxic," I said.

He slapped his cheek. "Huh. The power of suggestion."

"Oldest trick in the book," I said before turning back to Archer.

"Listen," I said gently. "As much as I'd like to dig into this whole thing with your icky sister-lover-mother-daughter, it might be better for you to find a trained counselor who deals with toxic family patterns. Right now, we need to find Morganna and stop her before she kills any more people."

My travel companions murmured in agreement.

Archer said, "I have a few ideas."

Griebel said, "I want to help. I need to redeem myself."

Zinnia said, "You mean you don't want us to leave you unattended now that the victim of your poisoning has identified you as the culprit."

"I knew," Archer said tiredly. "I knew the gnome was hiding here, in this clockwork art piece. I also knew what was happening from the first sip. I keep replaying that moment in my mind. I smelled the poison in the wine, and I drank it anyway. Have you ever heard of a genie having a death wish?"

"Save it for your therapist," I said. "This clockwork place is giving me the creeps. It reminds me of that machine Perry Pressman had in his attic. How about we go somewhere more pleasant? I saw a cute pub at the top of Lollipop Lane."

"Sure," Archer said. "I'll buy the first round."

"You'll buy *all* the rounds," I said. "We don't have local currency."

Everyone agreed.

We waited outside the house while Griebel used the washroom, then the five of us headed up the street.

I said to Archer, "What are you doing here, anyway? I thought when your kind died, you got reincarnated as a baby."

"It doesn't happen right away," he said. "If it did, Morganna would be an innocent newborn with no memories until she hit her teens and the evil kicked in."

"Why doesn't it happen right away? Do you have to get killed again in this world?"

"We don't usually end up in this world unless we are holding onto something, like vengeful anger, or..."

"Or what?"

He patted me on the shoulder. "Your guess is as good as mine," he said, and he skipped ahead to chat with Xavier.

I didn't have the benefit of my magic spells, but I still had my intuition, and my intuition told me Archer was lying. He was hiding something. There was a reason he hadn't passed through and been reincarnated yet. I had a bad feeling I wasn't going to find out why until it was too late.

We got to the pub, went inside, and took a moment to appreciate the unusual decor.

CHAPTER 22

The Olde Fishe and Grille Taverne, located at the end of Lollipop Lane, was exactly as charming as the name suggested.

It was, however, not an authentic English pub.

We took a seat in a large, dim booth in a corner. Xavier busied himself pointing out inaccuracies in the decor.

"That's supposed to be a Union Jack," he said, pointing up at the flag on the wall. "But it's got green where it should be red."

"Of course it's green," said the busty, blue-skinned waitress who'd just arrived at our table with menus. "Green, for the krakens who united the seven kingdoms."

Xavier stared at the waitress, mouth agape. He was not looking at her face, but her bosom, which contained more cracks than the usual bosom. There were two parallel lines, indicating she had three of something that the young man liked.

The waitress giggled. "You folks aren't from around here, are you?"

Was it that obvious? The red man had said the exact same thing to us before we busted down Griebel's door.

Xavier said, "Do we look familiar? We're from the new hit show, The Regal Riddles. I'm Xavier Batista."

She said, "Sorry. I don't watch the boob tube, but you are cute."

Xavier beamed.

Archer said to her, "They're big stars in the next village. They're also friends of mine."

"Should have known," she said with a knowing wink. "You know *all* the fun people, Archiekins."

Archiekins? The man had been there for all of twenty-four hours, and he was already well known to the local pub staff? He worked fast, but not that fast. He must have been living there before he'd showed up in Wisteria with flesh borrowed from Chet Moore.

Our genie friend—*Archiekins*—said to the waitress, "No need for menus, Dottie. We'll have three pitchers of elkspit ale, a platter of nachos, hold the squids, and a dozen blooming onions."

The lovely blue waitress said, "Crazy straws or regular ones?"

"Surprise us," Archer said.

After she'd left, he explained, "It's trendy right now to drink your ale with a straw. Don't worry about the plastic use. There's no plastic in this world. Everything is biodegradable."

"Seems to me you're not suffering here," I said. "It kind of makes all the grieving that folks are doing back home seem foolish."

"Please let them all know I'm okay," Archer said. "Tell them I plan to return to them soon. It will take about seventeen years for me to ripen in my new body and remember everyone." He gazed into my eyes, suddenly serious. "Our daughter will be older than you are right now."

"Kids grow up fast," I said.

"I'll miss out on walking her down the aisle." There was a tear in his eye.

"Bentley will do it," I said.

Archer glowered. "That guy gets everything, and I have nothing. It's not fair."

"Bentley has his fair share of challenges," I said.

"But he wasn't saddled with Morganna. Tied to her fate. Doomed to be swept away in her tide, era after era."

I said nothing. He reminded me of those self-destructive people who blamed everyone but themselves. Maybe I was being unfair. I wasn't soul mates with a genie who ruined everything, life after life.

Archer gazed at me earnestly across the table. "Please tell Carrot not to wait for me. She should find someone else. I don't even know if I'll come back as a man next time. I'm usually born male, but you never know. Carrot is open minded, and of course I know it's what's inside that counts, but she shouldn't throw away her breeding years."

My aunt made a choking sound at Archer's casual mention of Carrot's "breeding years."

Xavier said, "Tell her yourself, man. Come back over with us. We've got a working elevator key, no chameleon potion required, and I'll make two trips with the boat if it doesn't hold all of us."

Archer shook his head. "Thanks for the offer, but I'd melt before I even stepped out of the elevator. Once a genie is killed in your world, they stay dead. In that form, anyway. All I've got is this borrowed body, and I barely got it reconstituted after I melted through the barrier between worlds."

Xavier grabbed Archer's bicep and squeezed it. "You look solid enough to me. Are you sure?"

Archer replied, "Son, do you have any idea how old I am? You don't think I've tried everything? Sometimes I feel like I'm in that movie about the man who gets cursed by a groundhog."

"Groundhog Day," Zinnia said. "With Bill Murray." When we all looked at her, she said, "I'm familiar with all movies starring Bill Murray."

Gravely, Archer said, "I believe the director had some input from an actual genie." He waggled his eyebrows.

I said to Xavier, "He does this a lot. He casually mentions some era, or invention, or great work of art, and implies that he was a key figure, behind the scenes."

Xavier replied, "How do you know he wasn't?"

"It doesn't matter," Zinnia cut in. "Archer, can't you grow yourself another body? I know you grew this one by cloning Chet Moore, and you went right into it without having to lose your memories, so why don't you just do that again?"

I jerked upright in my seat and said, "No! Not again with the Erasure Machine."

Zinnia said, "Wasn't Perry Pressman involved with that?"

"He was." I turned to the gnome, who'd sat as far away from me as was possible while still being in the same booth. "Griebel, is that what Morganna's up to? Has she got someone building another one of those disgusting machines? Was Perry back to warn us?"

"I don't know about that," Griebel said. "But she does have someone in town working for her. I didn't put the poison into the wine, so someone had to do it."

My aunt said, "We need to find out who the agent is."

Archer said, "We need to stop my sister before she strikes again."

Xavier said, "Where is that cute serving wench with our drinks?"

"We don't call them *wenches*," Archer said in a warm, fatherly way. "You're in a foreign land, son, so you'd do well to mind your manners."

I said, "Did you just call him *son* again? Great. Just great. Don't tell me Xavier is another one of your illegitimate offspring."

Xavier straightened up. "What?" He looked hopeful.

Archer laughed and held his hands up. "It's just an expression. Easy, Zara. Don't shoot me with that gun of yours."

Just then, the blue skinned, triple-breasted waitress arrived with our chilled drinks and hot food.

"Wait a minute," I said before Xavier could take a bite. "Archer, is the food here a trick? Will it keep us stuck here? Like when Persephone—the one in the Greek myth, not my half sister—ate the pomegranate seeds and got trapped in Hades?"

"It's just food," Archer said, and we all dug in.

Zinnia didn't touch her mug of ale with its crazy straw, but she did do some serious damage to the food.

Griebel didn't touch anything, citing ongoing issues with his stomach. I didn't feel sorry for him one bit.

The strangest thing about our meal was that Archer didn't seem the least concerned that the gnome who'd imported the poison that had killed him was sitting with us. I concluded that being killed was a completely different experience for an immortal genie. It was just another thing that happened, like stubbing your toe really hard.

We had ordered another round of food when Griebel asked if he could be excused, holding his stomach and grimacing.

"You may go," Zinnia said. "I'm satisfied that the poison was denatured, as you said."

The small gnome was in the corner of the booth, so Archer and Xavier started sliding out to allow him to exit. Before they could get up, Griebel stamped his foot three times and disappeared into thin air.

"So cool," Xavier said. He asked Archer, "Is there any way a regular person like me can get powers?"

"There's Activator X," Archer said. "If you can get your hands on it. But I wouldn't if I were you. There are side effects."

Xavier said, "I don't care about side effects. I'd do anything to get powers."

Archer raised an eyebrow. "Anything?"

"Anything," Xavier said.

Archer leaned back and stretched. "Then it's a good thing there's no way you can do it, son. I don't like the idea of anyone having that much influence over you. It's bad enough you've been interning for Zara."

"Hey now," I said.

The other three shared a laugh at my expense.

More food arrived, and more good times. It was odd to be sharing a feast with the man whose funeral we would be attending shortly, but I was enjoying myself.

Xavier said, "Scoot over. I gotta hit the washrooms, assuming they have washrooms here."

"I'll show you the way," Archer said, and the two left together.

It was only me and my aunt left at the table.

I asked how she was feeling.

"Odd," she said. "We'll be at Archer's funeral next week."

"I was thinking the same thing. My psychic powers must be kicking in."

She pulled the twisting crazy straw from her untouched ale and played with it. "Do you think Archer is trying to protect his sister? What are the chances he hasn't told us everything?"

"It's possible," I said. "Hard to say. My natural lie detector went dormant a while back, thanks to having magic at my disposal. Getting the truth out of people was a lot harder without spells. I mean, it *is*." I sipped my ale from my own twirling straw. "Good job with your old pal, by the way. That thing you did, thwacking him on the forehead, did you come up with that on the spot, or is that a known interrogation technique?"

She leaned in and whispered, "Gnomes have sensitive foreheads. I used to date one back when I was in my twenties. *Not* Griebel."

"There's so much about you I don't know."

She looked away.

The pretty blue waitress returned with more food.

Xavier and Archer returned from their boys' trip to the washrooms.

"The hand dryers here are amazing," Xavier said. "They're like those Dyson Airblades, but cooler."

Xavier dug into the new round of food as though he hadn't eaten in days.

We ate and chatted merrily for a while, then Archer settled the bill and we left.

When we stepped outside, I was surprised to find the sun had set. Everything was cool blue, but well lit by a pair of enormous moons. It wasn't daylight, but we could see easily, and there was no need for street lamps.

I stared up at the two moons in the alien night sky.

"This is beyond cool," Xavier said. "This whole world is great, if you don't get eaten by a timewyrm the minute you arrive. Look at those crazy moons. I feel like I'm in a video game."

Archer said, "I guess you'll be on your way now. I'll walk you to the shore."

"Not so fast," Zinnia said. "Where's Morganna? We can't leave without talking to her."

"She's gone," Archer said. "She's not here."

"Don't lie to us," Zinnia said. "You're hiding her. I know it. Tell us where she is, or I'll tell Zoey you're willing to let her die to protect Morganna."

Archer clutched his chest. "No!"

"It's your funeral," Zinnia said, and she turned on her heel and began walking away.

"She's really not here," Archer said, running after her. "I'll take you to her house. Maybe there's something there about what she's planning next. Please, Zinnia, you've got to believe me. I would kill Morganna myself if I could find her. I've looked everywhere, and called in all my favors. She may have left. I heard rumors there's a hairline crack between the worlds. A female wyvern has been using it to visit your world and her offspring. Morganna may have slipped through."

Zinnia planted her hands on her hips. "How?"

Archer lifted his chin. "Trade secret."

She abruptly kicked him in the shin.

"Ow!"

"No more secrets," she said. "How would Morganna slip through?"

"She may have gone over as a wisp of smoke," Archer said. "It's a talent she has. She can even slip through and infuse a human host, or emerge as a talking specter from... ancient oil lamps." He turned his face away from us, as though embarrassed.

Xavier said, "Like in a cartoon movie?"

Archer muttered, "The idea had to come from somewhere, didn't it?"

Zinnia and I exchanged a look. Now what? Did we have to return home and look for wisps of smoke and old lamps?

Archer said, "Her house is this way. You can check it for clues."

Zinnia hesitated. "I have a feeling we should get back home as soon as possible. She may be planning her next move as we speak."

I said to Zinnia, "We might as well take a quick look inside her house for clues, since we're here already."

Xavier said, "I also vote we investigate the genie's house. That's two out of three."

Zinnia shook her head and said to Archer, "Lead the way."

"Right this way," he said.

On the way to Morganna's house, we passed several strange and fantastical sights.

One particularly strange and fantastical sight was a pathside booth selling advice. A green creature sat at the booth. The creature was the size of a pre-teen child, and looked a lot like a frog.

The frog was busy dispensing advice to a pink woman about my age. She was plump and had a stubby, upturned nose.

I got a serious Kermit and Miss Piggy vibe from the duo. Just a coincidence? The people here watched stories about me and my family on their televisions, so did the culture imports go both ways?

They both gave me a friendly wave and a wink as we passed.

We reached Archer's sister's place. It was both surprising and unsurprising at the same time.

Morganna Faire's home was an exact replica of her home back in our world.

The front was a hairdressing salon called The Beach Hair Shack. Exactly like the one Zoey and I had visited for a haircut the summer before. Well, not exactly. It was about half the size, and on wheels. But, other than that, it was an exact replica, which made me strangely homesick.

The door was locked, and there was a sign hanging from the handle: Closed for Renovations.

We stepped back and let Xavier kick down the door.

Archer patted him on the shoulder. "Good job, son."

Zinnia said to me softly, "That must be why Dawna's cards referred to Xavier as a son. It seems Archer has taken a fatherly shine to the young man."

"Is Xavier lacking a father figure at home? He doesn't talk about his family much."

"He grew up with both parents. His relationship with his father sounds fine to me. The only problem with Mr. Batista is he's just a regular human with no powers."

The guys entered Morganna's hairdressing shack. They switched on lights, making the place look cozy. Nobody screamed.

I held back, standing on the path in the bright moonlight.

Zinnia said to me, "Aren't you coming in? I'm surprised you didn't rush in ahead of the guys."

My feet felt like they were glued to the path. "I can't explain it, but I don't want to go in there."

"I can explain it," Zinnia said. "You don't have any magic. This place could be filled with traps, and you've got no way at all to defend yourself."

I made two fists. "No way at all?"

She smirked. "You don't have to come in with us if you'd rather stand out here and keep watch."

"Keep watch? Honestly, I have half a mind to double back and talk to that frog who was giving advice."

"Advice from a frog? We aren't on holidays."

"I know. I swear I'm taking our mission seriously, but I'd never forgive myself if I didn't take the opportunity to get life advice from a talking frog."

She said nothing.

"Blame The Muppets," I said. "I've got a soft spot for Kermit the Frog."

"That's no muppet back there," she warned. "But go ahead, if you must. Perhaps your natural intuition is working, and there's something to be gained by it."

"I promise to be careful," I said. "Save some ransacking for me."

"Don't be long." She entered the Beach Hair Shack, and I left, doubling back to the advice booth.

CHAPTER 23

As I arrived at the pathside advice booth, the pink woman who reminded me of Miss Piggy was just leaving.

She rode away on a pink bicycle.

The green fellow switched on an extra lamp, illuminating the sign above the booth.

"Hello," I said to the frog-like person. He was wearing pants but no shirt.

"Hello," he said with a deep, strange, male—by Earth standards—voice. "Walk-ins are welcome, as you can see by the sign, visitor from Earth."

A number of people had already pegged me as a visitor, so it didn't surprise me.

"What a lovely booth you have," I said. "I don't have any local currency, but I am a librarian back in my world. That's a person who helps the people in a town find books and other resources. Maybe we could do a trade?"

"Take a seat." He waved to the stool on the visitor's side of the booth. "No charge today. The first visit is always free."

"Zara Riddle," I said, offering my hand as I settled on the stool.

The frog shook my hand without hesitation. His palm was cool and smooth, but not moist, which was surprising but also a relief. Moist handshakes were the worst.

"My name is—" He made a croaking sound that wasn't translatable into an onomatopoeia. "Most people with underdeveloped vocal chords call me The Oracle at Dragon's End, or Toade for short."

"Nice to meet you, Toade."

He picked up a spray bottle and spritzed himself. "What advice do you seek?"

"General advice, maybe? Unless you know how to stop a genie from taking her homicidal rage out on the people in my world."

He took one long, slow blink, resetting the keyhole-shaped pupils in his large, green eyes.

"That, we can not prevent easily," he said. "Morganna is powerful, and she plays a role in the prophecy."

I leaned forward with interest. "You know about the prophecy?" My pulse quickened, but I wasn't frightened of Toade. If he posed a threat to me, he could have struck without warning. I certainly wouldn't be willing to leave the booth and travel to a second location with the green dude, but I felt safe enough to proceed.

"I am The Oracle at Dragon's End," he said. "My eyes see far."

A smaller frog came hopping up. No pants or shirt. In an adorable squeaky voice, the frog said, "Grandpa, come play on the tire swing at the pond with us."

"Later," Toade said. "I'm with a client."

The grandson hopped away.

I asked, "Which prophecy are you referring to?"

"The one that names your daughter," Toade said. "My people kept it at the ocean's bottom for millennia. I know it well."

"I really need to get a copy of that thing," I said. "Translated, of course."

"It is a shame you cannot read the original—" He croaked a sound like two cars crashing. "It's a beautiful language."

"What can you tell me about the prophecy? Is it true my daughter, Zoey, is some sort of soul catcher? Ugh. I hate the sound of that. It sounds like a dog catcher, but for souls."

"She is the *eater*," Toade said. "That is all I know. She is destined to consume the remainder of your world's souls."

"Why?"

His very large, wide mouth curved up into a very large, wide grin. "Someone has to do it. Don't tell me you believe in free will?"

"I'm not sure. I'm probably like most people. When it comes to the things that other people decide to do, I believe in free will, and that they should do the right thing. Otherwise, what's the point in punishing people who do bad things? If they didn't have any control over what they were always destined to do, what's the point?"

He was still grinning. "So, you see."

"And when it comes to what I do, I'm not sure I have any control at all." I shrugged. "Maybe there's a reason for that. I always have the feeling that I should be doing things. I can't sit still much. I'm always driving forward, working on something. Like coming here, for instance. I could have stayed home and let other people take care of hunting down a suspect, but I packed my suitcase and went without question." I rocked back and forth on the stool. "It must be the powers. I'm a witch over in my world. I figure the powers that be wouldn't have given me magic if there wasn't something important I was supposed to do with it."

"You are correct," Toade said. "It is all part of the prophecy."

"I'm fine with being in the prophecy, but I don't want my daughter in there. She's just a kid."

"The prophecy concerns her more than you."

"I knew you were going to say that," I said with a groan. "Forget what I said about my life being predestined. I want to believe in free will. I *choose* to believe in free will. That's what my aunt does. She says the alternative doesn't seem to be worth the bother."

Toade replied, "Destiny does not care if you believe in it or not."

"But there must be a reason the prophecy exists," I said. "See? This is the ultimate loophole. If everything is going to happen as predestined, why write a prophecy about it? Just to be ironic? Just to make a mockery of our puny mortal lives? For sport?"

Toade said nothing.

"Talk to me," I said. "I don't want my daughter to eat anyone's soul, let alone everyone's. There must be something I can do."

"Yes," Toade said. "If you wish to redirect the prophecy, the solution is simple."

I snorted. "Is this the part where the free sample ends and you want to get paid?"

"My advice until the close of business today is free for you, Zara Riddle."

I knew he knew my name, since I'd mentioned it during our introductions, so it shouldn't have surprised me, but I still jerked back on my stool.

"Great," I said, recovering quickly. "Hit me."

"The solution is very simple. To prevent the events of the prophecy, simply do not kill an innocent by your hand."

"Don't kill an innocent?" I shook my head. "What are you talking about? I'm a good witch. I may use my powers more than I should, but I don't go around killing innocents."

"Not yet, but you will," Toade said.

"I will not."

"You shall——."

I cut him off. "Shall not."

"You must—."

"I won't. I swear I won't."

He held up one webbed hand to stop me from interrupting. "You *will* use the divine powers of the gods, taking life and giving life as you see fit, and the ancient gods will witness your hubris, and they will smile, because you will have proven that your kind is no better than theirs. Your kind is no more worthy of those powers."

Though the moonlit night air was still warm, and it should have been cozy in the light of the booth, I felt cold.

"All shall be as written long ago," Toade said.

I replied, "Could you be *more* vague?"

"Sarcasm," Toade replied. "A language I understand but do not speak. Would you like more advice?"

"Is this general advice, or about stopping the prophecy?"

"It is what you seek," he said.

"Shoot."

"When the time comes, do not fly toward the wreckage."

"What?"

"Do not drop into the heart of darkness."

I crossed my arms. "Okay. Thanks for the vague hints. Since you're on a roll, do you have any good stock tips?"

"Buy low, sell high." He laughed at his joke. Grandpa humor.

"Figured as much," I said. "Well, thanks for the entertainment. It was worth what I paid."

"Did you hear what I said about not flying into danger?"

"Yes, but that's general common sense. That's not advice. Your booth advertises advice. You're just being vague and spooky. Is this how you reel people in? You scare them with a free reading, then you trick them into paying for more sessions?"

Toade said nothing as he spritzed himself with water, staring at me with those big green eyes with the keyhole pupils.

"You can't fool me that easily," I said. "I know about your new TV sets here, and the shows you people watch. I haven't seen every episode of the reality show about me and my family, but I bet one of them covers the prophecy."

Toade's mouth cracked open, and he caught a passing dragonfly with his tongue. It sounded crunchy.

"Whatever this is, it's been fun," I said, standing once more. "I should get back to my friends. Before I go, is there anything you'd like to ask me about my world? Fair's fair, and I did offer to swap."

Toade asked, "What word rhymes with orange?"

"Easy," I said. "There's Blorenge, a mountain in Wales. But places can be named anything, so that feels like a copout. The word you're looking for, the only perfect rhyming word for orange, is *sporange*. It's a real word. Sporange is an older botanical term for the part of a fern where spores are created."

Toade's enormous grin took over his whole face.

"Sporange," he said.

"Did you think you were actually going to stump me?"

Toade began to laugh, and he didn't stop laughing as I walked away.

I could still hear him laughing faintly in the distance when I returned to Morganna's miniature Beach Hair Shack.

I went inside, gave the others the barest report of my interaction with the roadside hustler named Toade, then asked what I'd missed.

Xavier said excitedly, "We found something."

CHAPTER 24

Xavier took me to the discovery.

It was a corkboard that had been hidden on the back of a framed poster of braided hairstyles for bridesmaids. The board was covered in drawings and maps, connected with pins and string.

"It's a classic serial killer corkboard," Xavier said. "As if we didn't already know Morganna was a bad genie, this is what they call in the biz *a cornucopia of evidence*."

"They do call it that," I agreed.

Zinnia was studying the pinned-up diagrams closely. "This is a map of the tunnels that run underneath Wisteria," she said. "And this—" She didn't finish. She just glared at Xavier.

He said, "What?"

"This is a 5C8027 Form," Zinnia said, ripping a sheet of paper off the corkboard and shaking it.

I recognized the form as the same one she'd been upset about finding on Xavier's desk back at the Wisteria Permits Department two days earlier.

Xavier said, "So? It's just a form for..." He grimaced. "Uh-oh."

Archer Caine joined the conversation, asking, "It's a form for what? I know thousands of languages, but I don't speak in Forms."

I raised my hand. "I believe it's for importing explosives," I said.

"That's right," Zinnia said, clenching her jaw. "Xavier, this passed through *your* desk, through *your* department."

"Uh-huh," Xavier said. "And?"

"And you would know if you paid as much attention to your work as you did to chasing around magic powers," she said angrily.

"Take it out of his hide later," I said. "What does it mean?"

Archer chimed in, "Yeah. What does it mean?"

Zinnia sucked in a breath. "By the looks of it, Morganna Faire has imported more than enough explosives to blow up the whole town."

I asked Archer, "Does that sound like something she'd do?"

He replied, "What do you think happened to the lost city of Atlantis?"

We stared at him.

"Yes," he said. "Yes. This does sound like something she would do."

"We must return immediately," Zinnia said. "We must stop her."

"Or at least warn everyone," I said. "Let's get going."

"Hang on," Xavier said. "What if we just give them a call?" He walked over to an old-fashioned, wall-mounted telephone, and picked up the receiver.

Zinnia asked me, "Would that work?"

"How should I know?"

"I've got dial tone," Xavier said, sounding excited.

Zinnia and I cheered.

Xavier said, "Does anyone know the direct phone number to the Department of Wacky Monsters? Uh, I mean the Department of Water and Magic?"

Zinnia said, "Not off the top of my head." She looked at me. "Do you know it?"

"I don't even know my own phone number," I said. "Xavier, can you dial the number for information?"

"We may have a problem." He was frowning at the number mechanism. It was a rotary dial—a circle with holes instead of the push-buttons of modern phones. "How does this work, anyway? Is this a magic phone?"

Seeing the old rotary dial phone brought back memories from my childhood. I used to play a game with my mother by grabbing the phone after she hung up a call. I'd use a code to redial the last number called, and then I would impersonate her. I didn't do anything awful. Just funny stuff. Like double the size of whatever it was she'd just ordered.

Xavier started to turn the old rotary dial.

"Don't!" I tried to blast him with magic, but I didn't have any. I jumped forward and pushed him away from the phone.

He gave me a hurt look. "I wasn't going to make the call," he said. "You can be the one to call and let them know. I'm not here to steal your thunder."

"It's not that," I said. "I remembered something about these old phones. Back before everyone had cell phones, and before every phone had call display and redial buttons, there were codes that you could use to do special functions."

"I remember that," Zinnia said. "When those functions came out, they were like magic spells. People could dial star-sixty-nine to find out the last number called. You had to do that if you missed a call and the tape on your answering machine got full."

Archer said, "I remember that, from my life in my previous body."

Zinnia said to me, "Are you suggesting we use star-sixty-nine to find out the last number that called Morganna? So we can locate her agent on the Earth side?"

"Can't hurt to try," I said. "What do you think, Archer? How do phones work over here?"

"Not many of us have phones," he said. "TV, yes, but not phones. Are you sure that's not just decoration? My sister recreated her old home here, down to the last detail."

"It's not *exactly* the same," Xavier said. "It's smaller, and this beach hut isn't anywhere near the actual beach."

"True." Archer smiled and gave the young man a pat on the back for being clever.

I was still holding the handset, and there was still dial tone on the line.

I reached for the rotary dial, which, unlike our young companion, I knew how to use.

There was just one problem. The rotary dial didn't have a star, or an asterisk.

Luckily for me, some seldom-used brain cell at the back of my head fired up—all thanks to my inner librarian —and I had the answer. Two ones could be used instead of the star.

I carefully used the rotary dial to dial the number one, one again, then six, then nine.

The line clicked, and a friendly recorded voice replied, "The last number that called this line was..." I waved desperately for a pen and paper. Zinnia understood what I meant. She handed me a pen, and the back side of the form for importing explosives.

As the recorded voice gave the ten digit code, I wrote it down. The first three numbers were the Wisteria area code, and the rest rang a bell, but I couldn't place it.

I asked the group, "Does anyone recognize this number?"

Zinnia, Xavier, and Archer shook their heads.

"Figures," I said. "Now that we have cell phones, nobody remembers numbers. I guess we'll have to call it and find out."

Everyone waited quietly as I dialed the number.

There was a click on the other end of the call, and a woman answered. "Dreamland Coffee, Maisy Nix speaking. How can I help you?"

"Maisy?"

"Yes. That's what I said. Who's this?"

"It's me, Zara," I said. "You aren't going to believe this, but I'm calling you from another world."

"I believe you," she said. "Probably because I'm talking to you on a phone that didn't exist before it appeared about ten seconds ago, when it started ringing in the back room. You startled poor Humphrey."

"Listen carefully," I said breathlessly. "I don't know how long this call will stay connected, but this is important."

"Duh," she said. "You made a phone appear out of thin air."

"Maisy, you've got to warn everyone in town. Morganna Faire, the genie, is behind the poisoning at the wedding, and she's not done yet. She's imported a whole bunch of explosives through a construction company. She has an agent on that side working with her. It looks like she's planning to blow up the whole town."

Maisy had a million more questions, but we kept it short so she could get busy alerting the authorities.

I hung up the phone so she could start making calls. I realized, too late, that I should have asked her to call my family first.

I picked up the receiver to call my daughter or my mother. I couldn't remember their numbers. I didn't even know Bentley's.

I hung up the phone slowly. My mind was reeling. I had to get back right away.

Archer said, "I'll escort you back to the crossing. I'm so truly, deeply sorry my sister is such a terror. This is all my fault."

My mind was reeling, but a new idea was bubbling up.

"Hang on," I said. "Star-sixty-nine was the big feature people loved, but there were other ones. There was a code you could use to redial the last number called." That was the one I'd used to impersonate my mother and double her orders.

"That's right," Zinnia said brightly.

"I bet we could use that to find out Morganna's agent on the other side," I said. "We contacted her from Dreamland Coffee, so we came up on the sixty-nine, but —"

Zinnia said, "Did we? I distinctly remember the phone ringing on our side."

"Sure, but we cast the spell, which initiated the call."

Archer said, "Magic sure complicates everything."

"Whether the other code works or not, it's worth a shot," I said. "Now what was that other code? Sixty-eight? No. I think it was sixty-six." I picked up the handset and waited to see if my mind would change itself again.

Xavier said to Zinnia, "We're just going to phone up the secret agent? Could it really be that easy?"

Zinnia said, "We had to travel to another dimension to get access to this phone. We could have drowned. I wouldn't call that easy." She touched my shoulder gently. "Go ahead and call the number when you're ready."

I dialed the one, the one, and then six, and another six.

There was a ringtone on the line.

"It's ringing," I whispered to the others.

After three rings, a breathless-sounding woman answered the call. "Hello?"

I'd been so worried about it even working that I hadn't thought through what I would do if it did.

"Hello," I said, as casually as I could. "How's it going, *hon*?" Telemarketers and surveyors didn't call you *hon*. It was a cheap trick, but I figured why not?

"Hon? Since when do you call me hon?" The woman on the other end of the call was partly buying it.

I coughed and said, "Just being friendly."

The woman replied, "Why are you phoning me on the land line again? I thought you were inside my head. I sniffed up all the smoke when it came through that crack in the elevator on New Year's Eve. Every last bit of it. I did what you told me to, Morganna. I thought you were going to live inside my head until the next part."

"Change of plans," I said, making my voice sound older, like Morganna's had sounded when she'd cut my hair. "It turns out I forgot something back here at my place, and I had to run back."

"Oh," said the woman on the line.

The others were staring at me with big eyes.

I improvised.

"Say, can you do me a favor and hold off on all the explosive stuff until I can make it back?"

"Wait," the woman said. "Now there's two of you, Morganna. Like feedback. I can hear you talking inside my head again. Wait. What's that? It's not you on the phone? But it's your phone number. I can see it on the call display? What do you mean? Oh. Okay. Calm down. I'm hanging up right now."

There was a click. The call had ended.

I pressed the button to get dial tone and redialled the number again.

It rang and rang.

No answer.

As I hung up the call, the others were dead silent.

"Did you catch all of that?" I asked.

They all nodded. I'd held the handset far enough away from my ear that they'd been able to overhear the whole thing.

"She's in a human host," Archer said. "Through the elevator crack, in a puff of smoke, and straight into a human host. If only we knew who it was."

"I know who it was," I said.

They all stared at me expectantly.

"Jasmine Pressman," I said. "Perry Pressman's widow, and Jo Pressman's mother. That's why those ghosts were hanging around." I pressed my forehead into my palm. "Why didn't I question her at the wedding? Why didn't I know she was connected to all of this? It's so obvious. Morganna needed an ally for vengeance, and who better than a woman who's lost everything? A woman with nothing left to lose?"

Everything hit me at once.

Archer, melting into the floor in front of me.

My daughter, grieving the loss of her father.

Even my own fearsome mother, looking worried about what terrible thing might happen next.

Then there was the loss of my privacy, with my life being displayed on TV sets in this strange world.

And that so-called oracle, mocking me.

I completely lost it, for the second time in the few days we'd gotten into the new year.

My aunt pulled my hand away from my face.

"Look at me," she said, calmly and firmly. "I know it feels like we're losing, because that's how life feels at times, but we are *not* losing. Look at the facts. We know about Morganna's plan. We even know about her accomplice. We've called Maisy, and she's doing her part over there to warn everyone. Maisy is an extremely competent woman. Zara, we aren't losing. Do you hear me?"

I heard her, but I didn't. How could we not be losing when I felt so hopeless?

"We should probably get going," Xavier said.

Archer said, "Should we use the phone to make a few more calls? I would like to speak with Zoey, if that is okay with you, Zara."

"No can do," Xavier said. "This phone is bye-bye."

We all looked at the phone. It was melting down the wall.

In fact, all of the items inside Morganna's house were melting, as were the walls.

The tiny Beach Hair Shack was collapsing in on itself, like a Styrofoam cup tossed in a campfire.

We all ran for the door.

CHAPTER 25

We escaped the collapsing house just in time.

The four of us stood on the pathway and watched the Beach Hair Shack fold neatly in on itself until it finished in the form of a bowling ball. Then the ball rolled away.

"Off to recycling," Archer said.

"There's so much magic around this place," I said. "Is that why our witch powers don't work? Is it like how you shouldn't light a match around gas pumps?"

"That's a good analogy," Archer said. "Save it for your memoirs. You should hit the road. Or the path, anyway." He took the handle of my aunt's suitcase. "Let me help you with that."

She made a face but let him help.

Xavier took the handle of my suitcase, and we were off.

We passed by Toade's advice booth. It had been shut down for the evening, and the green frog-like man was gone. I had an intrusive thought enter my head. It was about French cuisine, and the eating of frogs' legs, and how they reportedly tasted like chicken.

The thought wouldn't get out of my head.

I kept picturing Toade's enormous legs, roasted and served on a giant platter.

I had to force myself to imagine the whole town of Wisteria blowing up just to get the image out of my brain.

We made our way out of Lollipop Lane, and back into the forest, where more of the tiny people came out of their treehouses to gawk at the world-famous stars from another dimension.

They held lanterns, and pointed tiny flashlights at our faces.

We could still see the pathway thanks to the two bright moons, but the constant flashing of tiny lights did cause us to stumble around.

Finally, we got to the place where we'd left the boat.

It was still securely fastened to a tree—not that we needed it.

During the time we'd been there, the tide had gone out. Way, way out.

Off in the distance, a mile away over piles of rocks and sand, sat the familiar structure of Wisteria City Hall, now exposed.

"Tide's out," Xavier said. "That's a big tide. Is it because of the two moons?"

"It's complicated," Archer replied. "You see, the orbits —"

"Save it for your memoirs," I said. "Now give me a couple of hugs to bring back to everyone back home. I'll pass them along at your funeral."

Archer didn't move.

"Come on," I said, wiggling my fingers in the come-hug-me gesture. "Let's not make this more difficult than it needs to be. Nobody likes a long, drawn-out goodbye."

"I'll accompany you across the rocks, to the building," he said. "You can hug me there."

"Perfect," I said. "We can drag out our final goodbye for another half an hour."

Archer, my aunt, and I started walking over the moonlit terrain toward the building.

Xavier lingered behind.

I turned and asked, "What's wrong now? Do you see something we don't see? Like a big tentacle monster?"

He shook his head and made a few awkward movements with his hands.

"We don't have time for charades," I said. "Let's go. If my suitcase is getting heavy, I'll carry it myself."

He didn't move.

I doubled back to where he stood and took the suitcase.

"I'm not leaving," he said.

My aunt called back to us, "What's the problem?"

I yelled to her, "Xavier says he's not leaving!"

She put her hands on her hips. "We don't have time for this!"

Xavier said to me, his brown eyes gleaming with emotion in the moonlight, "Go on without me." His voice was husky.

"What are you talking about?"

"Leave me here."

"We aren't leaving you here," I said. "Don't you know the saying, *no man left behind*? You're the man, and you're *not* being left behind."

"There's nothing for me in that world," Xavier said, gesturing at the building in the distance.

"That's not true, and you know it. You're just in a sulking mood. Probably the fatigue of traveling. All the new information can overwhelm the brain." I nodded toward the other two, who were waiting. "Let's go. We can talk about your feelings on the way to the elevator."

"There's nothing to talk about. I'm staying here."

"Why? Because you're a celebrity here?"

"You wouldn't understand," he said. "Over there, I'm nobody. But here, I'm different. I'm special."

"Xavier Batista, that is nonsense. You're one of the most special people I've ever met. You're strong, and you're brave, and you're smart, and most people don't even get one out of three of those things. You've got all three. Plus you have a good heart. Even when you do dumb stuff, it's for the right reasons."

He pushed his hand through his glossy black hair, glanced up at the moons, then back at the forest behind him, and said, "This place wants me to stay."

"Oh, probably," I said. "You know what other places want you to stay? Shopping malls. Casinos. Nightclubs. Does that mean it's good for you?"

He frowned. "This isn't a shopping mall, Zara. It's a whole world. We've barely seen any of it, and you want to leave already?"

"Yes. Because there's an angry genie on the loose in our hometown, and she's going to blow up everything. We have to get back and stop her. Now, shut down the pity party and get your butt moving before I blast it with a double dose of..." I realized too late that my threat was empty. I had zero magic.

I reached inside myself for it anyway, like a person who knows the power's out but who keeps on flicking light switches and remote controls by habit.

When I reached for magic and felt nothing there, it was like tumbling through the darkness.

Xavier must have sensed my discomfort.

"Hah! You have no powers here," Xavier said. "How does it feel? How does it feel to be in a place where everything is strange, and threatening, but also wondrous, except you can't participate because you're just a *nothing person*?"

"You are not a nothing person," I said. "Dawna read the cards, and they told her about you coming here. You're important, Xavier. To this mission, and to me."

"To you?" He looked skeptical. "I'm only good at detailing your car and nearly getting us both killed." He clenched his jaw and looked at Zinnia in the distance. "I can't even do my job at the WPD. I'm the one who signed off on all those import forms."

"People make mistakes," I said, but I was losing my conviction. The kid had a point. Maybe he *would be* happier in this other world.

Archer called out to us, "The tide will be in again soon. It could be dangerous to dive down and access the elevator while it's underwater. I know you Riddles are tougher than you look, but let's not tempt fate."

"Xavier," I said.

He was silent.

I looked him in the eyes, which was hard, because every second I stared at his face, I felt some of the anguish he felt.

I pressed on with my speech, drawing on my recent experiences.

"Xavier, don't you think we all feel useless when stuff goes wrong? Do you think there's something special about you, that you get to beat yourself up more than the rest of us? That's pretty narcissistic. Is that what you are? A narcissist?"

Even in the moonlight, I could see his tan cheeks flushing. He clenched his fists but didn't move or say anything.

Archer yelled across the rocks, "I can see the tide rolling in. We should have enough time, but we have to leave now."

Xavier broke eye contact. "Go without me," he said, his voice thick with emotion. "Go back and save the world, like always. I'm better off here, out of the way."

Then he turned and ran into the woods.

Zinnia yelled, "This is no time for a bathroom break!"

I was about to run into the woods when Archer ran past me.

"I'll handle the boy," Archer said gruffly. "You two get to that building now, while the moons are cooperating." He paused to look back at us, and said, "Leave the luggage."

Then he took off into the woods, after Xavier.

With seemingly no other choice, I picked up my suitcase and jogged to where Zinnia was standing. I explained what was happening as we trudged toward City Hall.

Both of us stubbornly held onto our suitcases until we got about halfway.

We could see the tide rolling in. It was hard for us to judge the speed accurately, but as the glinting water got closer, the contents of our suitcases lost their value to us.

We thanked the suitcases for their service to us, and left them to their fate.

We carried on, stumbling over the craggy terrain in the blue light of the two moons.

As we got closer to the City Hall building, it became clear that it was not an exact duplicate of the one in our world. This one had an elevator that opened directly to the exterior, which explained why we hadn't had to swim our way out through hallways and stairwells.

I had a few choice words to say about Xavier, and how he'd endangered the mission.

I ranted angrily as we approached the building.

Zinnia said, "You're being pretty hard on Xavier. I can't say I blame him for wanting to stay. I'd stay here myself, if I thought you'd let me."

"Don't joke," I said.

"I'm not."

"I can't believe you two. How could you even think about staying? You can't abandon your friends when the going gets tough. Being an adult means doing what ought to be done. Isn't that what you're always saying?"

"Yes, but Xavier is little more than a child," Zinnia said. "He's barely twenty-five."

"So? When I was twenty-five, I was working two jobs and going to school so I could support my daughter."

"By yourself," she said neutrally.

"Yes. By myself," I said. "It was hard, but I did what had to be done."

"Alone," she said. "Independently. Without a man to help shoulder the load."

I realized what she was driving at, and I stopped in my tracks.

Exasperated, I said, "What do you want from me? Do you want me to say you should have this baby on your own? Do you want me to lie, and say that, out of all the possible options available, it's the very best choice? Well, I'm not going to. What I did was stupid. I had a child at sixteen, when I was barely more than a child myself. My mother would have helped me, but oh, no. My pride wouldn't let me. So, yeah, I did it all by myself. Do I think my choices harmed my daughter? Yes. Did she turn out great in spite of everything I did? Luckily for me, yes. But don't use me as a template for your life. I may look like I have it all together, but I don't. I'm barely hanging on by a thread. Do that kid of yours a favor, and don't be stubborn. Don't make your life harder than it needs to be just to prove a point."

She stared into my eyes, unflinching.

We were both standing still.

The tide was coming in. It pooled around our feet.

My aunt broke the staring contest, flicking her hazel eyes to the elevator door.

Neutrally, she said, "We ought to get going before the water rises much more."

We both ran the rest of the way, splashing ocean water noisily as we did.

When we reached the elevator, Zinnia pressed the call button.

The elevator dinged, and the doors opened.

The elevator car was empty, and brightly lit, like a beacon of hope in the darkness.

We stepped up and in. The base of the elevator was above the current water line, but not for long.

My shoes and socks, which had nearly dried, were soaked again.

My aunt took off her chain and prepared to use the elevator key.

She kept her head nodding down. "I can't look," she said. "Is he coming?"

With all the arguing, I'd nearly forgotten about Xavier.

I leaned out of the bright light that was illuminating the elevator car, and scanned the horizon for Xavier.

I could just barely make out a dark lump on the surface of the water.

It was Xavier, slogging through the water that was now up to his waist. He was alone.

"This isn't good," I said. "He's coming, but so's the water. He's not going to make it without swimming, and he can't swim. He could barely tread water."

"He'll swim," Zinnia said. "It's instinctive. Babies swim. We are descended from creatures of the sea."

Creatures of the sea.

That reminded me of Chessa Wakeful, and her powers, and of the Wonder family, with their chants about the *creatures of the deep*.

Xavier called out to us, "Hold the elevator! I'm coming back with you!"

"Hurry up!"

He kept walking through the water until it was up to his neck.

Inside the raised elevator, the level was up to our waists.

Xavier stopped moving, gave me one last desperate look, and then rolled onto his back. He began doing the backstroke. He wasn't very good at it, or very fast, but he was doing it.

We waited until he backstroked all the way into the elevator.

"I did it," he said, grabbing onto our shoulders with excitement. "I can swim."

I said, "Where's Archer? Did he decide against saying goodbye to us? Is he behind you, in the boat?"

"He's not coming," Xavier said. "He said he had something he wanted to take care of."

Zinnia put the key into the submerged panel, and turned the circular mechanism. The doors closed.

I said to Xavier, "I don't get it. What did Archer say to make you change your mind? What powers of persuasion did he use?"

Xavier wiped water from his face. "I'd rather not say. It's a guy thing."

My aunt made a disapproving tsk sound.

One of Xavier's eyes was swelling. His eyebrow was bleeding and making a mess on his face as it dripped down with the ocean water. I reached for his face.

"What happened here?"

Xavier flinched away. "Don't."

"Is this how Archer convinced you?" I asked. "Did he beat you up? Like a common street thug?"

"He didn't beat me up," Xavier reluctantly admitted. "But he did threaten to. And he gave me this shiner as a free sample."

My aunt and I exchanged a look.

She said, "Sometimes violence *is* the answer."

"Apparently so," I said.

The elevator began moving smoothly.

Zinnia said, "Is anyone else surprised that our mission has been so successful? Of course I'll have to replace my suitcase and its contents, which is a shame, but other than that, things have gone surprisingly well. We found Griebel, determined who was behind the poisoning, and even the identity of Morganna's human agent. All without bloodshed."

Xavier cleared his throat.

"It's just a bruise," she said to him. "And you had it coming."

He gawked at her with wide eyes, insulted.

"You really did," I said to him. "No more other-world missions for you. I'm not sure I can even trust you to detail my car. You might sell it for parts, or trade it for a ticket to another dimension."

He gave me a hurt look.

Zinnia was staring straight ahead at the elevator panel. "Honestly, I half expected some sort of sea creature to attack us when we were on the way here. Now we're already heading home, and we didn't even spend one night in this strange realm."

"We're not home yet," I said.

"True," she said, sounding hopeful.

"Aunt Zinnia, are you actually *wishing* for a disaster?"

She didn't say anything.

The elevator car abruptly lurched in a different direction. The water around us sloshed noisily, and we all scrambled to find hand holds.

Xavier gave me a frightened, wild-eyed look. "Are we going sideways? We didn't go sideways before, did we?"

There was another lurch, and the elevator went in the opposite direction.

Despite holding onto the hand railings, all three of us sloshed to the other side with the water.

With perfect comedy timing, I said, "Now I know how clothes in the washing machine must feel."

CHAPTER 26

The elevator shook us like we were grass-stained laundry for a while, then we were back in the no-gravity situation.

This time we floated along with half an elevator's worth of seawater, which was much less fun. I was glad we didn't have the suitcases. Xavier dubbed our ride the Vomit Comet before he was silenced by a mouthful of floating kelp.

When the elevator doors opened again, we clung to the railings while the water flooded out into the hallway at City Hall.

As the water settled, I'd never been so happy to see that familiar industrial carpet.

Mayor Paula Paladini stood there, arms crossed, looking stern and imposing in her black and white suit, with her icy blonde, nearly-white hair.

She was flanked by two members of the cleaning staff, both armed with mops and rolling carts full of cleaning supplies. I recognized the two men from the impromptu party in the building's lobby, but I didn't know their names.

"Good evening, Mayor Paladini," Zinnia said as she stepped out of the elevator onto the sopping wet carpet. "Or is it morning?"

Xavier and I followed, then stood behind Zinnia, as though using her as a shield against the mayor.

"It is past eleven o'clock in the evening," the mayor said. "Eighteen hours have passed since... the last time the plumbing in this region malfunctioned."

Zinnia shot me a look over her shoulder. Eighteen hours was at least twice as long as it seemed like we'd been gone, but I didn't doubt the mayor. We must have lost some time during transit, or the worlds weren't quite aligned. The portal went through space but also through time. Losing a few hours wasn't bad. If we'd taken a wrong turn, we could have turned up sixty years in the past.

One of the janitors, an older man with a bushy mustache, said, "This looks like sea water. Is that kelp? Hey! Something's moving in there!" He reached down into the corner of the elevator and picked up an octopus the size of his hand. The octopus, which was very much alive, wrapped its tentacles around the man's forearm and began climbing.

The janitor shrieked. "Get it off me! Get it off me!"

The other janitor, a man with a red beard and a shiny shaved head, gently scooped the octopus off his coworker, then bent down and dropped it into the crevice between the elevator and the hallway.

"There you go, little critter." The red-bearded janitor said. Then he calmly explained to us, "There's a sinkhole at the bottom of the elevator shaft. That octopus will return to the ocean in its world along with the water that drains out." He nonchalantly grabbed a mop and joined the other guy in the task of pushing the water in the carpet toward the drainage crack.

I looked over to the mayor for further explanation, but she was already gone. I wasn't too surprised.

Mayor Paula Paladini was a strange and mysterious figure. We had rarely interacted, so everything I knew about her came third-hand through other people. She did pop up now and then, whenever strange things were happening, always at a distance, observing. I'd last seen her at the town's Christmas tree lighting, but not since then.

"Sorry about the mess," Xavier said to the janitors.

He'd gone back into the elevator for some reason, and he exited again, both hands in his pockets.

Something about his body language wasn't right. The janitors were both male, so Xavier should have had his chest puffed up and his shoulders back. He was hunched, hiding something.

I stared at our young companion and asked, "What were you doing in there?"

"Nothing," he said guiltily.

"Did you swipe the elevator key?"

Xavier held his hand to his throat in offense. "I did no such thing."

"I've got it," Zinnia said, patting the key, which was back on the chain around her neck.

Xavier gave me a dirty look. Or perhaps it was just a regular look that seemed dirty due to one eye swelling shut.

The three of us made our way down the hall and into the stairwell, where we would have privacy. The building was very hushed. At eleven o'clock, we were likely the only ones there other than the mayor and the two janitors.

I reached inside myself for magic and found it there. I was so relieved I could have cried.

Without saying a word out loud, Zinnia and I pooled our magic and cast the spells to dry our clothes.

Xavier hadn't been expecting a drying spell, and let out an unmanly cry of alarm. He held his hands over the front of his jeans.

"For a minute, I thought I was having an accident," he said. "It's like when there's a seat warmer in a car, and you aren't expecting it."

I reached for his bruised eye and bleeding eyebrow. "Let me fix that souvenir you got from Archer."

He jerked away, giving me a wary look. "It's fine," he said, sounding surly.

I couldn't believe it. "You want to walk around town with a black eye? Why suffer when you don't have to?"

"It's fine," he said again. "Save your powers for someone who needs it, *witch*."

I took a step back. "I beg your pardon? What did you just call me?"

Zinnia put an arm across the front of my chest and cleared her throat. "Leave him be," she said softly.

But I couldn't.

"Xavier, if you want to go back to that world, I'm not going to stop you. Zinnia and I are back safe and sound now, as per Dawna's card reading, so technically we don't need you anymore. Why don't you head on back? In fact, why don't you go jump down the crack and flush yourself out of this world with that octopus?"

Softly, Zinnia said, "Ouch."

Xavier stared at me as though I was very stupid, which, at that moment, I probably was.

"I wouldn't fit," he said. "I'm not an octopus. I can't squeeze through a tiny space like they can." His swollen eye had puffed up enough to close his vision, so he glared at me with one eye. "Did you really just say that to me? Did you actually tell me to *flush myself*?"

"It was a metaphor," I said.

He jerked his head back. "I don't need this," he said. "I can't believe I ever wanted you as a mentor. You're a lousy mentor. No wonder Fatima doesn't like you."

His words stung. Fatima didn't like me? She told him that? Was it true, or had he made it up to hurt me?

Zinnia said sternly, "That's enough."

"It sure is," Xavier said. He turned and ran down the stairs, calling back over his shoulder, "Good luck saving the world and everything! Let me know how it turns out!"

Once he was gone, I said to Zinnia, "He's so temperamental."

"If you say so."

"He was the one who was out of line, right?"

"I suppose."

"Does Fatima really hate me?"

"He said she doesn't *like* you. He didn't say she *hates* you. There's a difference."

Her words stabbed into my chest where Xavier had taken the first stab. Was it true that Fatima didn't like me? After everything I'd done for her?

Zinnia started down the stairs wearily. "Has it only been eighteen hours since we climbed these steps? It feels like a hundred years."

I barely heard her. I was arguing with Xavier inside my head, getting in the last word.

My aunt snapped her fingers, and I felt the sensation of a wet towel snapping my backside.

"Let's go," she said. "We need to help the others make sure all the explosives are accounted for. We'll stop by the Permits Department and grab the 5C8027 Form so we can track down where it came from, how much is on the way, and where it's going."

We reached the bottom floor, and then the door for my aunt's department.

Through the door, I could hear Xavier Batista, talking loudly to other people.

"Who's in there?" I asked Zinnia.

She listened for a moment. "I hear Karl, and Gavin, and Dawna, of course."

"It's past eleven," I said. "What are they doing here? Did the mayor order them to work late?"

"They might be tracking the paperwork on the forms," she said.

"Or they waited around to make sure you and Xavier got back safely."

My aunt looked down. "They didn't need to do that." She cast another blast of the drying spell to dispel the last bits of moisture inside our shoes.

"Your coworkers love you," I said. "Isn't it nice to know that other people have your back?"

"We need to get to work," my aunt said. "You should check in with Bentley, and see if you can help with the investigation."

"So, that's it? We're splitting up now? Are you trying to get rid of me?"

She frowned. "That's not my intention. I'm going into the office to see about those forms. I shouldn't be long, and we can go check on Zoey and my sister after this."

I looked at the door. "I could help with the forms."

"It's complicated," she said. "Perhaps you would prefer to wait here in the hall. It might be easier for Xavier to focus without you in there."

"Sure." I tried to lean against the wall casually, but my body was too angry to lean.

"Hallways are good for sulking," she said.

"Just check on your stupid forms, and let's go."

My aunt went into the office.

I listened as they talked about the forms, the explosives, and what was happening locally with the investigation.

Down the hallway, the elevator doors opened. One of the janitors I'd seen on the top floor—the red-bearded, calm, bald one—came out, pushing his cart of cleaning supplies. He was a head shaver, and he didn't look much older than forty.

"Sorry about the mess up there," I said. "We had a delay on the way back. And I guess nobody thought to check the tide charts when we were leaving."

"This is nothing," he said with a Boston tough-guy accent. "Water, I can handle. I've seen worse. Anyway, I'm gettin' double overtime plus hazard pay."

"Hazard pay? You're smarter than me. I keep doing this stuff for free." I held out my hand. "Zara Riddle."

"I know who you are," he said. "Chive Bacon."

I did a double take. "I'm sorry. It sounded like you said your name was Chive Bacon. Like the toppings on a baked potato."

He grinned. "That's my name. I was supposed to be called Clive, like the author, Clive Cussler, but one of my uncles made a change on my birth certificate registration. Did they do the same to you? Was your name supposed to be Sara?"

"Maybe," I said. "I bet if I'd been named Sara, my whole life would have been different."

"You can still change it," he said.

"I've grown into it."

He held up his hand next to his mouth, as though telling a secret, and said, "Same. It's a good excuse not to be normal." He grinned, and his gaze wandered just enough to give away the fact he was checking me out.

I pretended not to notice.

"I'm not really a janitor," he said. "I work with the mayor. You've seen me around. I'm usually wearing a suit."

"Oh," I said. "Cool. Not that there's anything wrong with being a janitor."

"No, but you wouldn't go on a date with a janitor, would you?"

And there it was.

"I might, if I didn't already have a boyfriend," I said. "But thanks."

He shrugged. "Can't blame a guy for taking a shot, can you?" He reached for his phone, read something on the screen, and said, "Lucky you. There's another octopus on the loose." He went to the elevator, pressed the call button, and said, "Are you going to be okay on your own here without a weird guy with a shaved head hitting on you?"

"I'll manage," I said.

He grinned at me as he stepped into the elevator and pressed the button to close the doors.

He'd left his cart behind.

"Wait, Chive! You forgot your—"

The doors had already closed, and the elevator whirred as he went away.

My aunt was still talking to her coworkers.

I got bored enough that I walked over to the cart to check its contents.

It had the usual items you'd expect—a garbage bin, a supply of plastic bags, various cleaning sprays, a putty knife for scraping chewing gum, as well as mops and brooms.

There was one thing about the supplies that struck me as unusual. The broom wasn't the standard push broom with black nylon bristles. It was a handmade specimen, with a crooked handle and a brush made of straw. It looked like something out of a movie about teen wizards.

Suddenly, the floor beneath me dropped.

I grabbed onto the cart to steady myself. Everything in the cart was shaking and rattling.

The drop had been accompanied by a loud boom that continued to roll around me.

The whole building was shaking.

Dread filled my chest with blackness.

The explosives.

We were too late.

The door to the Permits Department burst open.

It was Dawna who came out first, with the bad news.

"Zara, we located most of the explosives but not all of them," Dawna said.

I was already reaching for the broom, as though guided by something much larger and more powerful than myself.

Next, Dawna spoke in a tight, strained voice, telling me what I already felt in my body.

"It was your house," Dawna said. "That was the first target."

With the broom in hand, I ran for the nearest exit, prepping my flight spell.

CHAPTER 27

There are rules to being a witch.

Most of them are for our own good.

The biggest rules are about not revealing the existence of magic, let alone your own personal powers, to the world.

Flying by broomstick, over a town, where anyone might see you if you don't have your glamor shields running perfectly, breaks those rules.

I should have known better.

But, upon hearing that my house had exploded, all the rules went out the window.

I don't think I even bothered to cast a disguise glamor, let alone check that it was working, as I flew over the town of Wisteria.

At least it was dark, so anyone looking up would only have seen a blur as I sailed overhead. It certainly helped that my outfit for the day was midnight blue, to match the night sky.

I didn't need an aerial map to guide me to my destination.

I followed the smoke, and the flashing red lights of the fire department trucks.

I pulled up on my broomstick and halted mid-air to get a visual of the whole thing.

For a hopeful moment, I thought I'd gotten the wrong street. There was no Red Witch House on the corner of the block. It must have been someone else's house that got blown up!

Then I struck something with the heel of my boot.

It was a metal cutout of a goat. The top of a weathervane. The weathervane that sat at the peak of the house next door to mine.

I was on the correct street, after all.

My house wasn't just damaged.

It was gone.

My house was gone.

My broom was losing power.

I landed clumsily on top of the Moore residence. I dropped the broom and let it slide away down the roof as I crouched to avoid detection. Belatedly, I cast a glamor spell that would help me blend with the background, chameleon style. It wouldn't render me invisible, but it was good enough, and better than turning into a bush.

Sitting where my beloved house had been—the lovely old red house with the delicious gingerbread trim—the house I'd moved my family across the country for—the house I'd grown to love as much as my favorite people—was gone. Entirely gone. As though it had fired up rocket engines at the base and blasted itself away like a spaceship.

Except it hadn't picked up and moved. As much as I wanted to believe the house was still safe, albeit somewhere else, there was too much evidence of its destruction.

Bits of lath and plaster were everywhere, along with red-painted siding, window ledges, and soft furnishings. The bathtub, with its familiar chicken claw feet, sat on its side in the backyard.

The house was gone, and in its place was a dark, smoking pit. It was a hole in the ground that extended below where the basement had been, and went deeper and deeper, as though it might go to the center of the world. Or straight to Hell.

All of this registered in seconds. Seconds that felt like an eternity, as I scanned for what I hoped I wouldn't see strewn about in the wreckage—my family.

Zoey and my mother might have been out of the house at the time. But it was nearly midnight on a weeknight, so they should have been home, unless they'd gotten the warning from Maisy or someone else.

The first firefighters on the scene charged toward the center of the blast. A rumpled segment of the front lawn gave way, the pit widened, and the first responder who'd been leading the way plummeted toward the blackness.

I shouldn't have been able to use my telekinetic powers to save that big man from his fall, but somehow I did. My magic worked. I groaned from the effort as I drew him back up and onto solid ground.

"Careful," said someone at my side.

I whirled quickly, stunned that someone was with me on the rooftop. Had my aunt tailed me from City Hall? Had she been on the back of my broomstick the whole time, and I'd blanked it out in my panic?

Was Ribbons there, doing a different voice?

No.

It was Maisy Nix.

"That firefighter was heavy," she said.

She'd pooled her magic with mine. That was why I'd been able to catch the man.

"Maisy! How did you get here?"

"Same way you did," she said. "By broomstick. Except I remembered to cast the cloaking spell. I was right below you, so I think you were shielded by mine."

I started to thank her, but my words caught in my throat. Zoey! Where was Zoey!

"She's not down there," Maisy said, answering the panicked screaming in my brain.

"She's not?"

Gently, she said, "I don't know where your daughter is, but she's not in the back yard or with the other... stuff." She waved a hand, casting a spell over the scene. "No blood."

"That doesn't mean she's okay," I said. "She could have been blown onto another rooftop, or she could be underneath a wall, or..." I trailed off, my mouth unable to keep up with all the horrible images in my mind.

"We'll find her," Maisy said.

"What about my mother? Did you check for vampire blood? It's different. I don't know if your spell will work on that."

"Blood is blood," Maisy said. "She's not down there."

I thought of the cat, and the budgie, but I fought back the tears and clenched my jaw. What was done was done. It was too late to change anything.

Something nudged my ankle.

It was my purse. I hadn't taken it on my journey because I'd taken the suitcase instead, and no phone, since they didn't work in the other world. My purse must have been blown onto the roof in the explosion, or maybe I'd called for it out of habit. Inside my purse, my phone was ringing.

I grabbed the phone with trembling hands.

It was my mother's phone number.

I answered, "Mommy?"

There was a long, horrible pause.

I tried again. "Mother?"

"Oh, good," she said. "It's you. Did you feel that big rumble?"

"It was the house," I said.

"Not again," she said. "What's it doing now?"

"Smoking," I said. "Someone blew it up. Morganna, the genie, blew it up. She's got an accomplice. Morganna came back into our world as a wisp of smoke and now she's inside Jasmine Pressman."

There was another pause as my mother took it all in. "Where's Zoey?"

"I don't know," I said, trying not to choke.

She said, "I'm coming over. Don't do anything crazy until I get there."

I dropped the phone into my purse and looked at Maisy.

She said, "I'm really sorry about your house. Hang in there. Maybe it will rebuild itself, and you won't even need to deal with the insurance. You do have insurance, right?"

Almost growling, I said, "I don't care about the house."

More vehicles with flashing lights were arriving. The red and blue lamps lit up Maisy's face and body.

Maisy glanced around. "We need to get down from this roof. Are you going to be able to control yourself, or do I have to incapacitate you, like when you have to knock a drowning swimmer unconscious so they don't kill themselves and the rescuer, too?"

I spoke honestly. "I don't know."

"Try to control yourself," Maisy said. "Whatever you do, don't make the situation worse. Don't abuse your powers. You don't want to kill an innocent by accident."

"Kill an innocent?" I remembered my advice session with Toade. Had Maisy been getting notes from him as well, or was it just a coincidence? "Who told you I would do something like that?"

She ignored my questions, busy with the task at hand. We had to get down from the rooftop without breaking any legs.

As we were finding a safe way off the Moore house, I saw my aunt's car pulling up behind the firetrucks.

The doors opened, and everyone from the Wisteria Permits Department poured out. It might have been comical, like seeing endless clowns emerge from a tiny Mini Cooper, if I'd been in a laughing mood.

One person emerging from the car broke from the others and launched himself at the smoking wreckage.

Xavier Batista.

He reached the edge of the pit, glanced around, and then jumped in.

I tried to catch him with magic, as I'd done with the firefighter, but I didn't have Maisy's powers witchpooled with my own. He slipped through my magical grasp.

I followed Maisy to the edge of the roof.

"Jump down here," she said. "You can't see it, but there's a cushion spell, like an air mattress."

Normally, I would have bickered with her and made her jump first—who jumps blindly onto an invisible mattress?—but I didn't have it in me to doubt her loyalty.

I landed on a cushion of air and bounced onto the lawn of the Moore home's backyard. I stepped on a framed picture that had once graced my hallway. The glass crunched under my heel.

I started toward the pit, but Maisy grabbed my elbow and held me back.

"Easy now," she said.

"Zinnia and the others from City Hall just got here. I saw Xavier. He jumped out of the car, and he ran straight for the pit and jumped in."

She stared at me in disbelief. "Xavier jumped into the pit? Why? That kid's always doing stupid things, but this is strange, even for him."

"He's in a mood," I said. "He picked a fight with me when we were at City Hall. He didn't even want to come back to this world."

She cocked her head. "Do you think that pit leads to another world? It would explain how your house has so many powers."

I didn't have any competing hypotheses.

I might have had ideas, if my cognitive function wasn't so hampered by my terror that something awful had happened to my daughter.

Maisy and I made our way to the disaster site, slipping easily through the crowd of first responders thanks to the camouflage spell she was able to keep powered up. She appeared to be chewing gum, her jaw flexing with effort, but I knew there was no gum. It was part of the spellwork.

I was genuinely grateful for her assistance. I would need her help when I got to the pit, found Xavier in a heap, and had to fix all his broken bones.

We reached the jagged wooden edge of what used to be my porch, and peered down.

The pit wasn't bottomless after all. It went down about three stories. The upper third was lined with the familiar stone walls that had once enclosed my cozy basement. Next was a layer of mixed materials—bricks, dirt, rocks —landfill. Below that was an open space with no visible sides. It had to be part of the rumored tunnels, the network of old sewer access tunnels that ran deep below the town. The old sewer system was nonfunctional, but the pipes had been left in the ground.

Standing at the bottom of the pit, next to a large, partly rusted-out pipe were two human figures.

One was Xavier Batista. He was standing on both legs, not visibly broken after all.

The other figure was my old pal, Jasmine Pressman.

The young man and the short, middle-aged woman were circling each other like boxers, fists raised.

Normally, Jasmine would have been no competition for Xavier. He could have knocked her out with a single punch.

But something else was going on under the surface.

Jasmine's eyes were glowing, along with her fists. Magic swirled around her.

Xavier's eyes were also glowing.

The young man didn't have any magic of his own—a fact he rarely let me forget—so it was someone else's magic inside him.

Xavier threw a punch.

Jasmine dodged it by leaning backward, defying physics.

Then, a blast of magic flew from Xavier's hand, soaring over the woman's face. The bright blast landed on the rusted pipe with a loud bang and an explosion of sparks.

Maisy, who was still at my side, said, "That's not Xavier. He's possessed."

"He is," I said.

We both stared in stunned silence as the two people in the pit took shots and dodged glowing missiles. They were arguing with each other, but I couldn't make out what they were saying from three stories up.

Maisy said, "How did he get possessed? It looks like they've each got a genie in them. Morganna and another one."

"Archer Caine," I said.

"Archer? But how? Are you sure?"

"I knew there was a reason he didn't say goodbye to us," I growled. "That sneaky trickster."

Just then, the female in the pit landed a blast on the male. Xavier staggered back, clutching his shoulder.

"Uh-oh," Maisy said. "Archer's going to get himself killed. Again. And Xavier. That poor kid."

"We have to stop them."

"How?"

"I don't know, but we have to do something. Cast one of those cushion spells down there. We're jumping in."

She held me back with one arm across the front of my shoulders.

"What about your daughter?" Maisy asked. "Aren't you worried sick about her?"

"Yes, but I can worry myself sick while saving Xavier. I'm a mom. I can multitask."

"But we are... mortals," she said. "We should not interfere in the affairs of gods and demons."

"It's a bit late for that now," I said. "Now, either cast the cushion spell down there, or get ready to help mend my broken legs. I'm going down there whether you like it or not."

I backed up a couple steps to get a running start so that I could jump clear of the rusting pipes and stream of dirty water.

As I fell through the air into darkness, I really hoped Maisy had opted for the cushion spell and not the leg repair.

As I plummeted, I had enough time for one single thought:

Wasn't I doing exactly what The Oracle at Dragon's End had specifically told me not to?

CHAPTER 28

Maisy Nix pulled through for me. I landed on her cushion.

With that problem solved, all I had left to do was settle a sibling dispute that had been raging since the beginning of human history, maybe since the beginning of time.

I stepped off the air cushion and got my bearings in the pit. The depths were lit only by the glowing fists and eyes of two furious genies.

Something shifted.

It wasn't like the explosion I'd felt all the way over at City Hall.

It wasn't something in the ground beneath me, or the craggy walls around me, but something definitely shifted.

The world went quiet.

I looked up to the edge of the pit. Maisy Nix was frozen in mid-air, one foot on solid land and the other foot over nothing. She resembled a wily-yet-unlucky coyote in an old cartoon.

It wasn't just Maisy who was frozen. The first responders who were ringing the pit were similarly locked in their poses.

The air around me felt thick and dense, like fog but not moist.

I'd experienced this before, at Castle Wyvern, the previous time the genie siblings had tangled.

That day at the castle, I had walked into a freeze-frame from a music video, the air filled with all the loose items you'd find inside a hair salon. Bentley had been there, frozen and helpless, wearing a plastic hairdressing smock.

Was he around to save the day again?

I searched for the vampire's face in the crowd above the pit. I couldn't see him—not that he'd be much help to me if I had found him, and he was outside of the field.

I was in a time-dampening bubble.

The warring genies had cast it around themselves so they could settle their differences without others taking a side. I must have dropped into it at the last possible instant. Lucky me.

Before me, glowing with magic, the battle continued.

Morganna Faire and Archer Caine, housed in their human hosts, faced each other, circling.

They each fired a few more sparking missiles, to no effect. There seemed to be an invisible barrier between them. Defense shields, I guessed. What was the game plan? Lob balls of energy at each other until someone's shield gave way? Sure, it took heart and courage, but there was no intellect to it.

The entity inside Jasmine Pressman called out to me, "Zara, it's me, Jasmine! From the dressing room at Mia's boutique! Something terrible is happening and I'm scared!"

"Jasmine?" I felt my heartstrings being tugged. Was it Mrs. Pressman talking, or the genie? It sounded so much like a regular human. A terrified human.

"Don't fall for her tricks," the man growled through Xavier's clenched jaw. "She's not what she appears to be. That's my dear sister, Morganna. She's stolen that woman's body."

"Archer, is Xavier in there with you? Is he still there? I want to talk to him."

"He's not in there," the woman said. "It's Morganna Faire inside your friend. I'm Archer. I'm inside the Pressman woman."

I was surprised to hear that. "What?"

The two genies continued to struggle against each other, locked in a physical tug-of-war that was starting to throw off some serious heat. If my seawater-soaked clothes hadn't already been dried by magic, they would have been drying rapidly now.

They didn't respond to me, so I asked, "What's happening here? Who is in whose body?"

"Zara, it's me," the male said. "I'm Archer Caine. I'm sorry, but I talked your friend Xavier into letting me hitch a ride here with him."

"That's partly true," the female said. "Except that's Morganna over there in your friend's body. When I jumped into this pit, she caught me by surprise and swapped us out before I could stop her." The female turned her head to make eye contact with me while holding off her opponent. "It's me, Zara. I'm Archer. You've got to help me out. My sister and I are too evenly matched. Do something."

The male shouted, "Lies! My sister is the queen of lies! I'm Archer!"

"Zara, you know me," the female said. "You know I'd never do anything to harm our family. What do I have to do to convince you that I'm Archer? Do I have to kiss you like that time I kissed you by the water fountain? Our first kiss?"

The male growled. "Stop it right now, Morganna! Take your defeat with some dignity, and resign yourself from this world!"

"You first, Morganna," growled the female. To me, she said, "Do something, Zara."

"Like what?" I got a powerful sense of deja vu. Maybe it was a side effect of being inside their time-dampening bubble, but I felt like a mere puppet going through motions that had already happened countless times before. Like I had no choice. No free will.

The female said, "Hit her on the head. Knock her out. Use your powers."

The male said, "She's in that body. Hit her, Zara!"

I wasn't going to follow orders blindly, but I did use my magic to reach for a nearby piece of broken pipe.

It was too heavy for me to even budge it, let alone pick it up.

My powers had been drained by the breakneck broomstick flight over, and then by lifting the man who'd fallen into the pit. I may have had some gas left in the tank, but it wasn't much.

I leaned down and picked up the pipe manually. It was heavy, and slipped through my fingers. That wouldn't work. I could barely lift it, let alone swing it.

"Try again," the male coached. "Pick up that pipe and bash her in the head."

"I can't do that," I said. "Even if that is Morganna in Jasmine's body, I can't kill Jasmine."

"Thank you," the female said. "It's me, Jasmine. I've got Archer Caine in here with me. He says you've got to take out Xavier. Knock him unconscious for his own good, before Morganna erases him and then he's gone forever."

"I can't," I said. "I'd knock you both unconscious if I could. How about you dissolve this time bubble thing and you let me get some help down here? Maisy Nix is right there." I pointed to where the other witch hung in the air above us. "Can you at least expand the bubble a bit and let her drop down?"

"I would do it, Zara, but my evil sister won't let me," said one of them.

"I dropped my side, but my evil sister, who's in the other body, won't allow it," the other said.

They continued to argue while I stood by, weak and helpless.

"You're evil!"

"You're the evil one!"

"Look at how everything you touch turns to death!"

"Look at the destruction that's always in your wake!"

"You are a curse upon humanity!"

"You are a shame to all djinn!"

They spat hateful words and ancient curses back and forth.

As their speech grew more toxic, the air inside the bubble got hotter. It wasn't just toasty now. It was like standing too close to a bonfire.

I tried to take a step back but I bumped into something invisible. The edge of the time dampening bubble.

There had to be something I could do.

I patted my pockets as I racked my brain for a solution.

I felt the hard lump of the weapon I'd carried to the other world and back. The cocoon gun.

Oh, how sweet it would have been to blast a couple of cocoons at the two warring genies.

Alas, the current iteration of the weapon only held a single blast. It was like an airbag in a vehicle, as it used some of the same technology. It had been fired at Griebel and Xavier, so now it was empty.

As I stared at the shiny gizmo in my hand, I recalled the short training session Rob from the DWM had given me on my porch the night before.

The new models had a secondary feature, to be used in emergencies, and only when the nonlethal cocoon had been expended.

I examined the small switch on the base of the handle.

I flicked it from C for Cocoon to B for Brain Blast.

The second feature was an electromagnetic shockwave that shut down the subject's brain and ceased ATP production within every cell of the body. Something to do with protons.

It was, not to put too fine a point on it, instant death.

Instant death that didn't leave any trace.

The genie siblings, or lovers, or soul mates, or whatever they were, continued to spar.

The last standoff I'd witnessed between the two had ended with gunshots—Morganna being shot by a bystander. The bullets from a regular gun had been highly effective. Of course Morganna had been in her own body then, one she'd been born into. It wasn't a host human that would have to die with her.

I flipped the switch back to C.

I couldn't kill an innocent.

Toade was wrong about me. His advice was worth what I'd paid for it.

I put the gun back into my pocket.

I couldn't kill Jasmine or Xavier, even if both of them had been complete idiots for allowing genies to inhabit their bodies.

That frog-shaped oracle in the other world had been *so* wrong. I wasn't the sort of witch who killed innocents. If anyone was going to fire a weapon in that dark pit that night, it wouldn't be me.

But then a shadowy form at the edge of the bubble moved.

It was an animal, with four legs. With red fur. Behind it was a dark circle that was blacker than the rest of the walls.

A tunnel.

A tunnel the animal must have emerged from a moment earlier, at the same time I'd been falling into the pit.

The fox climbed to its feet, struggling from the effort, and took two steps toward me, eyes dull and unfocused.

I cried out, "Zoey!"

A light flickered in the animals eyes. Recognition. It was her. My daughter.

One of the genies darted forward and grabbed the fox.

Everything happened so fast.

The two genies simultaneously screamed at me to shoot the other one before the fox got hurt.

It didn't matter which one had my daughter.

It didn't matter to me because it didn't matter to the gun in my hand. The gun that had contained only one cocoon, but up to ten electromagnetic brain blasts that killed instantly.

I shot one genie in the head, and then the other.

CHAPTER 29

For a brief moment after I fired both shots, everything remained frozen.

The two genies were completely still, their arms wrapped around the small body of the fox they were fighting over.

Behind me, Maisy Nix was still frozen in the air above the pit.

Then the hot, heavy air around me flashed cold.

Time started up again.

Three bodies dropped.

I turned in time to see Maisy Nix land on the magic air cushion she'd cast a couple minutes before. The cushion had been on the boundary of the genies' time bubble, and had partly deflated. Maisy landed with a heavy thump, but no cracking bones—at least not that I heard.

I whipped my head back to catch sight of the bodies of Jasmine Pressman and Xavier Batista dropping limply to the ground.

The magic glow that had been coming from genies dissipated, and we were plunged into darkness.

I had pretty decent night vision, but I couldn't see in the dark. What was that spell for a lamp?

A flickering torch came to life above me. Maisy, who was at my side once more, had already cast the spell.

I didn't even glance up to see which spell it was.

I was focused on the genies.

I had a flash of memory, back to when I'd first discovered what Archer Caine was. He'd told me his kind preferred the term *djinn*. I'd never called them that before, but now, in the pit, I realized that was what they were.

Djinn were demons. Powerful, destructive entities. Calling them *genies* made them seem like cute, harmless cartoon figures. But they were anything but harmless.

As I watched the limp bodies to see what happened next, two wisps of smoke emerged from their mouths.

The smoke was the disembodied djinn.

I still couldn't tell which one was which.

The two wisps of smoke wrapped around each other like twisted knots as they drifted up, up, up, and out of sight.

As the time bubble cast by the djinn rippled out and away, the noise of the world returned. There were sirens, flashing lights, and people shouting. There was commotion above the pit again.

Someone touched my arm.

It was my daughter, back in her human form. She was gently prying something from my hand.

"Mom," she said softly. "What did you do?"

I looked down at the shiny silver weapon in my hand. "I..."

Maisy Nix ran past me. She moved awkwardly, favoring one leg.

Maisy also said, "What did you do?"

I couldn't say what I'd done. I couldn't even comprehend it.

I must have done exactly what the oracle had warned me not to do. I had taken the lives of not just one innocent person but two.

Except that hadn't been my plan.

Before I'd pulled the trigger, there had been some thought. Not much, but I must have had an idea. There was always a method to my madness.

During the brief safety training session Rob gave me, he'd said the shockwave from the gun was only deadly if the person wasn't revived. During their tests in the lab, they'd used standard shock paddles to restart their subjects' hearts. It worked.

On the animal studies they'd done.

They hadn't tested it on humans.

But humans were animals.

If pigs and goats could be restarted, why not humans?

I joined Maisy Nix, who was kneeling over the bodies.

"They're dead," she said. "Zara, what have you done?"

"Dead isn't dead until they're cold," I said. "We need to shock their hearts."

"What spell did you use, anyway? When did you learn how to do that?"

"It wasn't a spell," I said. "It was a weapon I borrowed from the DWM."

"Oh, no," she said. "No, no, no." She reached for Jasmine and straightened the woman's body.

"Restart them," I said.

"I can't," Maisy said. "I can't heal someone who's dead. It will take me into the darkness. I can't." She made a choking sound, as though fighting back a panic attack. "Why am I here? Why did I let you drag me into this? I should have known better when I saw that look in your eyes. I should have incapacitated you when I had the chance. I should have—"

I grabbed her by the shoulders and gave her a shake.

My daughter stood off to the side, silent.

"Look at me and listen to me," I said to Maisy. "They're not dead. We just have to restart them. I would have done it already but I don't have enough power. You need to help me. Let your power flow into me, and I'll shock their hearts. I know how to do it. I've restarted

Xavier before. I know his circuits. My body knows his resonance. Trust me. We can do this."

From the sidelines, Zoey said, "Should we wait for the paramedics?"

Maisy's face was pale. "The paramedics," she said. "They'll be able to restart their hearts."

"We're in a pit three stories deep," I said. "We don't have that kind of time. You have to trust me."

Zoey went to Xavier's limp body and knelt by him, cradling his head tenderly. "What were you thinking, Xavier? You let Mr. Caine talk you into this, didn't you? Why are you such a stupid, stubborn boy? Now you've got yourself killed."

"He's not dead yet," I said.

Maisy placed her hand on my back, between my shoulders.

"I trust you," she said. "Do it."

I felt her power flowing through me.

They weren't dead yet, but they would be if we delayed.

I pushed my hands underneath Jasmine Pressman's shirt, touched her warm, sweaty flesh, and sent a jolt through her.

To my surprise, it worked on the first try.

Her eyes flew open, and she gasped for air.

She made eye contact with me and said in a croaking voice, "I don't like this nightmare."

"Close your eyes," I said. "It's almost over."

She squeezed her eyes shut.

Maisy said nothing as she followed me over to Xavier.

"You stupid boy," Zoey was saying, still cradling his head. "Why are you like this? Why do you have to try to be a hero, you big, stupid dummy?"

"Stand back," I told her.

She gently set his head on the hard-packed dirt and inched backward.

Xavier was still wearing the same clothes he'd been wearing on our journey. I unzipped the thick hoodie, revealing his T-shirt. It was the green one that said Kiss Me I'm Irish. Xavier loved wearing that T-shirt because he didn't look Irish, and the shirt was enough to provoke fights with the other guys around town he didn't get along with.

Why did he wear that shirt when it only caused him trouble?

Why had he agreed to let Archer possess him?

Why did he do any of the stupid things he did?

The shirt was tight on his body, so I grabbed the neck and ripped it apart so I could access his chest.

I repeated the same motions I'd done with Jasmine Pressman, but it didn't feel right. His ribs were thicker. His muscles would give his heart more insulation.

I tried not to think of the physical differences as I sent a lightning blast into his body.

The body jerked, but went still again.

His eyes were motionless.

At my side, with both of her hands on my back, Maisy Nix whispered, "Again."

I shocked him again.

Nothing.

I shocked him a third time. They say the third time's the charm.

But the third shock fizzled.

He didn't revive. He couldn't have. I had no charge in me.

"Don't hold back," I said to Maisy.

"I'm not holding back," she said. "I'm out. I can't believe I had as much power as I did, between the flight over here, and the air cushions, and..." Her voice trailed off into nothing.

I tried to jolt Xavier, but I had nothing left. Maisy had nothing left. There was nothing we could do.

Zoey shouted, "Mom! You've got to do something!"

"Maybe I can call for help," I said. "Go get your aunt. And Margaret. Get them all."

"No," Zoey said, her tone harsh and suddenly cold. "You killed him. You have to bring him back."

I met her eyes and immediately regretted it. I'd seen my daughter upset with me, but never like this. The magic torch was still flickering above us, keeping everything visible, but I was deep, deep in the darkness.

Through gritted teeth, Zoey said, "Bring him back."

"I can't," I said. "Maybe give me a minute. Sometimes if I jump up and down, I can get a little more power going."

"Bring him back," she said again. "Do it."

"Zoey, I—"

She grabbed my face with both hands, brought her face close to mine, and said, "Do it."

Something started to happen. Where her palms were touching my cheeks, there was a glow. Power.

I felt it flowing into me. From my daughter, to me. Like witch power, but different. Hotter and colder at the same time.

Her hazel eyes narrowed. "Do it," she said.

Without breaking eye contact, I adjusted my hands on Xavier's chest, increasing the space between them.

Maisy sucked in air audibly. Her hands trembled on my back.

"I'm out," she whispered, and the torch she'd been using to light the pit went out.

We were in the dark. The only light was directly under my eyes, on my cheeks, coming from my daughter. My half-djinn daughter.

I closed my eyes and summoned a positive image of Xavier, still alive, in the future. He was giving me a hard time about ripping his favorite T-shirt. Then the image ripped apart.

He was in a casket, his parents sobbing at his side.

No!

I sent the jolt through my palms.

There was a sizzle and a pop, like a lightbulb flashing its final death spark.

The pit filled with white light.

There was a ragged gasp, and the chest beneath my hands began to move.

I couldn't see anything. I'd been blinded by the light.

I squeezed my eyes shut and let my fingers do my seeing. I walked them up to Xavier's neck. There was a pulse under my fingers.

I walked my fingers up over his stubbled jaw, to his mouth. Hot air came out and cool air sucked in.

He was alive.

I'd killed him, but I'd brought him back.

Thanks to my daughter, and what had to be her half-djinn powers.

I'd done exactly what the oracle had warned me not to do.

I had taken an innocent life, and I'd used the powers of a god to undo my mistake.

CHAPTER 30

The Next Day
Tuesday, January 3rd

Frank Wonder was surprised to see me walk in the back door of the library.

"Yikes," he said, grimacing. "Look what the cat dragged in."

"Your warm greetings make me *so glad* to be alive," I said.

He grinned, flashing his bright teeth. Frank was an older man with pure white hair, impeccable style, and a youthful build. He had a strong sassy streak that got sassier with each cup of coffee.

The door opened into the staff lounge and break room, so the library's customers—we called them patrons—wouldn't have to see my miserable face until I'd dosed myself with coffee and sugar.

I grunted as I wrestled with the door. I was having a hard time thanks to the big cardboard box I was carrying in my arms. How did people without magic carry things while dealing with doors? It was next to impossible without a spell.

Frank finally strolled over to help. He held the door open for me as I lugged the big box in.

He said in his teasing, fake-Southern tone, "Zara Riddle, since when do you need a man to help you with a door?"

"Long story," I said.

I dropped my big box on the floor in the Grumpy Corner, next to the two space heaters and a beanbag chair, and made a beeline toward the coffee maker.

Frank said, "Have you taken a vow to not use your magic anymore, because of the whole thing where you killed two people, and then barely brought them back to life using other people's god-like powers?"

"I guess my story isn't that long after all. Someone must have filled you in."

"Bad news travels fast," he said. "Listen, I know you're probably sick of hearing people weigh in on the whole debacle, but if it had been me there, and those genies had been playing tug-of-war with someone from my family, I would have shot both of them without hesitation."

"Thanks," I said. "I am sick of people weighing in, but mostly because they're never on my side. When I saw Zoey there, about to get ripped in half..." I fought to push the emotions back down. She hadn't been torn apart. She was okay. I'd said goodbye to her moments earlier, when she'd dropped me off at the library. I had to stop imagining the worst possible outcome to something that was already finalized. I had to move on.

Frank opened a pastry box filled with fresh cinnamon buns.

"I'd have shot them if I'd had a weapon in my hands like you did," he added. "And if it didn't seem like there was any other solution."

"Exactly," I said.

He pulled out a cinnamon bun. "And if I was absolutely, positively sure I could revive the human hosts after the genies were out of them." He pulled a fork from the drawer. "And if I had some sort of guarantee I wouldn't be tried for the crime of murder." He gave me a cheeky grin.

"Give me that," I said, and I took the cinnamon bun from him using my hands.

"Thief."

"That's weird," I said, frowning at the stolen pastry. "Whenever I steal food from you using my magic, it feels hilarious and playful. Quirky. Adorable. But when I use my hands and take your food, like a common thug, it feels...*wrong*."

Frank raised one snowy eyebrow. When I'd met him, he'd been dying his hair bright pink, but he'd recently gone through a makeover in favor of the natural look. He'd also traded in his vintage tight-fitting clothes for slim, tailored suits. He used to get plenty of attention as the pink-haired guy in the corduroy bell bottoms, but he got even more attention now as the guy who could walk in runway shows or host a reality TV show.

"Zara Riddle, stealing pastries was *always* wrong," he said. "We only put up with it because we love you. And also because Kathy's food swiping is so much worse." He shuddered. "That tongue."

"I know I've been bad," I said. A familiar lump in my throat rose up.

"You've been through a lot," he said. "Eat your cinnamon bun."

"I'm going to make some changes." I stuffed a bite in my mouth. "I'm going to eat healthier, and I'm going to use the calendar function on my phone to stay organized, and I'm not going to use magic willy nilly."

"Good for you."

I took another bite. "Starting tomorrow. My aunt says the new year is a good time to change, and the fourth of January is particularly good because so many people are already abandoning their resolutions, so there's tons of spare change energy floating around." A third bite. "No more cinnamon buns after this one."

Frank wandered back over to the cardboard box I'd brought with me and leaned over.

"What is this junk, anyway?" Frank asked.

He didn't wait for an answer before he started poking around.

He chuckled and said, "You know, you did walk right past the library dumpster on your way in."

"Are you saying that's all trash?"

"Are you saying it's not?"

"That *trash* is all that remains of the contents of my house."

"Oh, dear. This is everything?"

"My purse blew free of the blast, unscathed, along with those items. Go ahead. Pick over what's left of my life, and mock me for it."

"As you wish."

Frank lifted the objects out of the box one at a time. There was the tub plate, a Frisbee I used for snacking while bathing, as well as a few other damaged household items I didn't feel any particular connection to, and one big item. It was the thing that had made the box heavy.

"Oh, my," Frank said as he lifted out the world's ugliest lamp. "This survived the blast? Isn't this the lamp your aunt gave you as a housewarming gift?"

"That's the one," I said. "Clearly it's quite evil. How else do you explain its survival? There's not even a scratch on it."

Frank said nothing as he plugged the lamp into a nearby outlet to see that it was still working.

It was. When the light came on, Frank's white hair flashed pink for an instant before going white again. It happened so quickly, I barely caught it.

"Frank, do me a favor and flick it off and on again."

He did. "Still ugly," he said.

"That lamp's got some magical properties," I said. "When it came on, your hair was pink for an instant. Like with a reveal spell."

"But my hair isn't pink," he said.

"Your hair isn't, but your feathers are." Frank was a flamingo shifter.

"Ohhh," he said. "Magic lamp. Ugly, but useful."

"Just like me," I said.

Frank rolled his eyes.

"You said it yourself when I came in," I said. "I'm a mess. I'm wearing my aunt's clothes, and my hair is possessed by demons. It turns out I became dependent on the leave-in conditioner that used to appear by magic in my old medicine cabinet. What am I going to do? Rub mud on my head and embrace the dreadlocks?"

He ignored me and flicked the lamp on and off a few more times.

"I wonder what else this does," he said.

"I guess I'll have plenty of time to figure it out, now that I don't have any other personal possessions to distract me."

Frank spoke in a serious, heartfelt tone, "Your hair isn't that bad. I'll give you the name of my stylist for a leave-in hot oil treatment."

"Thanks."

"I'm really sorry your house blew up."

"Thanks. I'm just glad Morganna didn't get her wish to blow up the whole town."

"How's Zoey?"

"She's fine. A little shaken up, but I'm so glad she was down in that tunnel when the charges went off."

"The house did its job and protected her," Frank said, tilting his face up and holding his fingers over his heart. "Good for you, Red Witch House. Bless your plumbing."

"The house was a hero, all right, but also the ghost of Mrs. Pinkman. My mother was out with the zookeeper, and Zoey was home on her own when she started getting calls from people about a threat. She must have been so scared. It was Mrs. Pinkman who led them through the new basement doorway into the tunnels."

"Them?"

"Zoey, plus Boa, and Marzipants."

"Phew!" Frank pretended to wipe his brow. "I thought for sure the cat and the bird didn't make it. I didn't want to ask about them, and make you feel worse."

"Everyone made it," I said.

"The wyverns probably enjoyed the blast. They like that sort of thing."

"Ribbons and Junior were out prowling for leftover eggnog, and missed it all. I got an earful from Ribbons this morning. He came back, and when he saw that everything was gone, he freaked out. Then he started in on me about what we were going to do next. Like it's my responsibility to feed and house him. He squawked at me for an hour about his requirements. He thinks we should get a place with a Jacuzzi tub!"

Frank said, "Speaking of which, where *are* you going to live?"

"How many bedrooms do you have in your apartment?"

He laughed. "You are welcome to stay with me as long as you need. We'll need more beds, though. How do you feel about bunk beds? You and Zoey and the pets can come, but this ugly lamp should stay here at the library. At least until we know what kind of evil it does."

"Thanks, but I was only teasing. My mother's already getting herself and Zoey set up at Zinnia's. It's going to be a full house with four Riddles."

"But you won't be bunking together for long," Frank said. "Right? That house of yours is magic. It moves its walls around, and creates portals to other worlds. It should be able to rebuild itself quickly. You probably won't even need to deal with the insurance companies."

"Maisy keeps saying the same thing, but..."

My stomach sank. Everything inside me was sinking, and the cinnamon bun wasn't doing much to help.

"The house is dead?"

"It does seem that way," I said. "There's no sign of movement, or magic. It's just a giant empty hole in the ground. The weird thing is there isn't very much material around. A few fixtures, and some sticks of wood and plaster, but not nearly as much stuff as there should have been. Bentley said it looks like a movie set that's been decorated to look like an explosion has happened. It doesn't resemble a genuine disaster site."

"Morganna blew your house to another dimension," Frank joked, except it wasn't that far-fetched. The material must have gone somewhere.

"Anyway, there's a restoration company coming by later today to put up a safety fence so that all the lookie-loos in the neighborhood aren't traipsing through there, falling into the pit and getting themselves hurt."

A minute passed as we ate cinnamon buns and stared at the ugly lamp.

Frank said wistfully, "Your beautiful house is gone, and you've taken a vow to quit magic. Kind of a rocky start to the new year."

"Plus Archer Caine is gone."

Sadness flickered across Frank's face. "Oh, Zara, I'm so sorry. In all the excitement, I forgot all about that. But isn't he just on the other side of the elevator? Hanging out in that other world? Zoey could go over and see him any time."

"No." I crossed my arms. "She's not going to have anything to do with him. I don't care if that makes me the worst mother in the world, but that man has been nothing but trouble in our lives. He almost got poor, sweet, stupid Xavier Batista killed."

Frank nodded. He understood. He was a good coworker and an amazing friend.

For a moment, it seemed like he might hug me, but then he turned his attention back to the lamp and started making fun of it again, which was actually much better than a hug.

Over the last several hours, I'd had far too many of those.

All I wanted to do was finish my cinnamon bun, report for work duty as a librarian, and do something normal again.

So that was what I did.

And, after my shift was over, I paid a visit to Jasmine Pressman.

CHAPTER 31

I arrived at the hospital and took the stairs up to the second floor.

Typically, I would have taken the elevator, but I wasn't in an elevator mood for some reason.

Only one of the people I'd shot the night before was in the hospital. Xavier Batista had been pronounced "as good as new" once the first responders had retrieved us from the dark pit. Jasmine Pressman had been checked over by agents from the DWM, then transferred to the regular civilian hospital for care.

I reached her room and knocked tentatively on the doorframe.

"Come in," she said from her bed. "Oh, it's you. My favorite librarian who's also a wizard."

The room had two beds, but the other was empty, so we had our privacy.

"That's right," I said as I took a seat in the visitor's chair. "You found me out. I'm a wizard."

Jasmine frowned. "I said that wrong, didn't I? You're something else. It's like a magician, but not a magician. What was it? You're not a fairy, but you do cast spells and make potions. You're..."

"A witch," I answered. "I guess they didn't wipe your memory during the patient intake at the Department."

"No use," she said. "I'm dying. All this town's secrets will go with me."

She didn't look like someone about to die. Her cheeks were flush with color, and her thick, mostly black hair looked lush against the hospital pillow. But there was something off about her eyes. They were slightly misaligned, as though something might be pressing the orb or the musculature from behind.

"It's a tumor," Jasmine said, though I hadn't asked. "They think it started growing a few years ago. Based on where it is, it might have been the force that made me push my beloved Perry out of my life. When it's in your brain like that, it can affect your whole personality."

"I'm so sorry." I wanted to take her hand and try to heal her, but I knew there was nothing my magic could do against that type of illness. Years ago, my aunt had tried to save a little boy, using everything she could, and she had failed. Witches had powers, but there were limits.

"It's okay," she said. "Don't be upset."

"I'm going to be upset whether you like it or not, but I will try to hide it," I said with a smile. "It's not fair that you should have to try to comfort me. That isn't how it should be."

"Are you mad at me?"

"I don't know," I said, which was the truth.

Jasmine had been the one who'd acted as an agent for Morganna Faire. She worked at a construction company, and she'd knowingly acquired a huge amount of explosives. Even though she had a tumor that affected her brain, she must have known what she was involved in was dangerous.

But I couldn't be too harsh on her for it. Genies could be very convincing. Morganna must have leveraged Jasmine's grief over her two lost family members.

As a person who had recently done bad things myself, I couldn't judge her too harshly.

"Thank you for stopping me," Jasmine said. "I've been hearing things about some of the stuff you've been involved with. You're quite the wizard."

"Thanks."

"It must be hard to have all those powers," she said. "Knowing when to use them, or not use them."

"It is hard," I said.

"I wouldn't wish your powers on my worst enemy. I sure am glad that fate didn't make me a wizard."

I didn't say anything.

Jasmine tilted her head and gazed out the window behind me. "Funny, isn't it? We think we have free will, but we don't. Everything we do is predetermined by a bunch of chemical signals running through a lump of fatty meat."

"You don't believe in free will?"

"We think we're making choices, but we're not. We just do whatever *this thing* makes us do." She turned her eyes back to me and pointed to her temple.

"What about the heart? There's more to us than just our brains."

"The heart is a rose." Her eyelids grew heavy. "The heart is a rose."

I waited quietly for a moment. There were multiple lines running to and from the woman in the hospital bed. She was tired, or sedated, or both.

My own body felt heavy and tired as well.

I had been reassured by doctors at the DWM that what I'd done to her in the pit—killing her and then restarting her—hadn't affected her condition, but I still felt responsible.

As I was about to slip away, her eyes fluttered open.

"Hello," she said, pushing to get herself more upright. "It's you," she said, as though her short-term memory had been wiped clean by agents. "The librarian. You're a wizard."

"I am," I said. "Is there anything I can do for you?"

She smiled. "Tell them to be patient. I'll be along soon enough."

"Who?"

"Them." She rolled her eyes. "Don't play dumb with me. I know you're all friends." She weakly pointed to the foot of the bed.

I followed her gaze. Standing at the foot of her bed were the transparent forms of her husband and daughter, Perry and Josephine Pressman.

I wouldn't have said we were all friends, but I *did* know them.

Jasmine asked, "Do you see them?"

"I see them."

She sighed. "I'm not crazy. I've felt them near me for some time now, but ever since I fell into that pit, I've been able to see them. Aren't they beautiful, Zara? Look at my beautiful family."

Perry and his daughter held each other and stared at their mother with love.

"They're beautiful," I said.

"Tell them to be patient," Jasmine said. "It won't be long now."

She reached for my hand and squeezed it. I had been looking at the ghosts, and was startled by her touch. I squeezed her hand right back, as though we were old friends ourselves, and I'd forgiven her for everything she'd done.

"Zara," she said looking at me. "The heart is a rose."

"That's lovely," I said. "Is it from a poem? Would you like me to look something up for you at the library."

"Yes."

I leaned in. "What can I do?"

Her eyes closed.

Her face relaxed.

She was gone.

The monitors attached to her began to beep their alarm signals.

Nurses and doctors came running into the room.

The two ghosts at the foot of the bed were joined by a third.

As the hospital staff fought to delay the family reunion without success, I quietly slipped away.

CHAPTER 32

Sunday, January 8th
Abernathy Family Funeral Home
Memorial Services for Mrs. Jasmine Pressman

My family and I attended Jasmine Pressman's memorial service at the Abernathy Family Funeral Home.

The funeral home was in the town's newest strip mall, which had been built so as not to resemble a strip mall, but an old-fashioned high street in a small town. Each of the buildings were separate, and designed to resemble freestanding homes with a business on the lower floor and family residences upstairs. Instead of canvas awnings or letterbox lighting, the shops and services had hand-painted wooden signs.

My daughter spent a lot of time at the Abernathys' home, and enjoyed going there, but I had so far only visited for memorial services. I was no happier to be there that day than I had been during previous visits.

Most of the people there for Mrs. Pressman's service were friends and coworkers from the construction company where she'd worked for many years.

Everyone who spoke mentioned being comforted in knowing that Jasmine was finally at peace, joining her beloved husband and daughter.

I knew it was just something people said, and they couldn't have known I'd witnessed it myself, but it was surreal to hear that phrase over and over again.

My family and I left the woman's memorial in the chapel, and crossed the hallway to a smaller meeting room, where a service was being held for Archer Caine.

There was little talk at that service about who Archer might be joining in his afterlife. He'd been a stranger to most in town. Everyone in attendance was there to support Carrot, whom we all considered a widow, despite the fact they hadn't officially been wed.

I thought I'd used up all my tears for the year already, but then my daughter got up and spoke of the man she'd barely gotten to know in their short time together.

She did a lovely job. I couldn't have been more proud, or more heartbroken for her.

After Archer's memorial, a group of us gathered at Dreamland Coffee.

Maisy closed the coffee shop early, and drew the curtains so that we had our privacy.

Agent Rob from the DWM produced a crate of tequila —no doubt arranged for by fellow agent Charlize Wakeful—and said, "Let's get this wake started!"

Drinking ensued.

Zoey sat beside me, holding a Dreamland coffee mug with a single shot of tequila in the bottom and not sipping it. She wasn't even seventeen yet, but nobody had batted an eye when she'd accepted the drink from Rob. If you couldn't have a tequila shot with a bunch of supernaturals at your djinn father's funeral, when could you?

Also, the girl was half djinn herself. She had powers beyond my comprehension. Probably. We hadn't talked about it much, and she kept telling me she didn't feel any different from before.

I put my arm around her. "Good job with your eulogy," I said.

"It was just a few words," she said. "Knox was the one who gave the eulogy."

I squeezed her. Knox had started things off, but she'd been the only family member to speak, which technically made her speech a eulogy, but I wasn't going to argue the point.

Ambrosia Abernathy came over and joined us, landing heavily in her chair. The bleached-blonde teen with the heavy eye makeup was still recovering from the wyvern bite on her arm. She'd been using her current lack of magic to feel sorry for herself more than usual. On a scale of one to ten, her ability to sulk was at least a nine.

By comparison, my own daughter, who'd just lost her father, was only at a level three. Not that it was fair of me to compare anyone directly to Zoey. But I did, all the time, and Ambrosia had been coming up short more and more.

"Easy now," I said to the young witch. "I think you've had enough of the spirits, by which I mean the non-ghost spirits."

"I only had two," she said, slurring her words.

"Then two is enough," I said. "Switch over to coffee. Maisy's still got some eggnog from Christmas, and she's pushing eggnog lattes on everyone."

"Mmm," Ambrosia said, her eyes widening. "I'll have one of those!" She raised her shoulders, then slumped in her chair. "My body is too heavy. Did someone put a hex on me?" She gave Zoey a suspicious look. "Did you put a djinn hex on me, you dirty half-djinn?"

"Easy now," I said again, waving my hand between the girls. "Ambrosia, I'm not sure if calling someone a half-djinn is an insult, but when you put the word *dirty* in front, it sure feels that way."

Ambrosia stuck out her tongue.

Zoey said, "Real mature."

Ambrosia laughed, tipping her head back in the wingback chair—the comfiest spot in Maisy's cafe—and then leaving it there. She was passed out, or asleep—what difference did it make? Her body had flipped the safety switch on her drinking, which saved me from having to put my foot down.

I asked Zoey, "Is she always like that when she drinks?"

Zoey raised an eyebrow. "Is this where I'm supposed to lie to you and pretend I don't know?"

"You would if you were a normal teen."

Zoey nodded. "She's always like this. Zero to one hundred in two drinks, then right back to zero again."

"What about you?"

Zoey took the tiniest sip of tequila. "I'm very careful around potions of all kinds."

"Good girl."

A horse walked up to us—Appaloosa with a chestnut base—and shifted into human form. The Appaloosa shifter was a middle-aged woman with long, wavy chestnut hair streaked with white. She wore earthy clothes and silver jewelry with turquoise.

"Wonderful eulogy," she said in a deep, serious voice as she shook Zoey's hand. "Your father spoke very highly of you."

"Thanks," Zoey said, politely choosing not to argue with a stranger over whether or not she'd given a eulogy.

The woman stared at my daughter with an intensity bordering on ferocity.

She said, "Did you know you are his only offspring? That is, the only child who didn't turn out to be... *the other one?*" People had been referring to Morganna Faire as *the other one*, as though speaking her name might invite her back to set off more explosives.

"People keep telling me that," Zoey said. "I'm not sure I believe it, but thanks anyway. Thank you for coming to the service. How did you know my father?"

"I'm not sure if I should say or not. I probably shouldn't, but it only becomes more uncomfortable when I don't, because people start to wonder if I'm being enigmatic for other reasons." She produced a business card and handed it to Zoey. "This is me. Call me sometime if you need someone to talk to."

My daughter thanked the woman, who put her hands together and bowed her head briefly, then walked away, still in human form. It was getting a bit hot and crowded inside the coffee shop for people to be turning into horses anyway.

Zoey handed me the card.

The woman was a therapist specializing in family counseling. Her name was Tallulah Swiftwater.

I tossed the card into someone's discarded mug of cold latte.

Zoey said, "That's not very nice."

"Were you planning to call her?"

"I don't think so."

"Good. She obviously takes herself way too seriously, and therefore cannot be trusted. Plus the last thing we need is more people in this town hearing about all our secrets."

She suppressed a smile. "Are we back to *this* again?" She was referring to the Regal Riddles, the hit show in the other world.

"Yes. We are. Our family is always the talk of the town, and it's got to stop. You will not be calling that woman, even if she is the best therapist in town. Isn't it bad enough that someone's been selling our stories to another world for entertainment?" I crossed my arms and glared at the woman with the Appaloosa streaked hair. "What do you want to bet that woman is in on it? We should set a trap for her. We should plead poverty, now that we're couch surfers without a house, and ask if she'll give us sessions for free. If she takes the bait, then we know she's a mole."

Zoey stood up, went to where Ambrosia was snoring in the wingback chair, closed the girl's mouth for her, then returned to her seat next to me.

"I think you may be overreacting," Zoey said. "So what if you have fans in some other world? It's sweet. Xavier said they're all really supportive."

"You've been talking to Xavier? When? Where?"

"He phoned to make sure I was okay."

"He's in his twenties, Zoey. He's an adult. He shouldn't be phoning you."

She rolled her eyes.

"I'll speak to him," I said. "He won't be coming around, and he won't be bothering you anymore."

"Then who's going to vacuum your car and run your errands?"

I didn't have an answer to that.

Ambrosia suddenly stirred back to life. She let out a "Whoo!" followed by "This is some party!"

Zoey got up again. "I'm going to take her home to the Abernathys."

"Good idea," I said. "Thank them again for all the beautiful arrangements at both of the memorials. They did a wonderful job on such short notice."

Zoey said, "Most funerals are on short notice, Mom."

"Good point. I'm glad one of us is smart."

"Still feeling sorry for yourself?"

"Yes. I mean no. I just attended two memorial services. I should be more appreciative of the life I have, shouldn't I?"

Zoey shrugged.

Ambrosia snored loudly.

"See you at home," Zoey said. She dragged Ambrosia out of the chair, and they exited the party.

I was alone in the corner. I looked for a more comfortable seat.

The wingback chair that Ambrosia had been passed out in did look very comfortable.

Before I could take it over, it was filled by another person—my aunt.

Zinnia sat heavily and said, "You're holding up well for a person who's just been to two memorials back to back."

"You know what we say. We Riddle women are tougher than we look."

"I understand you were in the room when Jasmine Pressman crossed over."

I nodded. My daughter and I, plus my mother, Boa, and Marzipants, and the ghost of Minerva Pinkman, had all been staying at my aunt's house for the past couple of days but she and I hadn't gotten much time alone.

Zinnia asked, "How did that make you feel? To be there?"

"Does it make me a terrible person to say that, on some level, I was happy for her? She lost her daughter. If that happened to me, and I had the chance to be reunited with Zoey, I don't know why I wouldn't want to go, too."

"What about Bentley?"

I squirmed in my chair. I loved Bentley, but he wasn't my daughter. He wasn't my flesh and blood.

Rather than answer the impossible question, I turned things around.

"How are you doing?" I asked. "Did you talk to the baby's father yet?"

"Why would I need to do that? I have a house full of nannies. Zoey's still at school during the weekdays, and you're at the library, but my big sister is always around, bragging about how much free time she has. Between the four of us, this baby will be very well taken care of." She patted her stomach, which still wasn't showing much of a bump, despite her issues with the fit of dresses.

"Zinnia, don't take this the wrong way, but you're being a real ding-dong."

She pursed her lips. "I believe you've had more than enough tequila."

"I've barely touched it," I said. "I'm stone cold sober, and I can see you much more clearly than you can see yourself, so it's up to me to tell you the truth. You're being a big, huge ding-dong."

"I don't need a man," she said. "I don't need you, either. I'll hire a nanny. Fatima has mentioned a few friends her age who are interested. Nice girls."

"Why are you being so stubborn?"

"Why are you?"

"I'm not stubborn," I said. "I'm just right, and you know it."

She blinked. "I may have a lead on the party who has been selling our stories to the other world."

"Don't try to change the subject. Why don't you tell me who the father is so that maybe I can see where you're coming from?"

Her nostrils flared. "That's none of your business."

"Do you have any idea how easy it is to get DNA testing done?"

"Is that a threat?"

"That baby's inside you now, but once it comes out, all it takes is a single drop of blood."

She narrowed her hazel eyes at me. "Secrets revealed are trouble unsealed."

"Yup," I said.

She looked away. "There's a load of towels in the washing machine that needs to be transferred to the dryer. I noticed it on my way out. It's fine for you to live with me for as long as you need, but you ought to be more considerate of the laundry facilities, and not allow them to gather mildew."

"Is that a hint? Do you want me to run back to your house right now and do laundry?"

"No rush," she said lightly, which was Aunt Zinnia's code for delay-this-task-at-your-peril.

I got up and grabbed my purse, which had been hanging from the back of my chair obediently. Ever since the explosion, my purse had stuck close to my side.

"It's been a long day," I said. "Maybe I will head back to the house. Would you like me to pick up anything at the store on my way?"

"We're low on eggs," she said. "And bread and milk."

"I'll pick those up. How about olives? I had strong cravings for olives when I was pregnant. I got my fix with Greek pizza."

Giving me a faint smile, she said, "Olives would be lovely. Thank you, Zara."

Smiling back I said, "No problem. We may disagree on a few things, but I'm here for you, Aunt Zinnia. Anything you need, say the word and I'll do it."

"Please wipe down the lid of the washer after you transfer the towels to the dryer."

"Will do."

I did a quick tour through the wake, said goodbye to a few people, and headed out.

Compared to the warm interior of the coffee shop, the street outside was cold and bitter.

I pulled my trench coat tighter around myself.

It was a new coat—bright red. My wardrobe hadn't survived the disaster, so I'd been rebuilding, one item at a time. My coworkers at the library had been surprised by the jacket. They pointed out that half of the popular thriller paperbacks featured a woman in a red trench coat running down a forest path, running into darkness, running from some unseen threat. Was I trying to court danger by dressing like one of those ladies?

It was a nice color, I'd told them. Plus it defied the unwritten rule that redheads shouldn't wear red.

And it was warm. Which was useful when a witch was no longer casting warm-up spells willy nilly.

I got into Foxy Pumpkin and drove to the grocery store, where I bought the items my aunt had requested, along with a few more things, then drove to Zinnia's house.

I brought the groceries inside and tucked them away, all manually—no magic.

Then I stood in the kitchen, uncertain what to do next. It wasn't my home, so I didn't feel at home. Zinnia had made us all feel welcome, but there was a limit to how welcome I could feel in someone else's place.

Also, there was something else I was supposed to do.

I couldn't remember.

All I could think of was Bentley, and how he might be finishing work at that moment.

I left the house, locked up, went back to the car, and drove over to Bentley's apartment.

He was just getting home when I arrived.

"Good timing," he said as we both stepped out of our cars at the same time. "I was going to call you. How were the memorials?"

"Nobody else died. Unlike the last wedding I attended."

He nodded solemnly. "Zara, I really am sorry Archer is gone."

"You don't have to lie for my benefit. You feel how you feel."

The wind picked up speed, fighting to get through the warm wool layers of my coat.

"It's freezing out here," Bentley said. "Are you coming inside?"

I suddenly remembered the errand I'd forgotten to do for Zinnia. I'd left the wet towels in her washer, where they would gather mildew.

Bentley was waiting patiently for an answer.

"If I come into your place, I'm not going to leave again until tomorrow morning," I said. "Which means I won't transfer the wet towels out of the dryer, and there will be mildew, and my aunt will be annoyed at me."

He said nothing.

"Of course I'm coming inside. I'm not crazy."

Bentley put his arm around me as we walked up his front steps. He lived in an apartment, so we would have to pass through a lobby to get to his place.

"You and Zoey could always come stay with me," he said.

"It's too soon," I said.

He unlocked the door. "But you need somewhere to live. Why not with me?"

"I don't know. Maybe because, deep down, I'm an old-fashioned sort of gal, and we're not married?"

"We can get married."

"We can?"

"I'm divorced. I'm free to get married." He walked over to the mailboxes in the lobby. "Hang on. I've got to check the mail." Without looking back at me he said, "What do you say?"

"Theodore Bentley, are you proposing to me while you check your mail?"

"Yes," he said. "Because I know you'd hate it if I took you to a fancy restaurant and put the ring in a glass of champagne. You're not that sort of girl." He snuck a sly glance at me over his handful of envelopes and flyers. "Well?"

"Let me think about it," I said. What made him think I wouldn't want a ring in a glass of champagne? I didn't even know if I would like that or not, so how could he know more than I did?

"You can think about it," he said. "Do you have any questions for me?"

"What kind of food do you have in your apartment?"

"Nothing good," he said. "We could go out. It's late, but a few places are still open."

He tucked the mail into his pocket, took my hand, and we walked to his apartment door.

"I'm not actually hungry," I said.

"You *have* had a long day," he said, almost smiling.

We reached his door, and he paused.

"Use your keys," I said.

He raised a dark eyebrow, his silver eyes glinting with curiosity.

"You're serious about not using your charms," he said. "Interesting."

"Don't make fun of me. I'm trying to be good."

"If you say so."

"Now open your apartment door," I said. "Don't make me use my forbidden powers."

"You want inside my apartment? What's the urgency? I told you I don't have any good food in there."

He gave me that stony, serious look of his. The one that drove me crazy.

I knew he would keep me out there in the hallway for ages, torturing me, if I didn't do something. Magic was out of the question, so I did the only thing I could.

I kissed him.

He got the apartment door open quicker than ever.

CHAPTER 33

Wednesday, January 11th

"Is it Friday yet?" I asked Frank at the start of the day at the library.

He smiled as he checked his teeth in the mirror next to the sink then straightened his sunshine-yellow tie.

"This job's a lot harder without magic," he said.

"It really is," I said. "They do *not* pay us enough."

He shot me a knowing look. "You love being a librarian. You'd do it for free."

I held my fingers to my lips. "Shhh. Don't let them find out."

"Are you still keeping up your new resolution? How long has it been?"

"About six or seven or a thousand days without casting spells," I said. "Very long days."

He glanced over at the ugly lamp, which had taken up residence in the staff lounge since I'd brought it in. We kept the light switched on at all times. It seemed to take the edge off the lamp's ugliness. Like forcing yourself to smile when you felt gross.

"And the house," he said. "Any signs of life?"

Frank had taken a few extra days off, so he had missed my updates for a few days. I was glad to have him back.

My life felt unreal sometimes, but talking to Frank made everything more real, and more bearable.

I shook my head. "The house is dead. Rest in peace, Red Witch House, with all of your mystical powers."

"It feels like the end of an era," he said. "What did the insurance company say?"

"They said nope."

"They can't say nope. Do they not understand the basic premise of insurance?"

"They said no to rebuilding. The site has been declared a hazard by the township. The town's engineers have to figure out where those tunnels go, and how to safely block them all off, and also make sure that a certain genie didn't plant more explosives in key areas."

"Sounds like a major undertaking."

"Oh, Frank. It's going to take *years* for the whole remediation process, plus the cost of materials and labor can fluctuate wildly between now and then, so the insurance company said nope. They're cutting me a check right now. A one-time cash settlement. Well, it won't be an actual check. That's just a figure of speech, but you know what I mean. I can use the cash to rebuild, eventually, in a few years..." I lost the energy to complain further.

"End of an era," Frank said, shaking his head.

"Let's talk about something else," I said. "How are you?"

"Hungry." He opened the pastry box on the counter. "How old are these cinnamon buns?"

"I'm not sure. How many are left?"

"Two."

"That sounds about right, if it's the box you brought in on our first day back after the Christmas break, which would make them about a week old."

"Perfect," Frank said. "I love it when they firm up."

"Me, too." I held out my plate.

"Zara Riddle, what happened to your resolution to eat better?"

"Frank Wonder, don't make me break my other resolution to not zap you on the butt."

Smirking, he loaded up my plate.

We got to work after that, and I was on my best behavior all day.

No magic.

No trouble.

I finished my shift eight hours later, and punched out my timecard with a loud KERCHUNK.

I said goodbye to the head librarian, Kathy, who was working late that day, and got in my car to drive home.

Except I didn't have a home.

I realized as much when I turned onto Beacon Street and rolled up to where my house used to be.

I pulled over and parked.

As the motor purred—it was assisted by magic, but not my own personal magic, which made it fine by my rules —I stared out the window.

The sun was setting, and the streetlamps were flickering on to illuminate the sidewalks.

The only things to look at beyond my windshield were the security fence and the Moore residence, with the For Sale sign on the lawn. I could just make out the phone number in the glow of the streetlights.

I pulled my phone from my purse and did what I'd been pondering for the last week. I called the listing agent for the blue house.

The agent himself answered the call.

"I've had a lot of interest in that home," he said confidently. "Tell me about your buyer. How do they feel about a multi-offer blind bidding situation?"

"I'm the buyer," I said, "and I do not feel good about a multi-offer situation. Also, I happen to know you're bluffing. That house has been on the market for months with no interest." It was true. The most action the house had seen was when I'd done a stakeout there on Christmas Eve, sleeping over with my mother on the living room floor.

"It's a new year," the agent said with an arrogant scoff. "Things always pick up in the new year, and it's a hot property. The whole block was featured on the national news after those domestic terrorists burned down the house next door. We've had a lot of interest from out-of-town buyers looking to move into the area. Overseas buyers, even."

"Great," I said. "My house blows up, and even though I'm getting a decent buyout from the insurance company, the fact that it blew up so spectacularly is the very thing that makes the house next door unaffordable. It may not be ironic in the classic sense of the word, but it's a real pickle!"

The real estate agent cleared his throat on the other end of the line. "Did you say you have an insurance check? Cash in hand? I have some other properties you may—"

I ended the call.

I turned off the engine and sat in the cooling car as my emotions washed over me.

What was I supposed to do now?

Buying the Red Witch House and taking possession of it had been some of the happiest days of my life. It was just a house, but it was so much more. It was comfort, and security, and the home I'd always wanted for my family.

As I sat there, I cursed myself for every little complaint I'd ever made about the house, from the magical rearrangements to the influx of pets and people who moved in and never left.

Why had I ever complained about being crowded? There had always been enough space for what we needed.

Why had I been grumpy about having so much life under one roof?

Why had I even quibbled at all, when it had been exactly what I'd always wanted—what I needed?

Why hadn't I appreciated heaven when I'd had it?

The car windows were fogging up.

I wasn't ready to drive. Given my mood, there was a possibility I might run people down. After all, that was something I did now. I killed innocent people. Sure, I brought them back to life, most of the time, but now I knew what I was capable of, and nothing would ever be the same.

I opened the car door and stepped out.

A walk around the block might clear my head.

I braced myself as I approached the spot on the corner where my house used to be.

The security fence surrounding it was eight feet high and covered in plywood. There was no way for me to see the other side without using magic.

Or was there?

I walked all along one edge and then the other. What would I see if I did get a glimpse? Would I catch my house in the act of rebuilding itself? Stranger things had happened.

Finally, I found a small crack between the sheets of plywood.

I peered through, and all of the hope that had been building in the top of my chest sank away.

The pit was still a pit. It looked even deeper than the last time I'd seen it, when the town engineers had allowed me to pick out the few possessions that had survived the explosion.

I heard footsteps. A woman my size, in boots, was approaching.

She looked like a tiny Grim Reaper, dressed in black, with a rain hood over her head. One wisp of bright-orange hair crossed her forehead.

"Carrot," I said.

She gave me a startled look. "Zara? What are you doing here?"

"Overseeing the renovations," I joked. "We're having a pool put in, as you can see. A very deep pool."

She smiled. "That's funny." The smile quickly faded. "Zoey did a wonderful job with Archer's eulogy," she said. A tear gathered in the corner of her eye but didn't fall.

"How are you doing? I mean, besides the obvious. Being a newlywed widow and everything." I smacked my forehead. "Duh. That was insensitive of me, Carrot. I can be so stupid sometimes. You caught me at an embarrassing time. I'm standing out here feeling sorry for myself over the house. It was just a house. It wasn't a person."

"This is the last place Archer was," Carrot said. "It's sad for any of us to be here." She looked down. "That's why I came here. To be sad."

Her words made me feel better and also worse at the same time.

"I shouldn't have done what I did," I said. Carrot, and the rest of our friends, knew all the details about what had happened that night in the pit. "I didn't need to shoot them. There must have been another way."

"Dawna says there was no other way," Carrot said. "That's why I'm not mad at you for killing him."

I swallowed hard. I hadn't really killed Archer Caine. He hadn't been alive. He had been a wisp of smoke, inside Xavier's head, and then I had... released him. Had I killed him? Or had Morganna killed him already, with the wine?

Carrot came to stand next to me at the fence. She leaned forward and peered through the crack.

"That's a deep pit," she said.

I kept my mouth shut so I didn't stick my foot in it.

Carrot turned and gave me a mischievous look as she pushed back her dark hood. "Want to go down there and explore the tunnels?" Her large, bulging eyes made her look so young and innocent, like a cartoon drawing of a little kid.

I had to laugh. "We'd get ourselves muddy," I said. "Plus we'd get in all sorts of trouble if people found out."

She raised an orange eyebrow. "What are they going to do to us?" She grabbed the plywood on the fence and gave it a tentative tug. "I bet you could use your magic to get through this in ten seconds flat."

"I'm not going to," I said.

"Why not?"

"Ever since what happened, I've taken a vow to not use my magic, except in emergencies."

"But won't your magic get rusty? I thought the point of using it all the time was so that you were ready when an emergency happened?"

I didn't have an answer for that.

Carrot took a step back and dropped her arms limply to her sides. "Ah, never mind," she said. "These tunnels just lead to more tunnels, and most of them are too small for humans, anyway. I was just looking for something to do to keep me out of the house, away from all of Archer's things. I haven't packed up his clothes yet."

"Do you want some help with that?"

She gave me an uncertain, worried look.

"When you're ready," I said. "Not right this minute."

She let out a sigh. "Yes. I would appreciate some help with that. When the time comes."

"It's a date," I said. "What are you up to tonight? Do you have dinner plans?"

"I'm planning to eat macaroni and cheese out of the pot while I stand at the stove."

"That's one of my favorites," I said. "How would you like to come to Zinnia's with me? We'd love to have you. Plus it's good for you to be with your family right now."

Her eyes were shining. "Family?"

"My daughter is your stepdaughter, so that makes us all family."

"But not officially," she said.

"Archer made us family. He connected us. Plus you worked with Zinnia, and you were her work-family even before I met you."

She chewed her lower lip. "What are you having for dinner? I don't eat meat."

"We can rustle up something. I'm a fantastic chef. People are always talking about my cooking."

"Sure," she said. "That sounds nice."

Carrot had walked there from her place, so she climbed into the passenger seat of my car, and we drove over to Zinnia's.

Little did we know, we were both in for a big surprise.

CHAPTER 34

When Carrot and I pulled up to my aunt's house, there was an unfamiliar car parked right in front of her home, so I had to leave Foxy Pumpkin further up the street.

As we walked up the front steps, I detected something in the air.

Not magic.

I detected a regular, standard thing that anyone might have noticed.

It was a man's aftershave.

And not the kind Bentley wore.

Who was in there?

"Zinnia's got company," I said to Carrot, and I pointed to the car that was parked in the front. "Do you know whose car that is?"

"I thought it was Bentley's," she said.

"It's not."

Her bulging eyes nearly popped out of her head. "It's your aunt's boyfriend," she said. "The one who knocked her up."

"We don't know that. It could be... a furnace repair man. Or a plumber."

"They drive white vans," she said. "Open the door. Let's see who it is!"

"Okay, but play it cool. Even if it is a man, we can't assume anything about him."

"Open the door," she said, bouncing on her toes with impatience.

I opened the door, and we stepped inside. The entryway had a thick rug, and was lined with plenty of coats that muffled the sounds of us entering.

I could hear a man in the living room, talking to my aunt.

Carrot or I would have announced our presence immediately, but what happened next unfolded so quickly.

Zinnia, who hadn't heard us come in, was saying, "You need only be as involved as you'd like to be."

Carrot grabbed my hands and we stared at each other in shock, mouths open, like little kids.

Then the mystery man said, "I'm the baby's father. I'm going to be very involved." Then, with wonder in his voice, he added, "I can't believe I'm going to be a father. This is... This is the best news I've ever heard."

Carrot squeezed her eyes shut and bounced up and down with excitement.

My heart lifted high in my chest. It felt so good to see Carrot happy that I barely registered how happy I felt.

My aunt called out, "Hello? Is someone at the door?"

"It's me, Aunt Zinnia," I said from the entryway. "Me, and Carrot Greyson."

We both stepped into the living room sheepishly.

Zinnia and the man stared at us.

"We didn't hear anything," I said. "We *definitely* didn't hear what you two were discussing."

The man shook his head and smiled. "Zara, you really are terrible at bluffing when you don't have any magic spells running."

Dramatic pause.

Wouldn't you hate me if I didn't tell you who the man was?

The father of Zinnia's baby, the man talking to her in the living room, was... her dear old friend, the man who used to be a detective before Bentley took that role, and was now the chief of police.

It was Ethan Fung.

Zinnia had claimed that she and Ethan were only friends. Old, good friends. She'd sworn there was no chance of a romantic relationship between them. She'd even gone so far as meeting with him to coach him on relationship advice with another woman.

They'd gone out for a few dinners to discuss his dating life, and, apparently, much more.

"Hello, Chief Fung," Carrot said, waving girlishly. "Nice to see you again under better circumstances."

"You can call me Ethan," he said. "Or Fung." He shot an adorable, tender look at my aunt. "Zinnia likes to call me Fung."

My aunt said nothing. She looked even more uncomfortable than when she'd been wearing double Spanx and a too-tight bridesmaid dress.

I grabbed Carrot's hand and dragged her with me toward the kitchen, calling back, "Can I interest anyone in a cup of tea?"

Neither of them answered.

As soon as Carrot and I got into the kitchen, we made childish faces and milked the moment for every last bit of happiness.

Zinnia had decided to tell the father, and it was Ethan Fung, and it was wonderful news.

My coworker, Frank, had been right about the destruction of my house.

It really was the end of an era.

And the beginning of a new one.

For the first time in a week, I stopped worrying about the prophecy.

It wouldn't last long.

For a full list of books in this
series and other titles by
Angela Pepper, visit

www.angelapepper.com

Made in the USA
Columbia, SC
30 June 2023